T0307919

SUTZKEVER
essential prose

Sutzkever Essential Prose was made possible
with the generous support of Emile Bendit
in memory of Tanya and Saul Bendit.

Yiddish Book Center
Amherst, MA 01002

Paperback edition ISBN# 978-1-7343872-6-1
Hardcover edition ISBN# 978-1-7343872-5-4

Cover photograph from the Archives of the YIVO Institute for Jewish Research, New York

Book and cover design by Michael Grinley

"Lady Job" was originally published in *Asymptote* in 2012.

"Green Aquarium" was originally published in *Jacket2* in 2014.

"A Funeral in the Rain" was originally published in *In geveb* in 2015.

"A Smile at the End of the World" was originally published in *BODY* in 2015.

"The Cleaver's Daughter" was originally published on yiddishbookcenter.org in 2016.

"An Answer to a Letter" was originally published in *Pakn Treger*'s Translation Issue in 2018.

"The Gopherwood Box" was originally published in *The Big Book of Modern Fantasy*, Penguin Random House, 2020.

SUTZKEVER
essential prose

Translated by Zackary Sholem Berger

Introduction by Heather Valencia

White Goat Press
A Yiddish Book Center Translation
Amherst, Massachusetts

yiddishbookcenter.org

TABLE OF CONTENTS

Where the Stars Spend the Night

The Prophecy of the Inner Eye

INTRODUCTION

"Di dertseylungen zenen ikh." (These stories are *myself.*) Avrom Sutzkever wrote these words on the flyleaf of a copy of his second prose collection, *Dortn vu es nekhtikn di shtern* (*Where the Stars Spend the Night*, 1979). The writer regarded his prose works as an absolutely central part of his oeuvre, but it is striking that his first collection of literary prose texts, *Griner akvarium* (*Green Aquarium*), did not appear until 1955, by which time he had been publishing poetry for almost twenty years and was regarded as one of the most original and important poets in the modern Yiddish literary canon.

Sutzkever was born in the town of Smorgon, in Lithuania, in 1913, but throughout his life he thought of his true birthplace as Siberia, to which his family was forced to flee in 1915; the Siberia of his childhood memory was a magical wonderland, the cradle of his poetic inspiration. In 1920, after the early death of his father, Sutzkever's mother, with her three children, came back to Lithuania, settling in Vilna (Vilnius).

The poet grew up, therefore, in the city revered for its centuries-old Jewish culture; Jews called Vilna the Jerusalem of Lithuania. He started writing poetry in Yiddish in the early 1930s, and by the time the Nazis entered Vilna, in July 1941, he had published two books of poetry and was already well known in the Yiddish-speaking world of Europe and America.

There followed more than two years of horror. Sutzkever's mother and his newborn son were murdered by the Nazis, but despite his personal tragedies, he was very active in the cultural life of the ghetto, organizing the theatrical productions and poetry readings that immeasurably contributed to the inner resistance of the ghetto inhabitants. His most important work was his forced labor for the Rosenberg Task Force in the so-called Paper Brigade: he and his colleagues were supposed to sort valuable cultural artifacts to be either sent to Germany (for a museum of Jewish culture after all the Jews had been annihilated) or destroyed as rubbish. He and the others managed to save a substantial amount of cultural treasures from the Nazis.

After escaping from the ghetto in September 1943 and spending almost six months as partisans in the Lithuanian forests, Sutzkever and his wife, Freydke, were airlifted to Moscow; he testified on behalf of the Jews of Lithuania at the Nuremberg Trials, and in 1947 he and his wife and little daughter reached Palestine, just before the creation of the state of Israel.

Despite the antipathy toward the Yiddish language prevalent in the young state, Sutzkever managed to found what became *the* greatest Yiddish literary journal, *Di goldene keyt* (*The Golden Chain*), which fostered the regeneration of Yiddish literature after the Holocaust. He became an icon throughout the Yiddish-speaking world and remained creative until almost the end of his life. He died on January 20, 2010, in Tel Aviv.

Green Aquarium was not Sutzkever's first published work in prose; his 1946 memoir *Vilner geto* (*Vilna Ghetto*) is a vivid, often harrowing account of his and other Lithuanian Jews' experiences in Vilna during the war years, and as editor of *Di goldene keyt* he published numerous articles on literary and cultural topics. Until the early 1950s, however, his literary creativity had been expressed entirely in poetry: short lyrical verse and longer epic poems. When he did start writing literary prose pieces, they usually appeared first in *Di goldene keyt* and were then collected in several volumes. The fifteen texts that make up *Green Aquarium* were published together as the final section of a 1955 volume of poetry titled *Ode tsu der toyb* (*Ode to the Dove*). (Interestingly, Sutzkever did not call these prose pieces "stories" but rather "short descriptions.") Sutzkever's pen was subsequently silent for fifteen years—as far as prose-writing was concerned—and then eight new stories appeared between 1970 and 1974. These were collected and published with the title *Meshiakhs togbukh* (*Messiah's Diary*), together with the fifteen previously published texts, in a volume also titled *Green Aquarium* (1975).

Sutzkever then assigned more and more importance to the medium of prose. The volume *Dortn vu es nekhtikn di shtern* (*Where the Stars Spend the Night*), published in 1979, comprises twelve short stories written from 1975 onward. These twelve, together with twenty additional texts, make up the collection *Di nevue fun shvartsaplen* (*The Prophecy of the Inner Eye*), which appeared in 1989. Six more short prose pieces written in 1989 and 1990 were published in a 1993 volume of memoirs and literary criticism, *Baym leyenen penimer* (*Reading Faces*).

It is interesting to consider why Sutzkever, a natural and spellbinding storyteller, only started writing prose after almost twenty years as a prolific poet. We can speculate that his inspiration to create stories evolved out of the Holocaust itself, which remained for him a defining, constant inner presence that could never be forgotten or ignored: "[T]he past is a real and tangible thing for me," he said in the opening sentence of "The No-One." But as the overwhelming experiences of these horrendous years gradually receded from immediacy into memory, he needed another, complementary medium to explore them again in more detail. In 1962 he wrote, "Death's kingdom is now a legend. The dead live there on the other side of life. I send them poetic signals, as to beings on another planet. I seek common words, so that we can understand and love one another." Through the prose texts as well as his poetry he attempts to bridge the present and the past, to mediate between the living and the dead. This theme is present at both the beginning and end of *Green Aquarium*. In the first text the narrator experiences a wonderful but tragic vision: the earth turns into a green aquarium, and behind its glass he sees those who have perished, including his beloved. He can communicate with her but not kiss her, and when he attempts to smash the glass to reach her world the vision is destroyed and the dead disappear. They depend for their continued existence on the poet's remaining in the world of the living. In the last text the bee, which represents the soul of one of the dead, "[stabs] its last fiery honey" into the heart of the narrator so that, symbolically, the dead become part of him forever. Thus Sutzkever emphasizes the complex relationship between survivors and victims—he carries the burden of their existence, which is both painful and sweet, like the fiery honey of the wild bee, and he must give voice to their stories even though he cannot ever truly reach them through the pane of glass that separates the two realms.

The "short descriptions" of *Green Aquarium* all relate, though sometimes obliquely, to the traumas of the Holocaust. They are teeming with strange human beings, magical happenings, and fairy tale motifs. The imprints of children's hands on a frozen windowpane can talk, and the story they tell brings tears to the eyes of a frozen horse's head; the gallery of a synagogue turns into a pair of bronze eagles that carry an artist and his portrait off into the clouds; a man in clothes made from the pages of holy books finds a skull in a casket and from that moment on wears it over his own head. Sutzkever's infusion of outward reality with strange and mysterious happenings shows his affinity with the magical realist writers of the 20th century.

—ᓃ—

During the 15 years between the appearance of *Green Aquarium* and the first stories of *Messiah's Diary,* Sutzkever wrote a large body of lyrical poetry in which there is a strong sense of liberation and poetic renewal. Though the Holocaust is never absent, it gradually undergoes a poetic transformation: there is a mellowing of the pain and grief and an increasing emphasis not on mere memorialization but on the integration of the dead into Sutzkever's present life and consciousness.

Once he started writing prose again, this change of perspective is evident. The later prose works, which Sutzkever was happy to call *dertseylungen* (stories), are mostly longer narratives, episodes from Sutzkever's childhood and youth, the war years, and his life in Israel—all re-created by the author in his eloquent, idiosyncratic, and fantastical prose.

The figure of the first-person narrator becomes more prominent and is closely identified with Sutzkever himself; he develops in his later works a portrayal of the poet as a custodian of the past. He is often seen as having the special gifts of a seer or magician—in the story "The Prophecy of the Inner Eye," the narrator, through the power of his imagination, enables a bereaved mother to *see* her son, alive and happy, in a far country, "he and his bride under a canopy of stars."

Within this imaginative world, real historical figures and events appear on an equal footing with miraculous happenings. In "Portrait with a Blue Sweater," the narrator—who is here unequivocally identified with Sutzkever himself—voices to his close friend Marc Chagall his deep regret that a youthful portrait of him (painted by the Vilna artist Chaim Urison in 1936) had disappeared while he was absent from home. As they talk around the dinner table, there is

[s]uddenly a knock at the door. Believe it or not, the portrait of the

blue sweater comes in and climbs up on the eastern wall, where his home is to this very day. The only one who wasn't astonished was Marc Chagall. With a movement of his hand he pointed to the portrait and congratulated me with a Vitebsk smile: "If you truly long for something, you'll get everything you long for."

This fusion of biographical reality with the mysterious realm of the imagination gives Sutzkever's prose its particular character; as readers, we suspend our disbelief and enter with the poet into his multifaceted universe.

In many of the stories, the convention of the framework narrative is used most effectively. The narrator—sitting at home or in a café, walking the streets of Tel Aviv, or in one instance while on a visit to Paris—encounters an acquaintance from his past. This acquaintance is often someone whose life the narrator has decisively impacted, and the meeting provides a chance to relate that person's story. These stories can be powerful and moving: a dancer tells how Sutzkever's kiss had been the "amulet" that preserved her mother's life during the Holocaust ("In Memory of an Amulet"); a surviving twin relates the story of her sister's courage and dignity in the death camp ("The Twin"). By setting their stories within the context of his present life, Sutzkever fuses the past and the present, Vilna and the land of Israel. He rescues individual identities from the anonymous mass of victims, a kind of victory over those who tried to wipe out all traces of the Jewish people.

He also honors these individuals by the way he depicts them. The cruel oppressors are deliberately left anonymous and are usually referred to metonymically—as an "iron hoof" ("The Prophecy of the Inner Eye") or "an echo of hobnailed boots" ("Between Two Smokestacks"). Sutzkever refuses to dignify them with names or personalities, which would immortalize them. By contrast, almost all the central protagonists have names and individual identities. None of them submits passively to their fate; each story centers on an act of resistance, rescuing something or someone precious from death or desecration. An old woman saves her granddaughter from an aggressive peasant: by the force of her personality she convinces him that God is behind her, watching him ("The Peasant Who Saw God"). Felicia Poznanski gave away her diamonds and existed as a beggar in order to save her husband's manuscript ("The Woman in the Panama Hat"). In "A Funeral in the Rain," Kolya carries the body of a young boy for miles in order to bury him in hallowed ground rather than leave him in an icy swamp. Some prefer to die rather than to continue with a morally or emotionally impoverished life, like "The Last Woman among the Blind," who deliberately chooses death over an existence without her lover and soul mate; her self-immolation while dancing is a challenge to a blind God.

The truth at the center of all Sutzkever's prose is that courage, personal integrity, and love are more powerful than death. His characters resist the forces that would make them lesser human beings, as in the story of Bomke, who, when he is finally given his longed-for opportunity to take revenge on the man who hanged his little daughter, rejects it. In his imagination he has been able to experience this revenge, but the act of going back to the house where his daughter was born, to kiss its ruined walls, is for him the better choice.

This central theme of personal dignity is nowhere more powerfully evoked than in the closing lines of "The Twin." A death camp commandant amuses himself by watching the starving musicians of the camp orchestra scramble for his discarded orange peels—everyone except for the violinist, Hodesl. For this act of "defiance" she was murdered. Her sister, relating this decades later, sees the scene being played out again in the sunset over Jaffa and cries out triumphantly: "Hodesl will not bow, Hodesl will not bow!"

The Sutzkever scholar Ruth Wisse asserts that Sutzkever is always and only a poet, and that his narratives "invite definition within some new category of poetic prose." This is true for all the stories in this collection. The denseness and proliferation of Sutzkever's imagery, the subtle nuances of his language, and the ambiguities in his descriptions, which create a sense of unstable, shifting reality, make Sutzkever's prose rich and multilayered. The abundance of powerful, sometimes grotesque and disturbing similes and metaphors, his use of assonance, and the cadences of his sentences—all this is intrinsically poetic.

Thus Sutzkever the storyteller is inseparable from Sutzkever the poet. Both with regard to his themes and the powerful poetic language through which these themes are brought to life, his lyrics and his prose form one great poetic whole. His status as a major twentieth-century poet is gradually being established internationally through translations into many languages. The publication of this volume, containing almost all of his prose in English translation, is a vital contribution to a wider knowledge of this genre of his work, so essential to our understanding of Avrom Sutzkever's monumental literary oeuvre.

Heather Valencia
November 2019

TRANSLATOR'S NOTE

Sutzkever's prose poems, like the genre itself, straddle multiple boundaries. They are narratives with plots that sometimes meander, sometimes double back, and often let the reader off some distance from where she thought she would end up. They are prose, but thickly planted with poetic imagery—or poetic imagery at the service of description and character-building. Life and death meet in each page, as do the undead and the dying. These are written in the aftermath of the Holocaust, but they are not about the Holocaust any more than the story of our ancestors' deaths is our story. They are less about the camps than about ghettos, partisans, refuge, escape, and the life after.

There are common difficulties faced by translators of texts from Yiddish: traditional religious language, Slavic idioms, phrases from lost worlds. Few of those apply to Sutzkever's prose poems. Yes, these are Jews (these stories are in Yiddish), but these are also people plucked out of their particular circumstance by the universal phenomenon of genocide. A narrator dashes through landmines. Children seek food for a dying grandmother. Memoirs are saved from a capsizing ship. Thus there is the common Jewish vocabulary but also the particular lexicon of wartime hideouts; glowing searchlights; schools festooned with barbed wire.

As the Yiddish poet who (perhaps to an extreme) has represented Yiddish poetic modernity for so many of those who care about that literature, Sutzkever as an object of translation has caused my soul to resound in awe like a bell. If my product is worthy of the task it is thanks to those who have helped me, from Bill Johnson, Barbara Harshav, Seb Schulman, and the other devoted participants and faculty of the 2013 Yiddish Book Center Translation fellowship; to the small but mighty fellowship of Yiddish translators who manage to be congenial, good-humored, and self-effacing around the globe; to the hardworking editors (especially Veronica Esposito), copy editors, and most of all Mindl Cohen, academic director at the Yiddish Book Center. Experts on Sutzkever including Avrom Novershtern, Ruth Wisse, and Karolina Szymaniak have been generous with their time. I was very glad Heather Valencia, whose translated anthology of Sutzkever's poetry is required reading, contributed an introduction.

I also believe that translation needs a source, and I find my life in that source: my Yiddishist comrades (especially Khane Eakin Moss, Binyomen Moss, Brukhe Lang, Marc Caplan—the Baltimore crew) and my Chasidic friends (especially Katle Kanye). And most of all Celeste, Beylke, Mikhl, Esterl.

It is customary to say that any errors are mine and any felicities due to other people. Even the foundational felicity of being interested in Yiddish is due to my parents' support for a language-besotted teenager and the support of my high school English teacher, Diana Donsky of blessed memory, in remembrance of whom I gave my youngest daughter her second name.

As the rabbis said in another context, there is much else that I have not recited for you here. Consider this volume an invitation.

Zackary Sholem Berger
March 2020

Green Aquarium

GREEN AQUARIUM

I

"Your teeth are bars of bone. Behind them, in a crystal cell, lie your enchained words. Remember the advice of the elder: the guilty, who drop poisoned pearls into your goblet—set them free. Out of gratitude, they will build your eternity. But those others, the innocent, who trill obtrusively like nightingales over a grave—those you must not spare. String them up, be their hangman! Because as soon as you release them from your mouth, or your pen, they'll become demons. If I am not speaking the truth, may the stars plummet from the sky!"

This testament was left to me years ago in the city of my birth by an old solitary poet, somewhat flummoxed, with a long braid in back like a fresh birch broom. No one knew his name, knew where he came from. I only know that he wrote rhyming notes to God in Aramaic, dropped them into the red mailbox near the Green Bridge, and then thoughtfully strolled by the Viliya, waiting for the mail carrier in Heaven to bring an answer.

II

"Walk through words like you'd walk through a minefield: one false step, one false move, and all the words that you have threaded onto your veins your whole life will be torn apart, and you with them . . ."

That's what my very own shadow whispered to me when both of us, blinded by the searchlights, traveled by night through a bloody minefield, and every step that I set down for life or death sheared my heart like a nail piercing a fiddle.

III

But no one warned me to be careful of words drunk on otherworldly poppy blossoms. Thus I became the servant of their will. But I can't understand their will. Certainly not their secret: Do they love or hate me? They wage war in my skull like termites in a desert. Their battlefield pours out of my eyes with the radiance of rubies. And children go white with fear when I tell them, Happy dreaming to you!

Recently, while lying in the garden on an average day under a branch of an orange tree—or maybe it was kids playing with golden soap bubbles—I felt a movement in my soul. All right, my words are heading out! In their victory, they vowed to occupy positions previously off limits: people, angels, and why not stars? Their fantasy plays on, drunk on otherworldly poppy blossoms.

Trumpets blare.
Torches like birds aflame.
Accompanied by musical lines, frames.

I fell to my knees before one of those words, apparently the overlord, riding ahead in a crown set with my sparkling tears.

"That's how you leave me, no goodbye, no see you later, no nothing? We wandered together for years, you nourished yourself on my time, so before we separate, before you go off to conquer worlds—one request! Give me your word you won't turn it down."

"Agreed. I give my word. But no long sentences. Because the sun is curving down the blue branch, and in just a moment it will plummet into the abyss."

"I want to see the dead!"

"That's quite a wish! Fine. My word is more important to me . . . look now!"

A green knife cut open the earth.
It turned green.
Green.
Green.
Greenness of dark pines through a fog;
Greenness of a cloud with a burst gallbladder;

Greenness of mossy stones in rain;

Greenness uncovered by a hoop rolled by a seven-year-old girl;

Greenness of cabbage leaves in splinters of dew that bloody the fingers;

First greenness under melted snow in a circle dance around a blue flower;

Greenness of a half moon, seen with green eyes from under a wave;

And celebratory greenness of grasses lining a grave.

Greennesses streaming into greennesses. Body into body. And the whole earth has now become a green aquarium.

Closer, closer to the green swarm!

I look in: people are swimming like fish. Innumerable phosphorescent faces. Young. Old. And young-old together. Every person I ever saw in my entire life, anointed by death with green existence; they are all swimming in the green aquarium, in a kind of silky, airy music.

Here the dead are alive!

Underneath them rivers, forests, cities: a giant plastic map. Above them, the sun floating in the shape of a fiery human being.

I recognize acquaintances and friends and doff my straw hat to them:

"Good morning."

They answer with green smiles, as a well's response to a stone is a series of broken rings.

My eyes slap with silver oars, they race and float among all the faces. They search, looking for one face.

I found it, found it! Here is the dream of my dream . . .

"It's me, darling, me, me! The wrinkles are just a nest for my longing."

My lips, swollen with blood, are drawn to hers. But—oh, no—they are stopped by the glass of the aquarium.

Her lips swim to mine too. I feel the breath of burning punch. The glass is a cold cleaver between us.

"I want to read you a poem, it's about you, you've got to hear it!"

"Darling, I know it by heart, I'm the one who gave you the words."

"I want to feel your body one more time!"

"We can't get any closer, the glass, the glass . . ."

"No, the border will soon disappear, I'm going to smash the green glass with my head . . ."

The aquarium shattered after the twelfth smash.
Where are the lips, the voice?
The dead, the dead—did they die?

No one. Opposite me, grass—and overhead, the branch of an orange tree, or maybe kids playing with golden soap bubbles.

THE WOMAN IN THE PANAMA HAT

Before the time of slaughter, I sat writing one day in a dark little room. It was as if the angel of poetry were confiding in me: "The choice is in your hands. If your song inspires me, I'll protect you with a fiery sword, and if not—you've got nothing to complain about. . . . My conscience will stay clean."

In the small room I felt like the clapper of a bell. A touch, a vibration—and the bell might start ringing.

Words were hatching in the quiet.

The knock of a finger bone was heard at the door.

The quiet suddenly spilled over the floor like mercury from a broken thermometer.

"Danger. A friend wants to warn you."

I drew back the bolt.

A woman appeared. She seemed like a beggar. No surprise there. In the pause between death and death, when hunger ruled in full skeletal glory, masses of beggars migrated from place to place like swollen locusts. But this beggar astonished with her clothing: a straw summer hat decorated with dried wild strawberries; a long, old fashioned crinoline—a rainbow of rags; a bag at her side; around her neck a thin strand of obsidian, which ivory opera glasses were hanging from; and on the ends of her patent leather shoes—two ravens with open, blood-red beaks.

I asked nothing but gave her a heel of bread, moldy at the edges.

She took a couple of steps forward, took the bread, put it on the table—and then, with the voice of a cuckoo:

"If I'm not mistaken, you're *that* character, and if so I won't take the bread."

"You can have a seat, auntie, you'll be more comfortable that way. The bread? Moldy, sure, but I give you my word that I don't have any other bread. We will live to eat challah again."

I showed the woman the only stool and set myself on the table across from her.

"Oh, that's not what I mean, in truth." Like a dancer, she lifted her crinoline so it wouldn't get wrinkled and sat herself on the stool. "Can I ask a small favor?"

"A small favor is a favor, auntie. You don't need to treat me with kid gloves."

"These sheets of paper with the ink still wet. Who wrote on them?"

"Me . . ."

"You're a writer?"

"A writer."

Tears started to flow not just from the corners of her eyes but from all her wrinkles. Pink, smiling freshness, like mist after a rain in May, blossomed from her soul.

"If so, good. Now let me unburden my heart. For these minutes the Almighty will pay you back in years."

She pulled from her sleeve a pink handkerchief bordered in silver and touched it to her lips. From the handkerchief—the dying breath of an old perfume. She started telling her story:

"My name is Felicia Pozansky. The writer I. J. Singer immortalized me in a novel. I looked different once, but that's not important."

From the other sleeve she pulled another handkerchief, this one of a multicolored peacock hue with a different scent of perfume, and she wiped the moisture from under her eyes and went on:

"This Felicia, let's say she's a different one, not the beggar who's sitting here next to you; once she was a rich woman, that is, my husband Ignaz was a millionaire. Nine factories, hundreds of looms. The president of the city lived in one of his mansions. Aside from that he was an honorary consul to Portugal . . ."

The sunset illuminated her wrinkles with the light of green fireflies. She was getting thinner, shrunken, and she seemed like a mummy or an ancient Egyptian princess.

"No one liked Ignaz, not even his family. People thought he was a misanthrope. Maybe. People shouldn't judge so quickly. There was a reason for his hatred of people. As a child he broke his nose like a clay pot, and the greatest doctors in the world couldn't put it back together. So he had to wear a replacement nose made out of rubber. Because of that, he lost the voice of a man and spoke really high, too high, like a newborn kitten.

"I did love him. Though not for his riches, or for his carriage. No. I loved him for his writing. He wrote a long poem in Polish about Job . . ."

At night, in his office, he would take off his rubber nose, so he could breathe more easily, and write the whole night through. Felicia was the happiest woman in the world. Pozansky the factory owner? No, a writer—like Byron, Heine! Byron was missing part of his foot, and wasn't he was the greatest writer of the century? Pozansky was also a writer, and he was missing a nose!

The setting sun lit up the sky outside my attic, which encased me like a copper bell. The crying of a child in hiding wandered its way to its Creator. The woman in the Panama hat kept on:

"On the first day of the war everything changed. A piece of shrapnel hit Ignaz in the head. Before he breathed his last he made her swear: 'Felicia, Felicia! Be sure to save my works. My whole life is there—both this world and the world to come.'

"Felicia fled the city with one suitcase. Inside was the long poem about Job, a packet of diamonds, and the costume she had worn to the masked ball where she had met Ignaz. She stole across the Lithuanian border. On the way across the river, her ship capsized and the suitcase fell into the water. Miraculously, Felicia swam to shore and told the border guard about the diamonds; he dove in twice and rescued the suitcase. He was an honest farmer, and they divided things up just as they had agreed: he got the diamonds, and she got—her husband's posterity, his work, and her costume. 'You can see it,' she said. 'I'm wearing it now, and I want to wear it at the masked ball of death.'"

The woman in the Panama hat suddenly stood up and curtseyed as she once had done at that heavenly masked ball. But something happened—what was it? She couldn't unbend. Her face went dark, her face shone like scorched paper, and on the edges of her straw hat the wild strawberries bled.

"I don't need any water—no water. It's just a twinge in my chest, such a silly thing. Where were we? Right, I'll make it short." Standing there, she peered at me through her opera glasses, and her voice began to sound as if a blood vessel of hers had burst.

"Now I'm a beggar, it's been a couple of years. There was a time when I taught Portuguese to two girls and got two potatoes for each lesson. But since the girls disappeared I don't have anyone to teach Portuguese to. So I beg. But just for a couple of pieces of bread. I wanted to find someone like you, a writer, and give him my dear husband's masterpiece. Because, dear man, I won't be here much longer. I'm going to meet the two girls . . . give me your word that you will preserve this poem about Job like your own papers, and after the war—maybe you yourself—give me your word!"

When her bony right hand with the elegant piano fingers closed itself on mine, the left hand took from her sack a pocket-sized notebook and put that on the table next to the moldy bread.

When the woman went downstairs, the bell sounded. It couldn't stand the quiet any more. The quiet of old people snatched off the streets.

CHILDREN'S HANDS

A single window in a basement, frozen over. On the pine forest of the window, the prints of two children's hands, like the priestly blessing. Between the hands, a forest opening to the outdoors, and the sun falling into the basement like a dead man into a grave.

The walls are covered with tufts of snow and glimmer like a salt quarry.

On the ground, in a corner—scattered rags from a bed, and among them, like gold teeth, hidden straw peeks out.

On the rags—a thick *Korbn Mincha* prayerbook, dripped on by wax bearing the imprint "The Widow and Brothers Romm."

Nearby, in a pot of sand, a frozen wax candle, twisted like a bird trying to pick out its own heart with a dead beak.

And in the middle of the basement, between the prints of the children's hands on the window and the *Korbn Mincha* on the rags of the bedding—a bronze horse's head, with a silver spot like a dagger at its temples and the cold, eternal eyes of black marble.

The children's hands in the window speak:

Dear head, our apologies. We did not chop you off a living neck. When the very last people disintegrated into ash, we found you in a butcher's shop, and slowly, under a stranger's long coat, we dragged you into the basement. We wanted you to satiate an elderly lady. The elderly lady lay here in the corner, just as lonely as you are now on the ground. A burning candle at the head of the bed. But all of a sudden—dogs, dogs, dogs. They attacked the elderly lady, your frozen flesh. Attacked the boy that we belong to. We really wanted to help him . . . we were dragged to the window, to the snowy forest; where are we, where are we?

When the children's hands in the window tell the story, the icicles melt from the bronze head. It becomes shiny, alive. Its left ear droops like a lock of hair. In the eyes of black marble, tears appear.

LADY JOB

From disintegrated clay nests, from barred windows and distorted doors, burning leaves of holy books travel to the sunset. Like children with their arms stretched out, as if the sun had given birth to them in the synagogue square and they're fluttering back to their mother.

When the sun hides her children behind a cloud, they leave their black tears, glowing soot, on the gallery of the city synagogue.

The two-story gallery, lifted in a pyramid above the ruins of alleys and byways, doesn't look the same as always.

Now the gallery has turned into an eagle on top of an eagle!

The top eagle, with the head of an animal and a blue breast, like a spring among roses that sits between purple wings, digs into the bottom one with the talons of his four bronze feet.

And the eagle underneath, with a head like an angel, a brilliant snake around its neck, and with its wings that are two boulders facing each other over a cliff, stands bent over the city synagogue. Its ten feet, columns hacked out of salt, wobble under the heavy wings.

Overhead, near the bronze legs of the top eagle, against the background of its blue breast, I see a little man hiding.

"Little man, who are you?"

"I'm the painter Yankl Sher, the painter of the alleys . . ."

He is standing before a canvas in his green velvet jacket. He got the jacket in Paris. It once was renowned in our city. People used to stop in the street and admire its beauty. It buttoned at the neck with a big brass hook. Its pleats shimmered like a peacock's feathers. It had dozens of different pockets full of paintbrushes, pencils, and notepads.

Now the jacket's hanging off him, swollen, covered with mold, as if worn not by a person but a rooster. And the brush that he's holding in his teeth looks like a cleaver.

His crossed, watery eyes bulge out over his nose, and two brotherly tears close them together.

Now the painter is looking at the crooked streets, then at the canvas, and he doesn't believe his eyes. He sees for the first time how the world has changed since he hid himself here in the gallery.

Who blew a church clear across the street? Why is City Hall suddenly here, at the slaughterhouse?

Who lit the lanterns in the synagogue's dead courtyard?

Wherefore then, oh dear God, was the Gaon's *shtibl* condemned to death by a hail of stones? For what reason, pray, was the little tree at the gate sentenced to burn?

Only the gutters didn't change.

Them too! Gleaming with blood . . .

Yankl Sher wants to rub the canvas clean. Where is the truth, on it or outside of it?

And maybe his palette is to blame, hmm?

Once he saw a little fiddle in the hands of a master. In the middle of playing— oh, no! The sounds were lost. The audience's astonishment was without end. The master was pale, like the dust of rosin under his fiddle's strings. Soon he put his ear up to it and said, "Ladies and gentlemen, the violin has breathed its last. Please rise and pay your respects."

He puts his ear up to the palette. It's alive, it's alive!

Clusters of soot from the burning leaves of holy books fall on his hair, on the canvas.

Now he grabs the brush from his teeth. The brush, as if it had absorbed the hunger of the artist, devours the paint. On the canvas, the spots of snow disappear. From the young, fresh, springlike earth an aged lady blossoms with ever more vigor.

That's how the eighty-year-old looks. She's come back, back to life! A black Shabbos dress with crystal buttons. White hair, dazzlingly white, like frozen milk. Her face—a tangle of silver wrinkles. Spring brooks quiver within them. Plish, plash. The sun's dancing in the brooks, tossing little rabbits with its cold bayonets. And the aged lady, just a touch bent over, is carrying a blond girl piggyback.

Behind the aged lady—faces, faces. A chimney with a slashed throat. On one knee, a window kneeling in the air. The gate over the alley, under which the aged lady is moving, is open with a black crack.

Yankl Sher took a big step back. "Yep, that's what she looked like, the eighty-year-old woman. All that's missing now is . . . hey, what's missing?"

His watery eyes bulged out even more. Overflowed and dripped onto the palette. A moist, passionate pink covers his face.

The aged lady is walking . . . with a *shel rosh* on her forehead . . . she had picked up the *shel rosh* off the ground, from a gutter . . .

"Yankl, if you're a painter, paint the *shel rosh*!"

He dips the brush into the fallen tears, into a spurt of red: and the aged lady, with the blond girl riding piggyback, is striding now under the split gate, between bayonets, with a little house on her forehead, where God lives.

"Lady Job, that's what the picture will be called . . ."

The gallery trembles. Both eagles rise up. Two pairs of stormy wings. Together with Yankl Sher the painter, together with Lady Job, together with the kneeling window and the alley, the eagles escape into a cloud filled with lightning.

THE LAST WOMAN AMONG THE BLIND

Her eyes do not take form right out in the open like other people's. They dwell inside, in a separate face: two magnetic needles.

These needles are attracted to blossoming branches, sun and shadow, colors like beating arteries, faces, and, above all, the face of her blind lover.

They met for two nights, and their stony blindness struck sparks.

When he, with a face like a windowpane in the rain, climbs over walls at night, the moon tossing him a silver herring, he plays a yearning melody on the long recorder that he inherited, a bird's dirge, and she, in the attic, sees her lover in the mirror of his sounds.

Once he did not return. A deaf soot covered the mirror, as if blindness again entered the blind woman.

She feels his shadow. The flowing hair of his shadow. No attraction to the magnetic needles . . .

Someone stabbed a dead body!

Her fingers, ten buzzing bees, encircle the gaping attics, their air burned out like white ash.

"Come, sister!"

Her small, sighted sister, half naked, a book under her arm, two braids like open scissors, flows out of the shimmering corner with a lamp in her hand.

"Teach me how to dance; I've never danced, never in my life."

The lamp, a one-eyed owl, hanging on a beam. Under it, in the light of the bleeding eye, the two sisters dance. Accompaniment: the vanished recorder; the birds' funeral.

"Thank you, darling. Now leave me alone, and I'll see if God is blind."

The attic was overcome by a tremor, a nest picking up the vibrations of a saw.

The blind woman approaches the lamp slowly, her buzzing fingers turning down the shade, dripping kerosene on her braids, her dress; and the owl's eye is flooded with fire.

Over streets like haunted caves—sun, sun, sun.

Sun at bandaged windowpanes. Sun in faces. Sun on corpses that don't find death.

People, split into two separate images, take on bones again at the rosy glimmer of her dance.

She herself, the blind woman, completely made up of firelit eyes, illuminates the streets with her dance, sets the city, sets the clouds on fire: "Since you're blind, God, take away my fire!"

BETWEEN TWO SMOKESTACKS

Like a half-forgotten memory, the moon floats to the ruins of a black street and hangs between two smokestacks.

Long, nefarious shadows well out from the moon's arteries, like black blood from a slaughtered horse, melting the snows below all the way down to the pavement.

A person appears from within a smokestack, like a wild duck from dark water: "SHEIN-DE-LE!"

A second one climbs out from the smokestack across the street.

"TZAL-KE!"

"Sheindele, we've got to live."

"Yes, Tzalke. How long have we been in these smokestacks?"

"Not long. Three moons all told. Are you cold, Sheindele?"

"Cold? When the moon is shining, the soot on me looks like a silver fox. I am not scared of the cold. But they shouldn't warm up the oven in the building down there. I think there are sparks coming from the smokestack."

"No one lives on the black street. And the sparks are stars, lucky stars."

"No, Tzalke. Stars are cold and the sparks are hot, needle sharp, hot as kisses, but a lot more dangerous."

"Sheindele, who are you thinking of? Let's be honest, I myself saw—"

"No one can see people kiss, how did you see—"

"Next to the pit, before we ran away, before we hid in the smokestacks, you smiled at someone, such a smile. Who is he?"

"Oh, Tzalke, to be jealous of a smokestack . . . Okay, I'll tell you. It was . . ."

An echo of hobnailed boots cuts through the exchange.

In both smokestacks, opposite each other on the black street, the faces disappear.

THE PEASANT WHO SAW GOD

In a half circle like a taut bow, the marksmen stand around the canal, sleeves rolled up, and aim at the wheel of fortune: a heap of the condemned.

The glimmer of a brass crematorium in the next forest, groves of half-collapsed skeletons, casts its shimmer on the burning shadows, bones of the living dead, all of which together look like one person: soil cut and turned by a plow.

Only the grandmother with both grandchildren at her sides, a gray-haired eagle with spread-out wings, only she maintains the eternity of her face.

The grandmother remained among the last people.

Both grandchildren kiss her hands with fainting lips.

"Grandmother, why are so many people falling here?"

The grandmother lifts her head; it's blue and pure. A giant moon. From the grandmother's eye a tear floats out, which she had hidden for many years. The tear swims, flows, and floods the moon.

It starts to cloud over, rain, with warm grandmotherly tears. Those tears extinguish the bonfire, fill the canal.

Grandmother closes her eyes, blindly grabs a grandchild—and starts running.

Which one did she save, Chanele or Mirele? Can't deliberate on it. The child sleeps and the grandmother whispers:

"Chana-Mirele, Chana-Mirele . . ."

She wanders in the drenched darkness. Chana-Mirele sleeps on her shoulders.

Grandmother comes to a village. Behind a hut's windowpane a fire flickers. Grandmother sloshes through the water, falls, picks herself up, and then knocks at the hut, like at the heart of an angel.

"*Kto?*"

"Good person, let me in."

The door opens slowly, and a peasant, half naked, with a lamp in one hand and a whip in the other, appears on the porch.

He lifts his whip over the old woman.

But then a voice emerges, like a white wing, from the old lady's lips:

"You, man, what are you doing, are you blind, can't you see that God is in the rain?"

Clutched in the peasant's hand, the long whip aimed at the grandmother instead deals him a bite like a snake. He can't raise his hand, and he can't lower it.

He sees in the shine of the lamp:

An old woman with long white hair as if coated in lime. Her eyelashes hung with small droplets—pincushions. She's carrying a child on her shoulders—a blue sheep.

Behind the grandmother, among the threads of rain lined with trembling pearls, a form floats out and points a long lightning finger at the peasant.

His knees collapse, the lamp drops from his hand, and the blue sheep on the grandmother's neck wakes up.

"Grandmother?"

THE RING

A gathering of panting shadows, we made our way at night over the half-frozen swamps, whose thin ice beneath deceptive moonlight cracked from the wolf's howl under our tired, cut-up feet.

The waters, rich and old, with all sorts of weeds, roots, submerged birds, and sleepwalking beasts, dazzled by moonlight and mixed with swamp ooze, gave off a sour sharpness, like cherry brandy that someone had put aside to age millennia ago.

The gathering made its way ever farther into the swamps. We barely glimpsed each other, everyone's desires converged in a secret language of pupils, and all of us, drunk with fatigue, stumbled up onto a mossy hill and sank into slumber.

Only the breaths, ripples in water, quietly undermine the resounding, empty space and fill it with floating circles.

No one issues orders to get up. Our lips, like amputated fingers, can't move.

A humid warmth mists out of the bodies, and their clothes, as icy needle brushes, stick to them.

No, I won't fall asleep; someone *has* to be on guard, like the moon overhead. It too is exhausted from wandering in the heavenly bog. There in that heavenly bog, there's a mossy hill, like the night chamber of a swamp king. But the moon is clever and doesn't let itself be enchanted . . .

My legs are submerged in a sweet freeze; I can't move.

As I press my body to the distended hill holding icy water in its swollen mushroom, water starts rising slowly from the depths, encasing my skull in a thin glass. Only then, the tips of my toes begin to feel a sweet, heavenly warmth. And opposite them, in the air, silver-green eyes smile at me, striped with the brilliance of the moon.

"That's no wolf." The thought flew through my head. "A wolf is the foe of all smiles."

It became evident that the smiling, silver-green eyes belonged to a girl's face, and the girl herself was warming my icy legs with the silken sun of her body. She was the one who pulled off my heavy, tattered boots and enchanted my legs into her warm nest.

"You, you," whispers the girl, her breath snuggling up to mine, face like blue marble in motion. "I've been sending out my glances, wandering tears, for three years to find you; when the earth closed over me I rose like a tree, and when a whip chased me into the bonfires, I devoured the fire and conquered it.

"With whose powers? With yours. There in the garden, when we separated, you gave me as a gift a ring, a golden ring of your mother's with a sparkling ruby. Admit it: you enchanted the ring, and my love—like its ruby—did not stop glowing. This is my good angel; all deaths bounced off it and melted like butterflies around the flame."

She pulled off the ring and brought it closer so that I'd recognize it, carving sweet words into the air like into a tree's bark. Only then I felt the reality that disguises itself in dreams.

The rhythmic *thwack* of a machine gun was heard, shaking the roots like an elephant's trunk.

The gathering of shadows rose from the moss and headed deeper into the swamp.

Among the thin, naked trees and deadwood, the day smoked like yellow sulfur.

A stork with long, red legs standing in the shimmering swamp, bill fettered in ice.

Behind us, people are falling. The eyes in front don't see it, but the ones in the back of our head do.

The girl stops suddenly: "I have to run back to the hill. I lost the ring."

Before I manage to stop her, her hand flew out of mine like a white dove.

I was left alone.

Alone as the stork whose bill was fettered in ice.

Some of the friends fell, some fled into the wilderness.

I scream, "Awooo!" I sniff out her breath like a wolf. Run barefoot there and back. And bam! I sink up to my neck in a pit of water.

The day went out like a match. The burned-out stick, in its thin, red smoldering, still illuminated the horizon for a time.

Then the night dropped like a scorpion.

The next morning, in unhinged wandering, I finally found the hill. But even less than a dream was left of the girl.

I barely was able to free myself from the net of water, and I dragged myself to the grove—inhabited only by birches.

Drunk from desperation, I ripped a stone from the earth and started pounding a bare birch with it, the oldest one in the forest. I hit it once with the stone. Again. Another blow, till the sounds of impact split into echoes portending thunder.

The stone fragmented with my last thoughts.

Then a form appeared.

Appeared among the tall, stripped birch trees. Like a birch tree turned into a person.

First its eyes came to be, salty amber, just out of the sea.

A while later, the disheveled head in a crown of thorns.

A snake around the neck.

Clothes on the body, tattered, unraveling, dangling strips. Somewhere in there the naked body flecked with poppy red.

"Hey, who are you, the swamp king's bride?"

The snake around the neck shook its head no. The form came closer. Suddenly a ring sparkled from her left hand, the ring with a drop of blood from the ruby.

From then on, when a yearned-for, beloved poem reveals itself to me, in the dream where sounds walk like people but vanish on awaking like the precious girl of those swamps, I start to pound my own heart with a stone made of words, pounding till the stone crumbles and I fall to earth with my last breath. In that minute it happens: the disappeared poem comes to me in reality, naked and bloodied, but with a golden ring of love, smiling through tears.

TO THE MEMORY OF A FUR COAT

When you became a fur coat you stayed a sheep.

When my mother bought you from a hundred-year-old Kyrgyz man for a sack of salt and delighted me with that gift for my seventh birthday, it was as if I imbibed my mother's breath, or if I had dressed myself in sunlight.

The days marched through the snow, cross-eyed and cut by daggers.

I made you my first poem. A snowman.

I was a spirit in your wings. Disappeared from myself. Seven dazzling doves brought me home.

You accompanied me through times, lands, with the melody of childhood, a warm fiddle.

You saw the North Star scratch me.

When I got too big for you, you gave me your two arms, the two sleeves, to lengthen our friendship.

I entrusted you, my coat, with my white scraps of paper the color of the moon, with dead-end, fragmented lines, like a drunk dancing in the snow.

Later, when my dovecote left for the clouds, who else but you and a flock of wounds accompanied me.

When my face looked like a giant wrinkled finger, you didn't let the purple ice freeze my smile shut.

One night, in a forest, on sinuous paths anointed with ice, a woman was beset by labor pains, and into you, my warm nest, the tiny blue child fell. As blue as you.

And again, naked, only you on my shoulders, I rode to the morning sun across a battlefield.

The snow, a pure nighttime sky. My horse, an anthem over the snow. Golden fish drop from the wound in his veined neck. My ribs are his relatives. Skin is superfluous. You became superfluous too, or perhaps you perceived my struggle, and like a sad glance, bluish in color, fell into the snow?

The horse rose up on his hind legs. His rider saw a blue sheep wandering into eternity: "Baaah—baaah—"

And a wolf, sharp in the snow, a dazzling four-legged knife slashing through the landscape.

DEATH OF AN OX

With burning horns—two crooked wax candles—under a radiant yellow halo, an ox issues out of the flaming stall with a hoarse bellowing as if a golden cleaver were stuck in its throat. The dried dung stuck to its hindparts steams with purple mist, and the flesh from its front legs all the way up to its head glows like torched weeds.

The first falling snow—as if someone dumped a huge flock of pearly white doves from their warm slumber in heaven's dovecote and chased them across the young earth—that snow can't hold the fire. When the sparks, flying red needles, wake the falling doves with their slender stabbing, those doves are devoured by the greedy fire in no more than an "Oh." The fire becomes even wilder from the power of the devoured snow doves, binds its victim even more joyfully in copper staves, sits on its back like a naked satyr, and flogs the ox with whips from a bonfire.

A mooing reaches his ears, a horrible yearning mooing, a thunder of clipped wings.

He can't answer. Mouth open, but he lost his tongue.

He keeps going with the same momentum. The fire rises from the earth, reaching from the dark swamps of sunset all the way to the lake.

Only when he storms into the lake up to his knees—and with his double-vision elliptical eyes, like multicolored, melted glass, he sees another ox in the water, upside down, with its burning horns facing into its sky—does a human smile appear on his face.

The copper staves break.
The snow pours down.

And the ox turns his head to the left, in the direction of his home village, where only a dark chimney like a dead hand remains. He doesn't move a muscle.

The horns flame for a while, like a candle at the head of a deathbed, and go out with the day.

BEHIND THE GOLDEN VEIL

The sun, a hovering bog with green spots, apparently decided never to set.

The steps of the shining spring were frozen. Its breath in the depth of the woods—a moist mirror.

Two people walking at the edge of the forest.

Joachim, the blacksmith from Zosle, was in front. A rope around his fur coat, on his back the stitches of a yellow star that vanished here in the forest. Carrying an ax on his shoulder. The ax is like a dazzling skeleton of a wolf, flat head facing backward. A wolf that ripped itself to shreds.

I'm the second person walking. A saw, serrated armor, protects my ribs. Joachim was the one who taught me how to put the saw on. "It's handy, and you can laugh at bullets."

Like hunters who sniff out an animal, we're stalking our victim, which happens to be a tree. The kind of tree people call deadwood, bark falling off like a leper's limbs, proud roots transformed into veins of ash, split naked body light blue like burning alcohol.

We're stalking a dry tree whose wood would burst into flame with the first match.

The ox lost in the woods, whose blood sated Joachim's ax, has lain frozen for a few days by our earthen hut, without proper wood for a tasty meal.

The dead ox is lying on its side in the snow, dark cherry-colored hide half stripped from the neck to the thick belly and no farther. Lying in a white bed under a white blanket.

"Hey!"

"What's going on, Joachim?"

"Right in front of us, a deadwood tree!"

"Your imagination."

"No, friend, you can tell those trees apart at night. Around it, you see there, a golden veil."

We come closer. Joachim had guessed it. A thick, old, gnarled and rotten oak, lifeless.

"This one'll be enough to roast a herd of oxen; it's dry as pitch." Joachim chops his ax into the tree.

I observe the victim again and my saw flies off of my body with wings of steel.

"Joachim, the tree is wreathed in smoke; I have tears in my eyes."

"A black cloud is smoke to him! In spring, the black clouds wander like people, and their tired legs rest on the trees. The saw! Let's play the violin!"

The saw bites its teeth into the oak and the snow underneath is saturated with purple sawdust.

"Joachim, can a black cloud be this nasty? A heart can, of course, but not a black cloud."

Joachim wipes his eyes with his sleeve and the saw sticks in the tree like a ship between ice floes.

We go a few steps away from the oak and wash our stinging eyes with snow.

"Joachim, what do you say now? In spring the black clouds wander like people?"

The blacksmith from Zosle doesn't back down.

"Nasty, dark clouds. Let's keep sawing!"

We're sawing and sawing. And, unbelievably, from the dead tree comes a living melody.

A Jew reveals himself, under the dangling bark, in a tallis, smiling with that same bitter greenness like the sun that doesn't want to set.

"We've lived in this tree for about twenty months. That's right, ladies and gentlemen, me and my wife. She's baking potatoes in a foxhole and I'm saying Psalms up here. Thank you, dear God, that I didn't fall asleep. A miracle, a miracle. If I weren't saying Psalms I would have fallen asleep, and that saw of yours would have cut me to pieces."

A FUNERAL IN THE RAIN

A man with a heavy bag over his shoulder approaches a dark city in a rainstorm. A bolt of lightning—the blood of a shattered mirror—sets alight the pillars of rain in the deluge.

In the middle, the man with the heavy bag.

He looks like a black half-moon rimmed in gold.

No, his tongue has never tasted rain like this. Actually, not really rain—the magician in heaven had melted time! Yesterday, today, and tomorrow—all gone. The spring of the first human being and the winter of the last were fused in a huge crucible forged from clouds. The crucible shattered. The melted time mercilessly floods the earth, devouring any minute now the traveler with his heavy bag on his back.

He can't deny it: his feet are *walking.* His feet are going and the rain is going along. It's a sign, friend, that time is still in its place, a splinter from time's soul is left somewhere. Not just any old where—literally in his chest. Lub-dub—time is working. Time and place love each other, obviously. Stupid brain can't separate them.

A gray corrugated wall, as if wolves are drowning in its midst, appears from behind the columns of rain.

Saint Paul's Monastery.

Here, in the monastery, in the vaulted, red-brick chamber of Sister Ursula, the forest dwellers meet. Occasionally a runaway convict finds his way here, with bullets in his body that changed their mind midflight; sometimes it's someone sick from typhus, in a raggedy soldier's coat like a bullet-riddled flag, borne on the sun-lit wings of the eagle on its single button.

Here, in the monastery, Ursula saved him. Later she became the forest liaison, and he, the man with the bag, would come this way for news.

He remembers that to the left, by the unkempt grove, there was a gutter under the wall, choked with stinging nettles, through which one could get into the courtyard.

Now he would very much like the nettles to sting and burn him, his hands, his feet, his memory—as long as they would hurt him somehow. But the glass-sharp needles had hidden themselves away from the rain . . . oh, sometimes you just miss pain. True delicious pain. Only someone who's numbed can understand that, someone whose fingernails have grown over his entire body.

The seventh window. Six. Seven. You have to knock seven times to get to Sister Ursula.

A lead door slowly opens.

A startled yellow candle with a wax flame—bees resurrected from their buzzing wax—wanders backward in the thin, fine fingers of a happily startled woman, tracing a watery, tortuous path on the square, red bricks of the corridor.

The young woman, his rescuer, in a mist-wreathed nightshirt, floating in the distance with her eyes facing the guest, looks like a mermaid in pearls as she comes down the corridor, swimming and glinting from darkly burning waves. And he, with the bag on his back—a fisherman with a net . . .

He leaves the bag in a hallway niche, and the narrow door of Ursula's chamber, a cover to an oaken coffin, slams behind them both.

"Kolya, what happened? Anyone would say you look like your grandfather!"

Kolya—or Kopl, as he was called at home—lays down on the floor in a corner with his hairy hands over his head so that his head doesn't escape.

"Right, Ursula, I look like my grandfather, since you now possess eternal youth."

She brings a towel and a pile of clothes.

"Change into these clothes. They're yours. You left them here last year."

"Ursula, what time is it?"

"Two o'clock."

"Thanks. It's not worth changing. In an hour I need to leave again. If you could, a glass of milk . . ."

When Ursula comes with the glass of milk, Kopl is already bound in sleep's sweet chains.

She puts his numb arms around her naked neck and brings him, as if he were a half-drowned man, to the island of her bed.

Her lips, sharp-edged and warm, jump across his bony face—like birds that can't yet fly making their way over thorns.

Her nightshirt mists away from her. Her sunny body dries out the rain from his bag of bones.

"Kolya, I saw you before in a dream. Are there one or two of you? No, just one of you. Only when you aren't there are there two of you."

The fire from the candle—a rabbit with a burning hump—sinks farther and farther into its wax grave.

"Only when you aren't there are there two of you."

The rain pounds the glass with its leaden fists.

Kopl gets hit.

His eyelids explode.

Who's caressing him? Who's sucking the poison from his limbs? Oh, no—he's going to be late!

He frees himself, Kopl, from her sunny enchantment, jumps out of bed, comes running with the bag that he left in the hall, and quickly lays it on the bed.

Ursula falls at his feet crying, "My bag of sins, my bag of sins!"

"Ursula, not your sins; you can convince yourself of that."

A young woman stripped bare, in the aged-gray, smoky gold of the sputtering candle, on the background of red bricks, choking on tears, opens the bag of plowed earth while in bed, and suddenly it repels her as if by an electrical current. The odor of corpses floods the room.

A dead boy—a broken sculpture of blue, transparent marble, his hair a crown of laurels woven around his forehead and his lower lip a supine question mark—directs grave glances out from the bag at the two figures.

"Kolya, who's the boy, who's the dead angel?"

He pulls the bag back over the broken sculpture and relates, "Who is the dead angel? It's Yulik, my ten-year-old friend. On an oak, in a snowy nest, I saw a snowy boy near Lake Narocz. His wounds shone through the snow, just as here, in the room, the lightning shines through the window. A wolf with a jagged shadow was hanging around the oak. I had barely approached when the wolf, with the shadow in its teeth, disappeared.

"I brought the boy down from the oak. He looked like a frozen owl, and if you can imagine, Ursula, we recognized each other: the one who was swimming around in my flesh like a needle was his sister. Do you know who saved him in the city before he got to the forest? You're not going to believe it: a dogcatcher! When a horde of two-legged fires chased my young friend down, a dogcatcher threw a noose around his neck and hid him in the wagon among some captured dogs.

"Since I found the boy on the oak tree he became the apple of my eye.

"Until a month ago, when the violet storks drew an autumnal smile over the forest, the enemy had surrounded our people in a horseshoe. It appeared that we had only one path: to link up with the forest people under Commander Czarnohuz on the other side of the Narocz.

"It is a phosphorescent, moonlit night.

"In a long line, like ants, we make our way over the ice on the lake.

"I'm carrying Yulik on my back. A living prayer. Both feet froze in the oak tree. Folk remedies didn't help much. His breath and mine—the same breath. No, we were alternating breaths.

"In the middle of the pond, away from the snowdrifts, the enemy suddenly rises up before us. The night, a violet conflagration sets our faces on ice. I had washed my eyes with blood, so that the sharpness of snow and fire wouldn't dull them, and with the living prayer on my shoulder, and with legs that had turned into animals, I dash among the bullets, ever closer to the pine trees on the other shore. Look now, a wolf, a green wolf shooting sparks, with its shadow in its teeth, chasing, chasing us both, and now he's leaped up onto the boy, who's clamped around my neck. But in that blink of an eye—it sounds like a Bible story—as the wolf was coming through the air, the foe's bullet smashes its skull.

"A few days after the battle, it was carved in the icy scroll, Yulik disappeared. How? He was barely able to stand on his little legs! I can't answer that. But I looked for him for a long, long time and eventually found him next to the dead wolf.

"Yulik was bewailing his savior. I couldn't take him away from the dead wolf.

"'It's not a wolf,' he argued, 'it's a dog, a dog!' One star protected both when the dogcatcher took mercy on the boy and hid him in the wagon. Later, together with the freed dog, he came into the forest.

"At night, when Yulik was sleeping on the pond, snuggled up next to the icy hide, I took the creature away from him and buried it somewhere, but the boy wouldn't stop sobbing, 'I want to go to *him*. He went to the moon.'

"Since then he ate nothing, took in nothing but ice, and himself turned into ice, a frozen melody.

"You tell me: should I bury Yulik in a swamp? Abandon his bones to rust? For a month I carried my dead brother on my back. I want to bury him in the city of his birth. Ursula, what time is it?"

"Three."

"I'm not late yet. By dawn I'll take care of everything."

"Kolya, the city is full of soldiers. Comrades have been hanged on the Green Bridge."

"Rain is good armor. The armies in heaven will chase away those on earth. A spade—do you have a small spade?"

Ursula dresses herself in Kopl's clothes that he left a year ago in the monastery. She comes with a spade and stands next to the bed.

"Kolya, the armor will protect both!"

Kopl lifts the bag onto his back. Bent over, he again resembles a black half-moon hemmed with gold edges.

Ursula unbolts the door. Before they head out of the room, she puts the bed-sheet under her coat.

The candle—a midget with a burning hump—accompanied the funeral in the rain with its last waxen tear.

THE GOPHERWOOD BOX

He no longer remembers who entrusted him with the secret.

Maybe a dream.

A dream hare, on quicksilver feet, stole into his soul through some window he forgot to lock and told him the secret.

It could also be possible, he thinks, that the old man—who lived in the mausoleum at the cemetery and waited for his purple beard that was like a branch of rowanberries to grow into the ground and root him to the dead—told him with his stammering lips.

And maybe—he can't swear that it didn't happen—a cuckoo keened the secret to him in Yiddish.

He doesn't remember *who*, but someone had whispered to him that somewhere over there, in a well on Tatar Street, a gopherwood box was hidden, full of the most precious diamonds, without peer in the world.

The fiery tail of the war was still dragging through the dead city, like a part of a giant prehistoric creature.

The black sites of burned-out walls were besieged by clay clouds, as if the clouds were descending to rebuild the city.

One night, the man, dressed in paper garments that he had sewn for himself from loose leaves of holy books, went from the cemetery to Tatar Street to look for the well.

Because though he was as alone as a finger, the story of the gopherwood box had warmed his bones.

He didn't have to look long for the well. The moon licked its walls with lightning-bolt rays of light, like spores of mold. Nearby lay the well rod, like a gallows kneeling before the hanged.

The man leaned over the mouth of the well to look inside and saw nothing because its mouth was covered with spiderwebs.

So he tore open the closed net of spiderwebs and threw a stone into the well to estimate its depth.

The stone answered him.

Then he untied a rope from the well, knotted it around a hook, and, like a chimney sweep down a chimney, lowered himself in.

The water was lukewarm like the heart of someone who recently died.

Just then, when the moon, like a purple turtledove, emerged on its wings from the well with a sigh, the man found the gopherwood box under the water, hid it in his bosom, and his bones sang as he pulled himself up.

The morning star hung over the neighborhood like a drop of blood.

The man ran over glowing embers all the way to the old cemetery.

Only there, his heart pounding, his eyes like wild poppies, did he pick up the treasure with both hands and hold it in front of him.

He saw a—skull.

A skull like old parchment, with two shocking holes and a clever, living smile, looked at him from the ruin without a word.

"Skull, what's your name?"

When the hard-bitten teeth of the skull didn't answer, the man couldn't take it anymore and hurled it to the ground like Moses did the tablets.

But he immediately thought of the fact that the skull looked like his dad.

He covered the living smile with kisses, and his fiery tears overflowed into the skull's holes.

Kissing it, he felt at home. A warm tune began to play in his veins.

Suddenly a shapeless force repelled him:

"No, it's not your father, that's not what he looked like."

He picked up the skull again with both hands and like a beaten dog let out a wail:

"WHAT IS YOUR NAME?"

Then the man finally heard his own name.

He felt that the head that he had been carrying on his shoulders for so many years—was not his.

So he put the skull on his head, and keeping it on with both hands, in the paper garments that he had sewn for himself from stray leaves of holy books, he set out through the dead city to greet redemption.

BOMKE

After a year of darkness, Bomke emerged from the sewers into the liberated city. He resembled a citizen of Pompeii, covered in a lava of melted diamonds.

His thin, transparent legs—a dead spider's living parts—stopped in a narrow alley: a black coffin.

The sun set upon him like a locust.

Walls on both sides of the alley: children's toys.

Pink, pink in a world of pink.

He responded to the tap of someone on his shoulder—a little mouse. "Oh, goodness, it's you. Did you miss Bomke? No one in the sewer could sing you a tune? Hey, we'll stay good friends here too. You see how pink the walls are? Where's the pink from?"

Bomke pets the little gray thing on his shoulder. He remembers that's how he used to caress his Blimele.

At the word *Blimele* the pink disappears. The walls are no longer playthings; they're clay skeletons, with a cloud floating over them, an angel with sooty wings.

"Bomke," the mouse plucks at him, "what now?"

His memory is a path between stalks. You cut the stalks, but as you clear them, the path disappears.

"Bomke, you're a mouse like me, the liberated city is not for you. What about revenge?"

The angel with sooty wings bears away the alley—the black casket.

In front of him, like the trough of a dry riverbed and its dead fish in their sandy silver, a broad avenue appears—but without any life in the houses lining it. Along it march new soldiers to orchestral accompaniment, the brassy music like thunderclaps dancing at a wedding.

When the orchestra disappears together with the soldiers, only its sounds remain—pillars of coal.

Barefoot boys, smoke curling from their short rifles, escort somebody between the columns. He is tied up.

"Who's that lucky guy?" Bomke stops someone nearby.

"Some guy with pockets, the city's former hangman. They're taking him to be hanged."

"Really, the hangman, my hangman?"

And Bomke takes off over the pavement, catches up to the "guy with pockets."

But one of the boys leading the bound man, a boy in a sheepskin hat, face covered with green freckles, as if the sun were illuminating him through a net, blocks his path with a gun.

"Where are you going, citizen?"

"To see the hangman."

"Not here. In the Bernardine Garden."

Memory, a painter, mixes its paints in Bomke. Mixes them on its palette like souls. And with a long lightning bolt it dips him in the colors and paints, paints:

On a night in March, a fire starts in the peasant hut where he's hiding with Blimele. Cats meow with unrestrained sweetness. Holding the child at his bosom like a kangaroo, Bomke jumps from the attic into a snowdrift. Their quicksilver shadows seek to catch the next world. The next world is on the other bank of the river. Tonight, though, it's the devil who's boss. The ice cover of their home river shatters. Shatters from laughter. Its floes roar like oxen that smell blood—and crossing over them, Bomke and Blimele. Their steps are weighed out and counted like treasure. An ice floe cries like a child. Just thank the devil. Cross, cross over!

Their shadows on the bank—who conjured with their shadows? A shadow with the eyes of an eel, a shadow with a lamp?

Hanging from a cherry tree like a chandelier—two gallows. The man who's now escorting Bomke, as Bomke is tied up, hangs Blimele first. Like a spring bloom she trembles in the festival blue. And above her—swallows. Chirping swallows.

When he strings Bomke up, the rope breaks, and a razorblade falls from his pocket.

"How did you hide the razorblade?" asks the hangman.

"It's my secret."

"Can you use it?"

"Yeah."

"I'll let you live. I need a barber."

So now he's soaping up his chin, the hangman's, and scraping it with the blade. When it gets to the hangman's goose-pimpled neck, Bomke's hand starts shaking.

"I bet you'd like to slice it open, huh?"

"I'm not denying it."

"Scared, huh? You're scared?"

"No. Such a revenge isn't any revenge. Too small."

He keeps shaving the hangman.

Until one day, while the hangman is enjoying himself at a ball, Bomke manages to flee into the secret city.

In the Bernardine Garden, among the acacias, Bomke hesitates. He's got a rope on a branch—and the hangman sentenced to death.

"Bomke," the mouse asks him, "what did you mean then, 'Such a revenge isn't any revenge at all, it's too small'?"

"I meant . . . I meant . . ."

The hell with it! He can't answer.

But soon after he has a strange idea, a thought like a falling star. He'll run up to the boy in the sheepskin hat and tell him about his connection to the hangman so he'll let Bomke shave the hangman a second time with the hidden razorblade, and he'll hear the triumphant voice: "I bet you'd like to slice it open?"

But when Bomke played out that revenge in his thoughts, the mouse started to laugh.

Right after that he left the Bernardine Garden, back to the house where his Blimele was born, and deeply kissed the red clay sinking into itself.

HONEY OF A WILD BEE

The night will stay that way: old, an unmarried woman whose long hair is going gray.

The moon, whom no one can see and who left behind on the earth all those close to her, recites confession on her marble deathbed for the only living thing in the city, the gravedigger Leime, curled up on Rudnicka Street in a pile of sighing leaves.

Leime, who has been a gravedigger for as long as he can remember, who sowed a half cemetery with mothers' sons, will not bury anyone anymore.

Children, old people, all locals, have entered the kingdom of the stars. First they became burning pyres. Winds of bone, in tattered shirts marked with Stars of David, carried their sparks in a bloody crown and draped them over the world's skull.

Left his cemetery alone.

Abandoned the gravestones.

That's why the gravestones are bending down, heads bowed, as if they were parents insulted when the bride disappeared from the wedding canopy.

Leime is also left alone.

"Spade, where are you, gotta bury the moon . . ."

Now he sees the moon with his glass eye. There's a lock on the other one. The silver key is no longer in this world.

Once, a half century ago, he lost his left eye from a wild bee's sting.

The story about the wild bee is recorded in a town register:

One fine summer day, when Leime was lowering a corpse into the grave, the soul of the departed flew into the pit disguised as a wild bee—needing to whisper a secret before saying farewell forever.

Leime, an average man, did not detect the play of spirits. He didn't appreciate such monkey business and swatted at the bee with his clay-encrusted spade.

The bee let out a childish wail. Its polished, sunlit face assumed the visage of the dead man. A minute later, a screech was heard. Leime grabbed at his left eye, where the wild bee had flown in—like into a beehive. The eye quickly leaked out in a red, hissing wax under the gravedigger's hairy palm.

The whole city was up in arms. The fate of gravedigging hung in the balance. They didn't let him touch any corpses of the esteemed. But Leime didn't let up, and the arms were laid down. A doctor by the name of Tzirulnik put a glass eye in him, as blue and almost as big as a chicken's navel. Leime buried the story about the bee, together with the clods of earth, in the Zarzecze cemetery.

Winds, like mating cats, meow at his head.
There is no redeemer. The dead are far away. Someone should bring him a handwashing cup . . .
"Hey, spade, where are you, the moon needs burying!"
But he can't lay hands on his spade, his cemetery wife.
Shh! His spade is wandering around. Wandering by itself among hanging sparks. It's digging, his spade, setting infinity a-ringing.
Leime stretches a long arm to the moon, presses a star to its nostrils.
The silver feather doesn't quiver . . .

Then—I saw this myself—the wild bee flew out from his glass eye and stabbed its last fiery honey into my heart.

1953–54

Messiah's Diary

THE CLEAVER'S DAUGHTER

I

She was my first love, the slender redhead with cute freckles on her pert nose, like a poppyseed topping. I even allowed myself to imagine that she had as many freckles as she was years old, a freckle every year for good luck.

When I made her acquaintance, I counted nine of those presents on her nose.

The street where we grew up panted its way uphill, starting from the Green Bridge over the clay banks of the Viliya, ascending to the Sheskin Mountains, where the street became a trail going all the way to Vilkomir. Most kids from my street, and even a number of adults, called the girl "the cleaver's daughter."

Why did she get that name? Why was an orphan labeled that way? Because her father, Reb Elye, was a shochet? If that's the reason, it would be fairer to call her "the butcher's daughter." But why should you expect fairness if no one's treated fairly?

Many years later I often wished to portray in words my first—or nearly first—love, but I was embarrassed for my writing hand, in which a girl was reflected whose true name I didn't remember. For that reason, she would always slip off the page like off a sheet of ice.

Praised be my memory. Today he heard my prayer and blew her forgotten name into my ear:

"Glikele."

My heart was relieved. Now I can tell about her, sketch her in words.

II

From now on my memory isn't my boss. I remember what happened just as well as it does.

It's neither winter nor spring. It's Purim season, the happy holiday coming along any time now, but it's not hurrying; it's trembling on the tip of spring's nose, though spring can't—for some reason—finally sneeze. The hamantaschen are not yet here. As a matter of fact, Mother planted them in the garden next door and they should sprout any time now.

Even before the hamantaschen grow, Mother sends me to Roize-Eidel to buy a herring. My good mother already had her eye out for one, and since Roize-Eidel the herring seller had started wrapping up her schmaltz herring in newspaper, I loved carrying out this mission: attracted not so much by the silvery saltiness as by the dear words of love from the hero or heroine in the newspaper serials. But the storekeeper didn't always give me the pleasure—instead of a fragment of that serial, I often had to go home, disappointed, with no more than a herring.

Today I was fated to have an out-of-the-ordinary experience: I met Glikele in Roize-Eidel's store. True, we'd already known each other a while. How would we not know each other? We spent our lives on the same street, and from my court-yard—over the gray split fence—her house wasn't far. But because her father is Reb Elye, and Reb Elye is a shochet (I heard the chickens curse him on the eve of Yom Kippur), another fence stood between me and his daughter.

But now, in Roize-Eidel's store, the barrier disappears. It's not Glikele's fault that the hens curse her father! Did she give birth to him? I was sure that the hens weren't cursing Glikele. It might even be possible that they blessed her. Last year her mother died from a bad whooping cough, and feeling sorry for Glikele, I accompanied the coffin to the high bridge. A miracle that this girl has a grandmother, Granny Tzviokle, who loves Glikele—and Glikele loves her Granny Tzviokle much more than her father.

Roize-Eidel crawls out from behind the counter like out of a herring barrel. She's wearing an apron the color of tin, and perhaps the apron is made of tin—no one dares touch it. On her mother-of-pearl hair, brushed over the ears, she wears a tichel woven from silver scales.

Roize-Eidel is famous in the entire region. On Friday market days, the store is ringed by horses and carriages, like an inn. Peasants come from far off. There are those—they say—who come to Roize-Eidel's store from as far as Vilkomir, a city in Lithuania. They came over the border illegally because a herring of Roize-Eidel's is famous for its taste and smell in both countries. The farmers believe that her herring is so delicious because it's kosher.

When the storekeeper sees her two esteemed clients, she turns her salted head to me because I'm older.

"What do you say, little boy?"

I want to lecture Roize-Eidel: that's not nice! First of all, she should have turned to Glikele first, because a girl is worthy of respect, and besides, how can she see me as a little boy? But I don't have enough chivalrous courage to lecture her, so I answer in a grumpy voice. "Give me the same schmaltz herring you gave me the other day."

Obviously Roize-Eidel got up on the wrong side of the bed today.

First she grunts, and then her words start pouring out. "Little boy, you've already eaten up that herring. What, you think the sea is a machine? How can it keep feeding you schmaltz herring? I'm hoarse from telling everyone that this year the rains were late and so the underground wells in the sea were clogged. Without rains, the roe doesn't hatch—and without roe, no schmaltz herring. Even a holiak, a simple herring, is worth its weight in gold!"

I probably turned all sorts of colors from her lecture, because Glikele interrupted all of a sudden, coming to my aid quite respectably.

"So tell us what kind of herring you do have, and we'll know what to choose from."

The word "us" entranced me, attracting me to Glikele even more, the tips of my fingers touching her cold little hand.

Roize-Eidel sank down underneath the counter and emerged from the other side among salted barrels, as if overgrown with hair, rummaging in them, feeling around, sniffing, and finding something with the appearance of a rotten carrot.

"What I have is what I'm selling: a herring that stinks."

"Eat it by yourself," I cried out, doubly insulted that the herring seller allowed herself such a rude turn of phrase for an orphan's innocent ears, and grabbed Glikele quickly under her arm as we ran out of the store into the Purim eve, accompanied in the rushing gutter by a sun shattered into fragments, like the young bones of a broken fiddle.

The story of the herring seller in the store started spreading up and down the block. Glikele and I had absolutely no part in this. Roize-Eidel was the one who exaggeratedly blew up the incident. She even invented an entire story to insult me—that I grabbed the yellow herring and smeared her face with it.

But as soon as you start with a romance, insults and shame are worth it: Glikele was now my love. We walked together by the brick factory and along the river, when the moon slipped into the pocket of a cloud.

lll

"Darling summer, oh my love, buzz-buzz-buzz . . ." Is a bee buzzing in my veins? In any case, from time to time we have to cool our blood in the Viliya, but not where everyone goes swimming, which swarms with boys like an anthill with ants. I would much rather they not caress my lover's half-naked body with their sly eyes. Especially since, whenever she jumps out of the river and goes striding along the shore, one could be forgiven for thinking that she is wearing not a shirt but a wave—and if she's running, it's because she wants to catch her breasts dashing off in front of her.

So we swim far from an evil eye. A couple of miles downstream, where no one is swimming, the river curves to the left—and when you swim across the river, you're in the Zakret forest with the tall, blue-black firs, where it's cool and dark there in midday, like in a well.

And though Glikele felt like we should swim across the river, I was scared, scared of the whirlpools in the river and the whirlpools in ourselves. We could be dragged in and plummet to the depths.

We can't help it, though. We can't think about it. Both of us are dreaming of summer, and we let ourselves dream of it day and night.

After going swimming, I lie with Glikele on the warm sand, radiant with sun and summer. Sweet tongues of water caress the soles of our feet. Glowing gossamer engraves itself into the echoing blue. Both of us in a delicious silence, I slowly cover Glikele with sand. Before you know it, her small body is completely buried. Just her head and flowing, sun-reddened hair are peeking out of the sand. Like a sunflower, torn apart by a storm, lying submissive among the grass in the garden. Above us, a steel sunray breaks in two. The firs on the opposite bank do somersaults in the water. Glikele's eyes are now bigger than they ever were, and their color is celestial pink like bird's milk.

I bend down my head over hers, scared to cut open the silence: "Since you can't move and your hands are all covered up, I can let my lips do whatever they want."

Instead of getting angry, the girl bursts out laughing with a laughter that is too loud for an orphan. The laughter is carried playfully over the water and bounces like a stone far, far away to where the sunset starts: "It's too bad that my arms are all covered up; I can't hold you."

I try to laugh along with her sassy answer, but my lips are taken captive. Instead of Glikele, now I'm the one covered up to my neck in sand, and she has to take pity on me to set me free.

IV

It's clear as day that a good angel has me in mind. He is fluttering over my attic, and when I have fun he does too. So, for example, he frustrated my enemies, convincing Reb Elye that he should become shochet in the town of Worniany, coming home only for the holidays. For me it's always a holiday when Reb Elye is in Worniany. Then I don't need to creep around in other people's gardens with Glikele, hiding out from the busybodies in the stinging nettles next to the tall fence posts, getting stuck in the sandy shore next to the whirlpools; I can come to her house when I feel like it, even at night, and pour out my heart to Glikele till the rooster on the roof starts crowing—out of joy that Reb Elye has left.

Her grandmother, Granny Tzviokle, is a granny without a mean bone in her body. Only a crook would have a problem with her. Full of stories like a poppy's full of seeds. The only trouble is that Granny Tzviokle is paralyzed, can't move. Poor thing, she's always laying there, in a black silk dress hemmed with sequins, in a small wooden bed.

I like coming into that house, even when I know that Glikele won't be at home because she's gone off to the tailor or out to buy food. A father is a father; he doesn't forget to send home a couple of crowns from Worniany.

Granny Tzviokle can tell I've come in from the sound I make opening the door. I open it both slowly and with boyish impatience. And the door creaks out my good morning or good evening like a saw sawing another saw.

Granny Tzviokle doesn't remember how old she is, because the year is faded on her birth certificate. But she recalls well that where the Viliya River now runs there once was a birch forest whose trees grew higher than the castle mountain. She was a girl then, younger than Glikele, when she went with a friend of hers into the forest to pick wild strawberries. Each wild strawberry was as big as a fist—not like the ones now. Instead of a basket she carried them in a bag on her back.

"When did all that happen?" I ask Granny Tzviokle, astonished.

"In the first peacetime." She shakes her head, and I imagine a gray child lying in a crib. "Then there was a great famine; everyone ate up everything except for one wild strawberry with its roots; later, Emperor Napoleon came and set the birch forest on fire because he needed the birch trees to build himself a palace; then came a rain that put out the blaze, and from that rain, the Viliya was born."

However many times I hear the story, it never bores me, just like eating bread doesn't get boring. And the fact that Granny Tzviokle remembers all the charming facts so well and tells them the same way today as yesterday and the day before— that's the best sign that it's all true, you know?

Another story I like to hear is how she and her groom eloped from under the chuppah.

"What was his name, your fiancé?" I act like I don't remember, just for the heck of it, and the tips of my ears tingle.

"When my fiancé was a boy he was called Kishke, when he was a man he was called Kishl, and when my fiancé became a grandfather he was called Kiss."

"A beautiful name, very beautiful."

"A name is nothing. A woman can be called Gute and be evil or be named Chaye and be an angel. But Kishke was an exception. These days you don't see people like that."

"It's a pity I didn't know him," I say regretfully.

"Yes, it's really too bad. Whoever spoke a word with him became wise that very minute."

I swallowed her criticism and continued the thread.

"If he was such a genius, why did you run away from him from under the chuppah?"

"Dummy, what are you talking about? We eloped together!"

"I guess you didn't like the musicians."

"Musicians? Ridiculous. Don't make us out to be fools. We were too shy to get married, that's all it was."

"And where did you run away to?"

"Troker Street, to the cellar of Shapsal the Karaite. But we didn't have any rest there either, because a lot of cats attacked us."

"How many, Granny?"

"Round about a hundred."

"How many? I can't hear you."
"Round about a hundred, though I didn't count 'em."

V

I made big plans, figuring that Reb Elye did me a huge favor by becoming the shochet in Varnian. I'll be able to be the boss in his city house undeterred, enjoy Glikele's presence as long as I want, and see what's up in the black boxes where his old cleavers lay. Those cleavers, Glikele tells me, are hidden up high, over the top of the oven, between the oven and the ceiling, and I have a desire—an improper one—to open up those boxes.

But like Faivke the dovekeeper says, in his chamois leather boots and easily the biggest heretic boy on my street: "I don't know if there's a God, but I'm sure there's *someone* who tries to screw things up." So from the time Reb Elye left his household and went off to seek his fortune in Worniany, the One Who Tries to Screw with Things has certainly gotten on my case. As if with a cocked slingshot from a hiding place, he takes aim at me with sharp gravel and always hits his target:

First, the One Who Tries to Screw with Things shoved the ladder while I was crawling up, like a spider on its web, to grab a cleaver from the top of the oven cover—and I fell, breaking my left arm. But that by itself isn't such a tragedy. One can make love even one-handed.

My broken arm has a cast, and I carry it suspended from my neck on a sling that I keep close to my heart, like a widow carrying a baby; but what does the Screwer-Upper want from Glikele? After all, she looks like nothing so much as a dove sprinkled with ash. Who robbed her smile? No longer the pink bird's milk in her flowing hair. Even the freckles on her nose are obscured by a black cloud. What happened? I can't find out from Granny Tzviokle, and Glikele is full of silence.

A humid summer night sucks my blood like a leech. I want to go to sleep—no matter what it takes, let it suck me to the last drop. That's what I want, but it doesn't matter what I want. Sleep went out on a walk in sleepland and can't find the path back. Under the cast on my broken arm there's an annoying itching, and I feel like laughing and crying, crying and laughing. From the grates to my attic room, enticing odors are seeping through. There are flowers that no one sees, and just their spirits, like ghosts, reveal their blossoms in a garden where you can't stick your nose . . .

Lightheaded from the entrancing scents, I descend the wooden steps like a sleepwalker. Spilled mercury bounces over the rooftops. Over the street, bats swing in black cradles. The vault of night has the same color as my arm cast. Sleepwalking, I swim to Glikele—she needs my cure.

VI

The window of the little room where Granny Tzviokle is talking in her sleep is dark as the inside of a chimney. But at the second window, behind which Glikele is breathing, a long flame flickers behind a curtain. How should I let my girlfriend know that I am on the other side of the windowpane without scaring her? Maybe knock and call out her name? I never heard such a knocking from my heart. It must be a woodpecker knocking in me. The idiot pecker thinks I am pine. Such a brilliant thought. Woodpeckers don't peck at night. The idiot is me.

And now the curtain is drawn away and my lips are right on Glikele's lips. Just a thin pane of glass between us. In a moment—the pane melts away, my left arm forgets its fracture, and both it and Glikele help my right arm lift me over the sill.

Glikele's apron hangs on the chair across from the bed, blue with red dots like berries—you almost want to gobble it up. She herself is dressed in a glowing nightshirt that looks like a wave of diamonds in which she's leaping out of the river. I sober up enough to grab her by the hand and ask something.

"How did you know that I was snooping around at your window?"

"I would have had to be deaf not to hear your heart pounding," she answers. At the same time I heard both our hearts pound like two clocks pressed up against each other and bound by chains, when one strikes tick, the other answers tock in agreement, and look, one clock is stopping, it must be mine, and I only hear hers, not knocking but breaking out in silence just before tears.

I imagined something terrible must have happened to Granny Tzviokle. Even before my intuition took on words, the grandmother's voice floated to me from behind the wall. She is talking in her sleep, telling someone in her dream the story about the Viliya when it was still a forest and she went there as a girl to pick wild strawberries.

Glikele's cold hand is still in my right hand and is not getting any warmer. Now I see the floor is sprinkled with fresh sawdust. I was thinking that snow had fallen and that's why her hand was so cold, but what do I notice on the lit-up snow? Bills, torn-up paper zlotys. The snowy path is covered with cash. Did a rich landowner lose it? A strange story—the money is torn up, ripped to shreds, you can't even make out on it the eagles and the likenesses of heroes.

She tears her hand out of mine and curls up in a corner of the bed. "I don't need his gift. Even if he sends me millions it's all the same. You think he went to Worniany to earn more money? Nonsense. He went to get married, obviously. I'll go be a laundress or nurse kids to earn an honest living. Nothing is uncertain now. You only get one mother, and if my father wants to drop in here with another one, I'll take the green broom and chase them out of the house."

The rest of her sentences are in fragments, held together only by her tears. In any case, I could imagine what happened here: under Granny Tzviokle's pillow, Glikele found a letter from her father saying that he had struck it rich. The woman whom he is fated to marry is the possessor of a distinguished pedigree, and a head taller than him. If God grants it, he—Reb Elye—will come home for *Shvues* and bring his brand-new mate.

VII

At this point it was right before *Lagboymer*. We still have enough time before *Shvues* to prepare for the battle. Let my broken hand wither if I allow my Glikele to wash clothes or nurse other people's kids. It's not the end of the world yet. She won't go hungry with me. First of all, I'll arrange to loan her my fortune: the five dollars that my rich uncle sent me from America. Afterward I'll sell my bar mitzvah watch (I'll tell my mother I lost it) and give the money to Glikele—the money will be enough to live on for six months; then I'll go to work and hand over my earnings to the orphan. Of course, I was sick of my teachers in school. The Hebrew teacher, may he forgive me, is a dummy who can barely get his words out. The gap between one word and the other is wide enough for a hay wagon to drive through. The math teacher is an angry type and a wuss, plus he's a midget and so the students call him Dwarf. The Galitzianer, the guy who teaches Polish, the kids call Giant, and no one knows if he has another name too. The only problem is the teacher with the glasses—him I actually like. The only one who is smarter than his students. I am especially excited that he knows the names of all the stars.

My standing without hesitation at Glikele's side, my sympathy for her desperation, helps soothe her wounds. A wind issues again from her eyes with pink bird's milk, and the freckles jump out on her nose—one more freckle than her age.

Yes, the wheel of fortune turns to my luck and I win a treasure: Glikele is Glikele again, and she is happy with my offer to take a trip out of the city for all of *Lagboymer*. A distant relative was just visiting then from Haydutsishok, a pharmacist, who carried into the house the odor of valerian, camomile, and something a dentist smells of. True, when she heard that Reb Elye is still slaughtering in Worniany, the pharmacist grimaced—nonetheless, she will stay here till after *Lagboymer*. She'll figure out what to do later. So we had someone to take good care of Granny Tzviokle, and we can be free as birds. And my left arm was speedily recovering, the cast was carved off, and the annoying itching was no more.

I say to Glikele, "Where do you want to spend *Lagboymer*, in the Zakret forest at the green pond or in Werki?"

Glikele scrunches up her face in a girlish wrinkle that I see here for the first time—it snakes down the length of her face, from the blond-tinged fuzz on her high forehead to the freckles on her nose. "There are too many black crows in the Zakret forest. The green pond hasn't blossomed yet, so you can't swim there. Werki then. The forest there is young and dense, oozing with warm sap."

"Right, Glikele, we think alike. We'll take along one of your father's cleavers, and there I'll carve two sticks with it, one for me and one for you."

Glikele is so happy with our hike the next day that she doesn't dare ask why I must cut two sticks not with a pocketknife but with a cleaver especially.

VIII

The kids from my street greet *Lagboymer* with a campfire at the Viliya. The campfire is the kind that isn't extinguished by water. The kind of fire that gilds the river's fish.

The campfire glows with the spirit of *Lagboymer* on the frightened windowpanes.

Now is the time when Glikele fulfills my unclear will, clambering up the rungs of the ladder to take down from between the oven and the ceiling a cleaver for tomorrow's hike. I stay below Glikele, holding the sides of the ladder with both my hands so that the ladder won't slip and Glikele won't, God forbid, fall. The toes of one of her bare feet drift into my open mouth, and my teeth don't want to release their honey. The longer I sate myself with their sweetness the stronger my hunger is.

"Which cleaver should I bring down, for cows or chickens?" I hear Glikele's little voice overhead, a muffled whisper so that Granny Tzviokle and the pharmacist from Haydutsishok won't hear in the other room through the thin walls.

"The one for chickens is enough," I answer with feigned calm, and at the same time I feel a needle dancing down my spine. I can barely wait for that second when Glikele comes down safely off the ladder.

IX

In the young dense fir forest, flooded by rills of sap, summer is also young and dense; light blond, foamy, shy, curled-up moss. Sun and shade play hide and seek. The trees glow from the inside. Their roots drink from underground green fire and shine from the inside.

Quietly Glikele sits down first on the moss and unwraps black bread and cheese for us both from a bag. I like to see her cheeks filling up, moving with rhythmic enjoyment. I only envy the bread, which the girl kisses and swallows with such appetite.

There among the grass, opposite us on a chalk-white rock, a lizard with a bellows neck and a diamond head appears out of nowhere. But maybe I'm with Glikele in the Garden of Eden. Then it wouldn't be a lizard but that mischievous snake, wouldn't it, urging us to eat that fruit that we shouldn't?

"Listen to my heartbeat." Glikele takes my left hand, recently freed from its cast, and brings it mercifully to a warm nest and a pecking bill.

Not only do I hear her innocent heart beat, I even hear the echo afterward. And hot rills of sap from the young, dense forest pour into my veins.

Everything's the lizard's fault. Stuck itself onto that white rock casting dazzling frozen-spell glances our way. There's a twig on the ground, and I try to smack the lizard away with the twig: enough of your barefoot tricks. Get outta here! Whatever; it doesn't notice, plays dead. And then I have an idea: it's too bad that I don't have me a good little stick; even the devil is scared of a good thwop.

And that was the lizard's clever scheme: as soon as I thought of the stick, I immediately remembered the cleaver in the black case, which Glikele extracted at my request from its hiding place under the top of the oven, between the oven and the ceiling, for me to whittle out two sticks—for me and her.

I hadn't seen the cleaver till now. Glikele brought it to the forest exactly as she had taken it down from over the oven: in the longish black case.

When I open the case, something is torn among the trees, as if silence plummeted into a pit: a blue stream between violet banks sparkles on my palm. I hear an "oh" and I don't know if it's coming from me or Glikele.

I am a sinner, a sinner. In the pine forest, I discovered a naked secret sealed in a case. As soon as a living eye glimpses it—you can try pushing a mountain on top of the secret and you'll never cover it up again.

Now I know that the lizard followed us the whole way into the forest. The same one in the city that convinced me to play with cleavers.

No, I won't give in. I am a grown man. I'll look pretty silly if a little lizard ruins my radiant summer day and my fun with Glikele. I search about carefully and find a pine with moist, light-green bark and fresh buds. This is the kind it's good to whittle shapes out of.

"Glikele, first I'll carve one for you . . ."

She turns her face to me with a curiosity just this side of scared: "Why do I need a stick? I'm not a boy!"

"If Faivke the pigeon keeper hassles you, you'll have something to break his bones with."

I never heard such a salvo of laughter before. Not just the freckles on her nose laugh but also her bare feet and her breasts too; the sun-reddened hair over the pinkish breeze of her eyes; the hummingbirds laugh, as well as the warblers, though they should be singing; and the pine trees, overflowing with rills of sap, shake with laughter.

Glikele is laughing. The crowns and roots laugh, and higher than them all the lizard laughs. Let it laugh, let it die laughing. Meanwhile, I take my cleaver and cut into the chosen tree.

Suddenly, someone lets out a scream. Slaughtered laughter. Red bursts out of the cut branch like from a throat. The cleaver is not blue anymore. The blue brook is overflowing with sunset, the same color as Glikele's flowing hair.

A storm in the forest. A swarm of burbling shouts. Roosters crowing, geese honking; a mooing and babbling of cows and calves disturbs the forest and breaks its branches.

In the grass, the cleaver overlaid with the same color as Glikele's flowing hair.

After the lizard's magic and the disturbance in the forest, an invisible cleaver hung between me and Glikele. I kept loving her, but it was love at a distance. I was afraid to get close to her because of the color and the shine of her hair. How can I caress her? I'll cut my fingers open.

A little later I forgot her name. I called her the same name the kids on my street did: the cleaver's daughter.

Reb Elye came home for *Shvues*, and he brought home a brand-new spouse from Worniany. But the new householder no longer needed to drive out the cleaver's daughter with her green broom. That green broom had gone up in smoke the day before.

Here's what happened: the cleaver's daughter left to go swimming. The pharmacist from Haydutsishok left the house for a while to bring sawdust to sprinkle on the floor for yom tov. As it would happen, right then from under the trivet a burning spark fell onto the ground and the wooden shovel caught on fire.

The fire screamed to be put out, but because it was choking on the smoke, no one heard it at first. When the people with hoses and brass hats came running, half the house was already up in smoke.

The wooden bed where Granny Tzviokle had slept burned from the very bottom, from its four legs. She herself was lying in it, as black as charcoal.

When the people in the brass helmets came running up, she turned her sooty face to them: "I guess it's still smoldering."

Those were her last words.

1971–2

THE VOW

I

On a night of miracles in the year 1942, I took a vow.

The echo of my memory can relate that I took the vow in a snowy fir forest, where I covered myself with fresh snowdrifts so the celebratory neighborhood wolves would content themselves with my head, the sole owner and settler of all accounts for the sweet and bitter sins of my body. For that reason, the wolves should not disturb my head's guiltless messengers underneath the snow: hands and feet and their limb brothers. Leave them huddled in their warmth, like sown seeds, sprouting with fresh sap when the sun radiates on them.

The night of miracles began earlier, with the letting out of day. She began to turn the hands of her clock from Thursday to Friday.

On that night my soul was weighed and measured. I was born on a night like this, and on a night from Thursday to Friday I will breathe my last line. On a night like this the Angel of Death draws near and tries to lure me into his snare with mischievous tricks, but the Angel of Life suddenly stands in his way; both draw gleaming swords and struggle in a kind of cosmic duel. But the Angel of Life can't beat the Angel of Death to death, unfortunately. He manages to wound him. And by next Thursday that character has again become healthy as an ox, and he slaps himself on his skeletal belly, like a charm for quick triumph over his desired victim.

II

The night of miracles began in a cellar.

A night of miracles in a cellar smelling of potatoes. An odor of potatoes with a night of miracles in a cellar—one and the same, indivisible. A single human life might be too short to conceive of what the earth entrusted to a simple potato (I won't say a stupid potato) in its depths. Hidden away maternally in the cellar by the elderly gentile woman, I detect in the earthy odor of potatoes a gnawing closeness. Yes, my bloodhound's nose remembers and could swear: it's the smell of my childhood, and I get so warm, like a child, inhaling my own smell.

Right away, however, I hear a thin unraveling nearby in the cellar, like the cry of a lost bee in the hollow of a violin. "Don't stay here any longer. Run away; a hand will protect you . . ."

A hand. I have already seen hands where every finger is a gallows. But now I see very clearly fingers of mild blessing. They are stretched out like the priestly blessing from the bimah and the color of amber before the fire. They remind me also of the chalk-pale tendrils that sprout in the dark from the buried potatoes, revealing themselves in the cellar when the sun is no longer afraid of breaking through the sole crack in the door to the outside.

Even before I manage to answer the stillness's unraveling, the door to the outside, that one over there (my armor against the evil men), is thrown open, and I'm already on my feet with their suppurating wounds, into the unnerving, steely out-there. I observe now that the hand that just extracted me from the cellar has lit up the pitch-black, forested horizon facing me, its sharp, serrated treeline pointing into the ice of space. Out there, however, the blessing hand looks quite different than in the cellar: it has the shape of a half moon made out of parchment.

This is my password: I must run away into the forest that the parchment hand created for my sake.

III

Like an arrow I flew into the forest, traveling a couple hundred paces from my hiding place, with my breath following some distance behind, and it is only here that I find that because of my great hurry I didn't manage to (or forgot to) put on my military boots with heavy soles like horseshoes. Ever since I became a man of the cellar I always lie on top of the potatoes with the boots on my feet. Only tonight, between Thursday and Friday, did I take them off. The festering foot wounds pleaded with me to have mercy and free them for a moment from bootish captivity. So I had pity on them and freed them. Thus I am now barefoot. A barefoot cellar dweller in the snow.

Wait—not true. I'm not barefoot at all. Instead of boots I'm dressed in wounds. And on top? On top hangs a fringed fur coat like a tallis-koton in which I sleep and hope.

It stands to reason—a lit match courses through me—that someone didn't want me to wear the boots. Patience; the miracle night isn't over yet, and if it does end, God forbid, in this forest, the dramatic epilogue will take place in another forest.

And as soon as the match is extinguished in my bloodstream, just then—can my eyes believe it?—a horde of shadows with guns on their shoulders surrounds the hut, under which is the cellar from which I had just fled. Their orders to surrender ring out in three languages. But since no one crawls from the cellar, the hut is quickly traced with a golden brush and its roof turned into a fiery chariot, wheels revolving over the forest, whirling far, far above among terrified stars.

Now I understand that the boots in the cellar sacrificed themselves for me: if I had put them on, or if they had put themselves on my feet, I sure as hell wouldn't have been able to run away into the forest. The evil men would have caught up with my limping shadow and captured both of us alive.

Perhaps my shadow wouldn't have surrendered. He wouldn't have let himself be chained. But the evil men would have forced me to admit that I'm a person. Who knows if I would have withstood the temptation? I can't guarantee it. Maybe I would have admitted to it.

In the meantime I've transformed from a cellarman into a forestman. What next? If that's the question, there's got to be a next. Hop to it, guy, under the stars, don't let your feet freeze. Then the mind remembers the heels and I swaddle my wounded feet in strips of canvas from my warm shirt. Could it be—I'm a kid in swaddling clothes again?

Meanwhile it's still meanwhile, and the evil men sniff out my tracks in the fluffy snow. They light up the signs of my steps with green lights in the direction of the pine forest. They bend over the signs as if picking berries. Glimmering cranberries without fear of the cold. But the night of miracles did not leave me: it advances the glowing hands again, and a thick snow once more begins falling—a marble palace collapsed into empty space. The bad men can illuminate the snow with an X-ray machine—it's pointless; they won't find my tracks.

The green lights retreat and disappear under the hot ash of the burned-out hut.

IV

Whose life is so valuable that I happily accept salt in my wounds? I don't want to save only my own bones; that's impossible. Here's proof of that: I unwrapped the canvas strips from my feet, knotted them into a rope, hung them on a pine branch, and tried that redemptive noose on my neck. But a life that is more valuable to me than my own suddenly illuminated my desperation with its power, and instead of my body—a black wind was left suspended in the noose.

Now I know that the illuminating force was you. Your form flew past me in a vision.

I said to myself these words: "I must not extinguish my breath with my own hand, because a life more valuable than my own smiled into my veins. I will render myself unto the night of miracles—so that she will keep turning the phosphorescent hands."

V

New grass-green fires emerge from the snowy darkness. But not like the fires before, when one fire was cleaved out from another, and each—together and separately—dug around in the snow for my wounded steps. Now they are running among the bundled-up fir trees with heartbreaking howling and in pairs—in pairs, each small fire joined together with another.

Wolves, celebratory wolves—I'm the reason for their celebration. Are the wolves hungrier than my love?

Then I lay down underneath the tree on whose branch the black wind was suspended in a noose, covered myself up to the neck with fresh snowdrifts, and took a vow.

The vow consisted of three parts, or three vows. This is what I said: "If the night of miracles will protect me from the wolves in the fir forest, then even if I am later anointed as the head of all heads, I will leave my homeland and knead my lips into Jerusalem mountains."

And I said further: "If the night of miracles will protect me from the wolves in the fir forest, I will wander from city to city and search till I find the true form whose reflection flew by in my vision. We will both become one, like two pupils."

The third part of the vow I took is actually a vow by itself—I can't put it down on paper for strangers to read.

Then the tree at my head bent down low over me; I felt over my brow its protective wings.

The wolves came swimming up to the wings and were extinguished in the snow like clouds snuffed out by lightning.

This is the story about the vow that I took in the forest; I carved out an amulet for you from this very vow.

So many secrets, quite dark and with a reflected, merciful revelation, are engraved into the amulet; so many interconnections and images; such a holy music, which one hears only once in life. The third part of the vow, as well, which only God heard, was engraved by me into the amulet too. Now I will hang it on your heart, and it will sway over you like a water lily over a wave. Vanished, I will witness from a distance.

JANINA AND THE ANIMAL

While you were alive, Janina, I didn't write you any letters. Now I can defend myself: I would have had to write differently to you than to all my other friends, and I wouldn't know how; or, and this is more believable and closer to the truth, I didn't have your address. I knew to whom to write, but I didn't know where to write to. Right after our meeting at the end of the war, you disappeared from your little palace with the red terra cotta bricks in Zakret, on the high banks of the Viliya. I heard you were in Krakow, they said you entered a convent, took orders. I didn't know what was true. Now I know the truth: Janina is no longer. Now I know your address: where all human children meet for their last rendezvous.

I was struck by a desire, a tortured yearning, to tell you right now what you know yourself. I could have told it differently, just with my lips, so that no one could hear except you. I could have tossed it into my memory, like a jewel into a smooth river, one extended, elongated sound—*ya-ni-na*—and its radiating rings would make it all the way to your spirit. But I can't cure myself of my longstanding paperholic nature. A good angel will be the bearer and will bring you the letter at your otherworldly address.

It was, to name the earthly date, April 1943. The stream of melted snow could only flow in one direction, and it traveled all the way from the mountains of Ponar into the valley. Similarly, the stream of humanity couldn't manage a diversion and was carried with the force of nature ever downward into the valley.

On my right, Tzerne was carried along with the stream. From her backpack, sleeping hands were sticking out over her head—those of her baby girl born a month ago. Tzerne's hair was black on black, with a black reflection like a dazzling cleaver at night.

Floating by a stand of pine trees, quite near the electric Angel of Death, desperate Tzerne threw the backpack into the soft arms of a pile of snow, which the spring had left on purpose under the branches of the trees. I heard her whisper without turning her face to me: "God of my grandfather, protect my little baby."

The terrible picture next to the wires of the electric Angel of Death is something that I will depict some other time, Janina: when we will meet and our time will be eternity. Now, just a couple of thumbnail sketches: the fire went out before it could attack me. Tzerne's breath, separated from her lips, curled warmly, fresh as milk in the crystalline blue air. I picked myself up, drew her breath into myself, and I-don't-know-whose wings appeared on me, lifted me out of there.

Tzerne's backpack must still have been lying at the stand of pine trees in the soft arms of the pile of snow, and in it her baby girl born a month ago. I put it on like armor, and mercifully, I warmed up.

I hiked without fear back toward the city. The molten sealing wax of the path was stamped in its entire length and breadth with human footsteps, all in the opposite direction.

I walked—where to? And who did Tzerne's baby girl in the backpack belong to?

That's when I thought of you, Janina, and at the sound of your name I saw the both of us several years ago, me escorting you home from Vilna University. The whole way I was silent from joy. I didn't want to interrupt your improvisation on the topic of Mickiewicz's "Crimean Sonnets." You compared them to Chopin's music. Not to his "Wiegenlied," his barcarolle, but specifically to his short preludes, which are worlds in themselves, more artistic and well-rounded than his overloaded compositions.

You recited by heart a fragment of the sonnet "Sea Stillness":

> The wind barely touches the pavilion's ribbon
> The breasts of the illuminated water breathe quiet
> Like a young bride dreaming of happiness
> Wake up to sigh and then sleep again

You wanted to convince me that it's the most beautiful poem in all of poetry; Mickiewicz's crowning work isn't "Forefathers' Eve," not "Pan Tadeusz," but this sonnet.

When we got to your little palace in Zakret, by the high shore of the Viliya, evening already hung from the three birch trees. From their branches at the gate you asked me to come in and not turn on the light. You fluttered to the piano and tapped out a prelude of Chopin's with your bony fingers:

"In his music I wander among my own unclear feelings. When I return from the warm, joyful wandering, I am gifted by God with the fresh scent of the open field."

Now, with the backpack on my back, wandering brought me to you, to your little old palace with the terra cotta bricks.

The three birch trees at the gate bent obediently, like three queens in chains wearing rusted crowns.

You again sat down at the piano and your refined fingers prayed over the keys.

I unwrapped Tzerne's unconscious girl from the backpack and placed her on your lap.

You read my face and understood everything. Your hair cascaded out and fell over the chair. You were wearing a round silver diadem on your forehead with a ruby in the middle. Like lightning playing in terrified rain.

I am sorry, Janina, in those sublime moments I sinned against you. Me, or someone in me, but it's the same thing: I didn't expect it, but a dark thought pricked at me: who knows, maybe you'll regret it. I hastily growled out: "Janina, remember, the child's mother was called Tzerne." And I ran away.

Ran away without a goodbye, like a thief from his conscience.

I'll try to remind you what you lived through afterward. Though most details you told me yourself, and others I filled in, it was a year later, in the same palace of hours, when I came to you again; and now, while writing you this letter, it seems to me that otherworldly bees are buzzing the words into my brain, and I'm not the one telling it but them, the bees. As a legacy they leave me red poppies of memory.

When Tzerne's baby girl woke on your lap, her crying mixed with the Chopin-esque prelude still hanging in the air. From the other side of the window an animal was panting. A hoarse cry was intermingled with a human laughter rolling out of its mouth. You closed the shutters, bolted the oaken door, bathed and fed the child, said your prayers, and went to bed with the child at your breast.

But the animal was as awake as death. Its eyes glowed through the cracks in the door. It jumped over the roof and whistled down the chimney, and the thin layer of nighttime ice shattered under its lurking paws.

The animal was everywhere at the same moment.

The next day you got up with added strength. Inspired, you told the housekeeper Salomea that you gave birth to a lover's child and his mother brought it to you yesterday. Salomea loved you more than herself; you had been orphaned very early. Your father, the landowner Karol Szpinak, was killed by a stampede of bison in the forests of Białowieża. A very close friend of your father's, a character with the name Kotla, who played a suspicious role during the bison stampede, ran away to Italy with your mother right after the event. Wherefrom she used to send you money as Salomea took solicitous care of you.

You named Tzerne's daughter Tzerna. You and the faithful housekeeper watched over her.

But the animal didn't leave your little palace. It menaced with her claws from under the bed and terrified Tzerna's dolls.

When you went to church it shuffled after your footsteps, and once inside it sniffed after the tears of your prayer while its face clouded over amid the thorns of the crucified one.

The animal also accompanied your housekeeper, tore her handkerchief, chewed the fringes of her dress. When Salomea walked by, the animal stuck its nose into her basket, squealed, and scratched a gallows into the sand with its claws.

As a charm, the old woman set up a broken mirror at the threshold of the little palace. The devil isn't scared of anyone. He is only scared of his own face. When he approaches the threshold and catches a glimpse of his own devilish countenance in the broken mirror, he will be seized by trembling. He'll do three somersaults, go to hell, and break his back.

—൘—

This happened in May. Exactly a month after I dropped Tzerne's Tzerna on you. The air was pink like the baby girl's cheeks, full of the color of lilac and tangy scents. The three birch trees at the entrance were clearly set apart from each other in the scattered moonlight. Strings of pearls hung down from their stiff branches, and fragments of wind hung on them.

For the first time the animal went into your palace, then your room. The doors opened at its coming. It went in politely, elegantly, dressed like a mannequin.

"My name is Hans Oberman. I want to have the honor of your acquaintance."

He pulled off his white gloves, walked closer, tapped his boots together rhythmically, took your hand into his, bowed, and glued his thin lips to your trembling fingers.

This was the first insult, the first stain on your clean skin. But you were even more insulted by the black shine from his boots, which had the same glimmer as the polished lid over the piano. The observation flitted through your head—these are boots that trample music. And music and Tzerna were one and the same.

The officer Hans Oberman wasn't satisfied with his first victory. He strode to the open piano and dragged his hand over the keys, like a mouse scampering over them: "Miss Janina Szpinak"—he dragged his hand the other way—"I heard that you are alone, and aloneness in wartime is both sad and full of danger. I am ready to entertain you and protect you."

"Not 'Miss' but 'Mrs.,' and also not 'Janina Szpinak' but 'Janina Galinska,'" you answered. "Clearly you were misinformed. I am already the mother of a two-month-old baby daughter, healthy, thank God, and for your readiness to protect me, thank you. There is a Lord who protects his creatures."

"That you're a mother is news to me," Oberman said with crafty astonishment. "Is your husband at home?"

"No, I haven't heard any information about him for half a year. It was actually you Germans who ripped him away from me. I heard he was in a camp somewhere."

"Do you know, Mrs. Janina, what your husband's offense was?"

"His only sin: he was and remained a Polish patriot."

"That sort of thing can happen. It's war," said Hans Oberman, shaking his head with cold sympathy. "I will make an effort to seek him out and release him from the camp."

———※———

Such a terrible dream as you had that night could never before have occurred to you, dreaming or waking:

Hans Oberman jumped out of the piano on four feet and approached your bed, where Tzerna was cuddling up to you. He wore white gloves on his paws.

He was as hairy as a bear, and on his animal head was an officer's cap with a silver skeleton. He stretched out his paw to you, offering a bouquet of roses—dark red, alive, like a sunset in a storm.

"It's for you, Janina, for the birth of your daughter. I would have done it earlier, but I just found out about your happiness. I brought a present for the baby too. Can I know her name?"

"Tzerna."

"A lovely sound: Tzer. Na. Is she named, my lady, after someone in your family?"

"Yes, after my grandmother. I loved her very much."

"Your grandmother's name was Jadviga; you are clearly mistaken."

"No, I'm not mistaken. A person has two grandmothers."

"Oh, indeed, interesting. I will tell the priest to dust off the birth certificates in the archives."

When you woke up, Salomea was sitting on your bed. She was putting ice on your forehead and crossing herself. Tzerna was playing with the spring, her little voice hatching like a songbird from its egg.

In the real world, Hans Oberman came in. He left two paws behind the threshold at the entrance. He wasn't wearing his uniform now or the black boots. He looked different in his gray civilian suit.

"Dear lady Janina," he said, bowing to her, "please pardon my coming unasked, all the more while you are lying in bed with a headache. I brought candy for your daughter Tzerna."

"How do you know what my child is called?" You jumped out of bed, distressed. "I didn't tell you her name!"

Hans Oberman sat down on the piano stool facing you and spoke very slowly: "Janina, you think I'm not a human being, right? But I am! I am! We are all woven of the same stuff that dreams are made of—that's what Shakespeare said. So I found out in the dream that your daughter is called Tzerna."

You thought it was a continuation of your nightmare, but you had never been so awake. You bit your hand to arouse pain, but your hand was actually his and the bite didn't hurt you.

Oberman tried to calm you: "I was kidding, Janina; the kids outside told me your daughter's name is Tzerna."

Hans Oberman apologized again, left the bag of candy on the piano, and hastily left.

—⊡—

A month passed without the animal reappearing, but his shadow slinked around outside and in the little palace. Driving out a shadow is even harder than a living creature. You threw the candy into the oven: if Tzerna were to get sick, God forbid, you'd think she was poisoned by the gift.

I don't know what you went through that month. I only know the details that you told me: your mother returned from Italy. You barely recognized her, old as Salomea. You felt for her the pity one feels for a dead person. She wanted to make it up to you for your suffering. You were an orphan twice over, with a dead father and a living, unseen mother, so she brought you a little box of jewelry. You didn't want to take it. The will to save Tzerna won out.

Yes, you didn't tell your own mother that Tzerna is someone else's, Jewish. You told her the same thing you told Hans, and she eagerly took to looking after her own grandchild.

The same month Salomea felt that two mothers were too much, and the old lady breathed the last gasp of her refined soul.

—⊡—

This time he came in—Hans Oberman—with a wolfhound and in full officer's uniform. His face was dull yellow and powdered. Pink spots like fingerprints were traced under the powder. His wolfhound, on a chain made out of nickel, was proper and obedient. His sharp, purple tongue hung out in its whole length—a wet, vibrating sickle with teeth underneath. His head, with its perked-up ears, was attentive to his master, ready to perform whenever Hans Oberman gave the sign.

Tzerna was playing on a tiger's skin. Her eyes were the blue of genesis. The ancestral blue of all blues. And the fresh braiding of her moist, spare hair fit wonderfully into the composition of the three birch trees in the open window and the young ray of sun, which mischievously skipped over their branches like a squirrel.

You interrupted the officer's stride and haughtily took his measure: "How dare a proud military man visit a child with a wolfhound!"

The officer defended himself: "Janina, the hound won't do anything unless I order him to. I brought him with me today for one reason only, to guard me."

"Whom does the dog need to guard you from?"

"There's an enemy. Invisible."

Hans Oberman trembled as if a rain was suddenly attacking. The pink spots under the powder became clearer: "You know, Janina, I look at your daughter and I get this very weird feeling—she hasn't even a bit of resemblance to her mother."

"You're right. Tzerna is the spitting image of her father. But her soul is the same as mine."

Hans Oberman raised his voice: "They've searched all the camps, and her father is nowhere. Maybe her father wasn't Polish?"

You burst out laughing like a true actress: "Not Polish? You're right. My husband is a Negro. I thank you, Hans Oberman, for the good news that my husband wasn't found in the camps. Bravo, my dear Staszek, you ran away!"

The officer looked into your eyes with the gaze of his wolfhound: "Miss Janina, let's stop the game. They've done the research. There's no Staszek. Tzerna is Jewish."

The laughter was stuck in your throat. But the laughter continued of its own accord.

Hans Oberman put his hand on your shoulder: "Janina, I know that you are a pious Catholic. You go to church three times a week. Jesus is there hanging over your bed. When you kneel before him, cross yourself and swear that Tzerna is not a Jewish child—then I'll believe you."

You went down on your knees, crossed yourself, and swore.

Then something happened that you hadn't thought of before: Hans Oberman, the officer in the black boots, started crying. The beast started crying human tears. He took out a small revolver, a Walther, and shot three bullets into his loyally crouching wolfhound. The report of the shots was mild, like the knock of a thin summer hail on the windowpane. Tzerna didn't even get scared. Her mother's deadly fear was enough for her little daughter for a whole life through. The wolfhound circled around Hans with the rhythm of a dizzy carousel, and he was left sprawled out as quiet as a kitten, opposite the tiger skin. It looked like the dead tiger had torn the living wolfhound to pieces.

All this lasted no more than a few seconds.

Then Hans Oberman fell down at your feet, kissed them, and beat his head against the floor.

Janina, do you remember the seconds afterward?

You helped him bring the dog into the basement. Hans buried him there, covered him, and laid rotten beer barrels on top.

When you both went back upstairs into your piano room, his face was chalk white, as if leeches had sucked out his dark blood. The pink spots had disappeared, like the stains from the shot dog that you washed away with hot water.

It was fortuitous that your mother was not at home. She would have tattled about the incident to her neighbors, even without meaning to. She had lost her equilibrium recently, your mother, and found in the city a past frequent visitor to your house, a pharmacist, then together they busied themselves with summoning the spirit of her husband, the murdered landowner Karol Szpinak. Karol's spirit will be revealed in good time, and she'll tell him the secrets of his last stampede in the forest of Białowieża.

You were still shaking from the strange experience. A kind of earthquake of the soul. Reality was rebelling against itself. But at that moment Hans Oberman came to his senses and started talking familiarly to you: "Janina, you've got to run away today—you, Tzerna, and your mother. Tomorrow'll be too late, since there's an order to arrest the three of you. The same fate awaits you as did the Jews. Get ready. I'll come this evening with a car and take you all away from here. Where to—you'll think of by tonight. You must have a relative somewhere, a friend with an estate. I'll try to run away somewhere as well; the forests need military men. I thank you, Janina, for turning me into a human being again . . ."

This happened the following spring:

In the Ushachy forest, in the hideout of the commander, Trofim Belousov, there was the fresh scent of pitch, which was dripping from the moss-covered fir trees out of which the hideout was built. The roof was barely noticeable, blending in with the freshly resurgent grasses among the blue pools. The spruce firs had grown there in groves for their whole lives, but now they had realized that they could grow just as well lying down and cuddled up fir to fir in their mosses.

Trofim Belousov, the commander of a troop of partisan fighters in the Ushachy forest, wasn't in the hideout yet. His adjutant Grishka Molodyets, an energetic, blond young man with a face that looked like it was overgrown with corn stalks, brought me there and asked me to wait. I had made my scrabbling way from my guerilla base between Kobylnik and Myadel, about a hundred kilometers away. Under my shirt, I was bringing Belousov an important piece of news from Brigadier General Fyodor Markov, written on a strip of canvas.

The sunset penetrated down the earthen steps into the hideout. The door stood open, a black coffin without a bottom or a cover. This is how it looked: in one half of the hideout a bonfire was burning, and in the other half, where I was sitting on a log, its shadow.

Now Trofim Belousov and Grishka Molodyets came in. In comparison with the solidly built, stocky adjutant, the famous commander seemed a bit of a wimp: short, thin, in a round sheepskin hat that was on crooked and crammed down onto one ear, making his face seem even smaller and narrower—skinny and bony, with a meager, unkempt beard and a grumpy moustache. From the right corner of his mouth hung a pipe like a barrel tap. But his eyes—pointed, narrow, under the prominent furrow in his forehead—could penetrate a stone and extract the sparks from its insides.

I stood up, saluted, and stated my name. Then I took out the canvas letter from under my shirt and gave it to him.

The commander punched holes through the canvas with his needle eyes and, as if the letter was unfinished, stabbed me with them as he read. Then he doffed the sheepskin cap, thought for a moment, and twirled his moustache: "Ładno, ładno…"

Suddenly the furrow in his brow cut even deeper, more zigzag, and Belousov bent to me over the table: "Tell me—do you know the language of the Germans?"

"Somewhat, you could say so."

"Ładno, ładno." He knocked out the baked tobacco from his overstuffed pipe onto the edge of the table, then slowly turned to the adjutant: "Grishka, bring in the officer. If you have to hang him a bit later it won't be a tragedy. To hell with him really—but we'd waste his tongue. Maybe we can still milk it for something."

When Grishka exited, Belousov added a couple of sentences so I'd better understand the whole business: "We captured a high-ranking figure in the forest: a German officer. A spy? A decoy? Hard to say. He had disguised himself as a partisan and even demonstrated heroism. A refugee from Ponar recognized him—a boy from Vilna. The officer doesn't deny it, but he's hiding something. Plus there's no one here who understands the German language properly."

———ֆ———

The sunset stepped out from the earthen hideout in red boots. My shadowy side spread out over the entire square space among the lying fir trees. Trofim Belousov lit a lamp. As the scent of pitch absorbed the odor of kerosene, Grishka came in pulling the captive by a rope.

When I questioned him, the officer told me the same thing that Belousov had heard before: his name was Hans Oberman, born in Koln. It's true he killed innocent people. In June 1943 he fled from his military unit, and here, in the Ushachy woods, he wanted to atone for his sins.

"*Ładno, ładno,*" said Belousov, cutting short the interview with a sharp rap of his pipe on the edge of the table. "That's exactly the issue. Ask him, the brave officer, this Hans Oberman, why he fled from his military unit and betrayed his Fatherland."

When I translated Belousov's unexpected question, he started like a loosed spring: "Allow me to take that secret to my grave."

———ֆ———

Janina, I'm ending the letter. A good angel will bring it to you. You'll read it and remember that most words are *yours.*

PS: Yes, I didn't write you about Tzerna's wedding. Another time. Another . . .

1971

THE GRAVEDIGGERS' STRIKE

I

For a bunch of years now my alarm clock in this country has been a paper bird. I could swear that every dawn the paper bird is both the same and different.

Except for the Sabbath and holidays, when he keeps my people's commandments and doesn't tweak the swimming black pearls of my barely salvaged dream with his dull beak, he wakes me up daily with the punctiliousness of fate.

Once upon a time, in my boyhood home, it was different: a wild turtledove, washed in the night's tears, used to wake me up on Shabbos and yom tov. She used to fly from her nighttime hideaway to the pink folds of my attic's lone window, swing onto the highest branch of my one-footed neighbor, the hoary gray and occasionally hoary red cherry tree, and trill out her good morning, good Shabbos, and good yom tov.

She also always used to bring the first rays of sun in her polished beak.

The dove started her good-tidings trill when I became bar mitzvah. And it kept going this way during spring and summer like clockwork. Fall and winter, on and on—until . . .

Until the caretaker of my hilly courtyard of clay—like a plowed-up graveyard—was struck by madness, grabbed from the billowy weeds by the fence the broad ax with which he used to slaughter pigs, and with a raw impulse hacked down the aged cherry tree from its rough, tangled copper roots.

From then on the turtledove no longer came to greet me. No longer brought the first ray of sun in its polished beak. A dove, like a person, seeks a place to rest, if not on earth then in air.

But the caretaker didn't do any less to himself. At the same time as the old cherry tree, he hacked himself down with his hundred years, which he had carried locked in the safe of his bony hunchback. Together with the branched victim, he too fell down onto the moaning roots, holding in his hand the mighty ax, and he did not rise again. Neither living nor dead.

But that's a story in itself.

II

Hey—look who's here! My paper bird. The soft threads of my dream were torn open by his blunt beak at my glass balcony door on the third floor. The pictures and symbols that were captured in the night through my fully synchronous second soul, which is youthful and dominant only when I'm sleeping, escape from the torn net. Now that soul will drowse off and the other soul will take over all my activities: the real soul, the everyday soul.

I see through my eyelids as through a rain: all my captured treasures are escaping through the torn nets, and they fall with a mocking splash into a terrifying chasm.

Slow and careful, I open up the balcony door and let the paper bird into my bedroom.

I'm still observing the newspaper delivery boy with his leather hat down there on the empty street. Yes, the guy who first thing every morning manages to artfully toss the newspaper, tied with a red thread, onto my balcony. I admire his precise throw. I'm sure that even if I lived on the thousandth story, the kid in the leather hat would be able—with a single magic throw—to toss me the newspaper, which in his hands turns into a fluttering bird.

I've gotten superstitious. If it doesn't land on the balcony, making him throw it again—a tragedy will occur . . .

I free the bird from the thread that binds it and lie back in bed to feed my morning eyes with the good news of the world.

III

A man on the moon? The man and the moon should both forgive me; I'm not impressed. Me? I've been farther, higher, and it's not my fault that the newspapers have not reported on it. No one knows that I've got interplanetary talents; I've been as far as Mars. But try to tell everyone "I'm as great as King Solomon" when your name is Abraham. And as far as politics, orders, and declarations from the world's rulers go—I'm embarrassed for the printed words. They are poured in lead against their will. What is truer than the word? Apart from God Himself. And here? May the word not punish me—but when things start to be told, then the lies start.

The obituaries are the only things that are true. The black edges. Another eighteen-year-old casualty . . .

I want to get away from the newspaper now. When conscience sticks its little horns outside its shell, it becomes terrible. The long summer day won't go well, and my date this evening will be a failure, but right when I'm about to push the newspaper away I'm stopped by a short blurb on the last page:

GRAVEDIGGERS ON STRIKE

> We have learned that the gravediggers from the City Jewish Cem-
> etery have declared a strike. Their demands aren't yet clear. One
> thing is clear: they will not bury the dead tonight.

My day, new, dreamed into existence, is all upside down. I am lifted by a strange macabre force, like skeletons' laughter. Now I won't work today. My date is buried. Let's go see and hear the gravediggers strike.

IV

The gates of the Jewish cemetery are thrown open and bent over like an invitation to a dance. Sure thing, come closer, come in—but just the living. No entrance for the dead, like an erotic film to minors.

Mercilessly, I give myself a masochistic pinch on the cheek to feel my existence, and the sharp echo of my pain confirms that I belong to the living. The pain sends out vibrating, associational rings: I recall my blond rebbe Itzik-Moyshl. When he used to fall asleep over his *shtender*, I'd play a prank and glue his beard to the Talmud with gum arabic. He didn't even say boo when detaching himself from the Talmud. Rarely had my rebbe smiled so good-naturedly. But he caught the guilty one right away. With the pincer of his two tobacco-stained fingers, he grabbed a piece of flesh from my face, and together with that pain the incense of his burning tobacco penetrated me for many years to come.

Hey—who do I see? My rebbe himself, not aged a bit. The same face from a half century ago, framed in beard and *payos* like a wreath of onions. Except that instead of a beard, transparent peels are hanging down . . . and the hat got older, the brim—wider.

Goodness gracious sakes. How is this possible? I myself followed his coffin in the Jerusalem of Lithuania. Asked for forgiveness for gluing his beard. I remember the funeral horse, decked out in a black horsecoat. His two loudspeaker ears poked out through two holes, and through two others—icy pupils. I even remember the hoarse gurgling of the hearse's wheels. The spokes turned in a slow to-and-fro like the hands of an otherworldly clock. Snow greeted the black horse, and the snow was the soul of my rebbe.

Was he resurrected in the land of the forefathers? Itzik-Moyshl is now the spokesman here. The gravediggers are standing around him in a group like a circle of funeral wagons. Each one has a spade on his shoulder like a rifle. He is holding forth before them in a strange tongue.

I notice among the group of beggars near the main avenue a sitting figure like Rodin's *Thinker*. No one thinks to be astonished at *him*; I give him a coin and ask him a question: "That guy who's blabbing away at the gravediggers, you don't happen to know his name?"

The bronze face of Rodin's *Thinker* wakes from lethargy: "Reb Yoelish, the gravedigger Reb Yoelish."

"Pardon me. Do you also know where he's from?"

"Of course I know. From Munkatch."

I keep grilling him: "What language is that he's talking in? I'll be damned if I understand a word."

Dark bronze furrows start racing on the forehead of the *Thinker*. "In gravediggers' slang, my lovely. It's an underworld language, a mix of *loshn-koydesh*, Yiddish, Arabic, and Aramaic. The gravediggers weren't born in this graveyard. Only the dead are born here. They've assembled here, my lovely, from the entire Earth. From Poland, Yemen, Hungary, from the Atlas Mountains, and from the other side of the Sambatyon."

Rodin's *Thinker* lowers his heavy head and is consumed by frozen silence. I go to the circle of shovels again and prick up my ears—till I think I'll burst—to catch what Reb Yoelish is saying.

With patience and careful investigation, and with a sense of ancient awakening, I succeed in decoding his flying hieroglyphics: "Gentlemen, the situation is dire. I tell you there's no choice—understood? A strike is a lot more than a strike, understood? The heroes, such as they are, will set it down and pick it up, understood? Here's a comparison: How are we lower in estimation than the bakers? Just like you can't live without bread, you can't live without the dead." He finishes up with a rhyme, like a badchen.

In the middle of the heated preaching, behold a solitary locust the color of green glass, like a vibrating arrow, which comes zooming into the cemetery and then stops, hanging there over the preacher's full, fleshy nose. It occurs to me that the locust is a secret messenger from the thousand-eyed angel. He's carrying instructions to Reb Yoelish about how to lead the strike.

As I surmised, the single locust was just a spy. Behind it, a glowing cloud devours the sun and the sun's bastard shadows. As happens during a solar eclipse, the high-blue summer day scatters in ash. Masses of locusts attack the trees, the tombstones. I hear them chomp with a terrible hunger. The air is humid, barely breathable. How long, oh Father, will the war of Gog and Magog last? But I hear a whispering in me: time does not exist in a cemetery. Only the foolish humans from the other side of the divide entertain themselves—fool themselves—with a clock. They don't have the least idea that a tiny Angel of Death is hiding inside, slaughtering them continually with his cleaver clock hands: *tick tock, snicker-snack.*

I manage the thought that if I were King I'd issue an order to throw all clocks into the sea together with their tiny Angels of Death. As I'm thinking that, the cloud of locusts lifts off from the cemetery like a sandstorm in the Wilderness of Zin, the summer day unveiling itself in pure sapphire blue, everything that just happened no more than a mirage.

Far, far away though, in the westward throat of the horizon, one can still see its marks—the strand of its wound.

Where is Reb Yoelish? Where are the gravediggers? Where should they be? They're here. A time to speak and a time to be silent. A time to hunger and a time to eat. They're actually sitting right here on a fresh mound of earth and having a snack. Someone is skinning a herring; someone else is slurping curds. Two Jewish women have joined them, both in white robes and with white caps over their hair pulled down to their foreheads. The robes are stabbed through with needles. In some, white threads are moving around like worms. These are the matrons who perform ritual cleanings. They are on strike too.

I guess the locust taught me something. I become courageous, bold. Go right up to Reb Yoelish and—right to the point: "Mister, who are you striking against?"

My question catches him off guard. "What do you mean 'who against'? That's the kind of question an intelligent person asks?"

"Who told you I was an intelligent person? I am actually ignorant about these things. It's just that curiosity is nagging me: Who are Jews on strike against in a cemetery?"

His eyebrows get more hedgehoggy; first he throws a darting look in the direction of the spade people, and then with their silent agreement, his triumph, quick to come, is made even easier: "Obviously a new *oleh*, come from a country where one can't go on strike. A pity."

I get even more in his face, our noses almost touching: "So old and still no excuse not to answer the question. Who are you striking against? Against death, or against life? If we were all to go on strike against death, life would look different. And another question: People are just people. So it could happen, God forbid, that you might get a little twinge in your chest and here's-your-hat-what's-your-hurry. Who would bury you then?"

A hubbub among the shovel people. Probably no one expected a question like that. A gravedigger spits out a herring head; a second one gives up on his curds and tosses them aside with the jug. The two women who perform ritual cleansings burst out wailing like they're tearing canvas. Their falling tears look like their needles. And as far as Reb Yoelish goes—he was most taken aback by my expression "here's-your-hat," because he doffs now his hat with the broad brim, sniffs it outside and inside, and I sense that he is scared to put it back on over his yarmulke.

Surprised by my own heroic role, I leave the battlefield and walk back to the main avenue.

V

The *Thinker* is still sitting bent over on the stone, his veined fist under his chin, wrought in the bronze of his heavy thoughts. If I were to throw a coin at him, he might be insulted. So I throw one of my thoughts into the bowl at his feet. He can think it up. He can do with it what he wants.

I am reading gravestone inscriptions. Little and big people. I remind myself of one wise man's words: "Great people die twice, once the person and then their greatness." I am surprised that all the tombstones next to the main avenue are completely bare, no flowers or wreaths. I solve the puzzle immediately: the locusts devoured them. The grass has been chewed down to the earth's bare skull.

I stop by a freshly shoveled-out grave by the edge of the main avenue. Although it's noon and the sun has loosed its leopards, the grave is full with sober darkness like a country well. Who's it waiting for—a man, woman, young child, elder? Don't tell me that the new occupant will never in his whole death change his place of residence, never take a trip out to London or Paris? Can you imagine the human spirit knocked flat on its back like this? Movement completely dominated by rest? Perhaps the home is the resident's for no longer than a millennium, which for the eternal lasts just a blink? And afterward? Afterward they'll move into a more proper structure. I recollect a wise saying of Seneca's: We don't worry about death but our imagining of it.

I also think of a neighbor of mine, far away in the distant ago: Ayzikl the Snowman. He looked just like what they called him. He was about eighty years old, I was just the eight without the zero, but we were the same height.

Ayzikl the Snowman had a fiery wife. Amazing that she didn't melt him into water. He loved her, and he loved telling his stories to her just as much. All the stories were about the Garden of Eden—how great it is there, how big and beautiful, she won't need to scour the floor or patch his clothes, and she won't use up all her energy blowing into the broken oven for it to get warm.

And his woman of valor answered him with a fiery sigh in the middle of one of his stories: "Sure, my husband, it's fantastic there, but the gate into the Garden—the black grave—is not to my liking . . ."

I'm now standing alone at the gate to the Garden of Eden. Waiting impatiently for the newest human being to open it. Maybe the Tree of Life, the Tree of Knowledge, is still blossoming behind it? But the new human isn't coming, doesn't open the gate, because the gravediggers are on strike.

I think about the two trees behind the black gate. A portal to their fruits must be found.

VI

A wet wind, just sprung free of the nearby sea waves, unwraps itself and extinguishes the humidity of the cemetery. The locust-devoured acacia trees beef up their branches. They are loaded down with blossoms, like they're covered with purple hair.

What is life, what is death? If life is the sun, death's an unilluminated moon. It can only be illuminated by the person who is a part of the sun, maybe through creating it. The sunlit poet will yet be born who will light up the moon. Then skeletons will listen to his language. Applaud in the graves. As long as poetry is only for the living reader—it has no actuality. In truth, such a poet has already been revealed: Ezekiel. He prophesied in the valley of the dead; breath entered into his audience and they became living. Baudelaire also had a musical relationship with the dusty shadows. He appeals to his friend, to whom he dedicates his book *Artificial Paradises*: "I would love to write only for the dead . . ."

VII

A paper-thin music cuts open my thoughts. They break off from the ground and become soap bubbles. Someone operated on me, a little thing is missing and a little thing was added.

Over my head, within arm's length, a songbird no bigger than a thimble swings on a Garden of Eden branch. Providing a concert that Jascha Heifetz could envy him for. How does such a tiny little bird manage to be the hybrid of such a maestro and a Stradivarius together?

No fun should be had at a cemetery. The musician turns its little behind around and anoints me, in the midst of my admiration, with its comforting shit—

1970

A SMILE AT THE END OF THE WORLD

1

Maybe a law of gravitation was in force here too:

Suddenly I found myself attracted to a strange, unknown city. This city wasn't included in the itinerary of my voyage round the world by air. I didn't even know its name or whether such a clime was to be found on Earth at all.

It happened this way:

When the airplane slid out of the slanted air and onto the silky smooth runway, on its way to kick out some passengers to their connecting flight, glugging itself full of gas or some other drinkable, en route to another nonstop across the sea—I nonchalantly grabbed my bag and in a daze followed the few passengers off the plane.

I miraculously got free of the high, transparent aerodrome, where the people looked like flies under a huge glass.

I left without saying goodbye to my stewardess, the beautiful daughter of Bengal, with a glowing ruby above the delicate meeting of her brows.

In the airplane I also left behind a half day of my life; who knows if eternity will return the loss?

Jumping into the best car I could find, I said to the Chinese man with the cheeks of a mummy: "Take me to Main Street!"

As the car zoomed off to the main street—though no main street, of course, was to be found, and no main man either—two black cleavers from the airplane rendered molten by the sun quickly sliced into the car, like the half day that was choked up in my insides.

As we drove down an endless, narrow street like a swollen vein the color of a cloudy blue sky, I asked the driver to stop at a post office.

According to the calendar it was spring. But it seemed to me a fifth season. The four seasons of the year, like four wheels of a wagon, rolled off the axles and went to hell. Only a fifth season was left: the whipped horse.

The steamy air between the walls was imbued with an in-between sort of color, like when the Moon takes over guard duty for the Earth from the Sun.

The narrow street was lined with trees; the sidewalks, swarming with people, were covered with a mosaic of smashed shells. From the trees hung fruit that one could have mistaken for plump birds.

I went into the post office and considered this situation, new for me: Should I telegraph my friends that I had had to stop in such-and-such a city, or find a hotel first and let loose a cold waterfall over my head?

I fingered my address book, which opened up by itself. My eye, or subconscious eye, fell on Buk. William Buk. A long-forgotten name; his address: in this city where I was now. Buk, Buk—oh, I remember: a year ago and maybe more, I got a letter from an unknown William Buk who was publishing a dictionary of modern world literature. He asked me to send him a bio. I satisfied his request, receiving an elegant thank you note in return.

I tried my luck and rang him up.

A soft voice, like the smoke of a Havana cigar, curled out of the receiver. When I uttered my name, I sensed a smoky smile issuing from the telephone.

"What hotel are you in?"

"None, for the moment."

"So where are you calling from?" the voice asked with the same fatherly tenderness.

"From the post office, the post office where the sidewalks are covered with smashed seashells."

"I'm coming soon. My self-portrait: a short beard, a cigar in my mouth, an orange hat with a broad brim, and a black walking stick."

Not ten minutes had passed when I felt a friendly slap on my back, as if he was the one who had recognized me over the telephone.

"William Buk. You're my guest. A room is waiting for you in the Gong Hotel."

A brand-new Cadillac folded both of us into its soft, rocking plush, as if into lukewarm water.

"I must warn you," said William Buk, treating me to a cigar, two of which together could make a walking stick, "that in this city, which is, by the way, the city of my birth, just turning around is frightening. The inhabitants, albeit not all of them, have X-ray vision. Even if you could hide your money in your appendix, they would be capable of detecting and extracting it." His face donned a smile like a smoky mask.

"My appendix was taken out a long time ago," I smiled back through the tissue of smoke.

"Nevertheless, you must remember where you are. Please turn around and look behind you, out the rear window. Do you see that little red car following us? Those are my guards. I can't allow myself the luxury of traveling without an escort. I'm like the director of an insane asylum who doesn't have backup." We both burst out laughing like two jealous thunderbolts—and our laughter stopped suddenly when we got to the Gong Hotel.

William Buk took me by the arm:

"Wash up and get some rest. I'll take you out to dinner later."

11

William was here. A different William. His face was pink, pink like a carrot, wrinkle-free like a freshly washed corpse.

"I wasn't clever enough to ask you how long you were staying in our city," he said, taking me by the arm and helping me into the Cadillac, "but you're my guest as long as you're here. I have already arranged a banquet in your honor in my villa—for tomorrow. There you will meet some remarkable people. I have already spoken with the mayor. He will come too."

It was quite late at night. The red car floated after the Cadillac like a trained seal. And the hands of my watch displayed a nonexistent hour.

Flowing streams. Slender, naked centaurs with feathers on their heads and bells on their necks leaped while racing, bells tinkling, trying hard to act like real horses and amuse the couples embracing in the floating carriages. On the walls, fiery dragons in red and blue. The screaming advertisements, seen from the speeding car, dazzled and enchanted like a swarm of microbes under the powerful ray of a microscope.

The Cadillac stopped. We were surrounded by cherry trees. The boulevard led downhill. William broke off a cherry twig, first bringing it to my mouth, then swallowing the rest of the fruits.

The boulevard ended in a small door—we had to bend down to go in. The light was like sunset in a storm.

Two girls with long eyelashes like butterflies, their porcelain bodies barely wrapped in pink, shimmering silk, came running up with flasks of water, knelt before us, took off our socks and shoes, and washed our feet. After washing them and drying them with a towel, they put purple slippers on us. It happened so unexpectedly that for a moment I was sure they had stolen my old feet and put new ones on me. William reassured me: "This is the custom here. In Europe people wash their hands before eating, and here—their feet. In your honor I chose a restaurant where, in addition to the other curiosities, the dishes are very tasty. In Paris and London you can stuff your belly with mud if you like."

It was obvious that William Buk was in his element here. People bowed to him and stepped aside to let him pass. He barely had a chance to acknowledge the porcelain smiles of the guests and waitstaff.

"Do you know why everyone's smiling here?" William Buk gazed at me mysteriously while the maître d', who looked like a Chinese Napoleon, led us to a table. "Because everybody wants to show everyone else that he has teeth—sharp teeth." And he gave a capacious smile to show the meaning of the symbolism.

III

William Buk inserted a monocle in his left eye, used it to make a dazzling scan of the menu, and arrived at a professional determination: "We will start with the spectacled cobra. A delicate dish. The art is as impressive as the artist. I mean to say that the art of preparation plays the main role here. The cobra is cooked together with its deadly venom. The venom is neutralized in the heat—the Angel of Death's needle stabs no longer but caresses like a girl's tongue. After eating cobra one should wash it down with hummingbird wine. Here is the bottle."

While William was praising the exotic delicacy, I concocted an elegant excuse—pulled it right off the tip of my nose—that I had a stomachache and I must, unfortunately, make do with, I don't know, a bowl of rice or a cup of curds.

But William knew his way around lies and excuses even before they came to be. He got out ahead of me.

"Actually, this very dish is a treatment and relief for those suffering from stomachache. Yes, my friend, just as the head feels brighter after a revelation, the belly feels brighter after tasting cobra."

Fingers snapped like castanets. I heard my friend mutter something to the maître d', the one who looked like a Chinese Napoleon.

"Chu chu chu . . ."

My watch still showed a nonexistent time, or maybe it did exist, just not for me.

A chef with a white boot on his head brought our table a vase of Tibetan green glass swarming with spectacled cobras. It looked like a display window at an optician's. But here the spectacles were swimming around in the vase together with the spotted slippery faces. Behind the spectacles, zigzag eyes were shining.

William pointed with his cigar at the viper he wanted and the chef grabbed it by the neck with long, silver tongs.

It got darker in the dining room. The sun's wick was turned down lower and lower. A small theater lit up across from us. A midget raised the curtain.

On stage was a violet aquarium. A seashell opened up on the floor and the mother of all pearls swam out of it. The pearl began dancing to the sounds of a flute, swimming out of the aquarium and dancing into the crowd, her belly contracting or swelling with the flute's louder or softer notes.

When the dancer pearled back into the shell—our plates were already filled with viper. Steamed in hell, it was the color of red pepper. Only the spectacle frames, without their glass, were still dark around the deep, skeletal eyes, like an eternal tattoo.

William couldn't get enough. He washed down every bite with hummingbird wine. And as for me, to be tactful, I faked eating, moving my lips with pleasure, like the angel in the Bible . . .

The lights went up onstage again and the midget raised the curtain.

For the audience's delectation a set of Siamese twins appeared: two little sisters in one dress. Both with the same faces, sweating together in a figure eight. They sang. It grated like electric music. The gluttons whinnied.

I felt my throat closing up. William didn't let me have a second thought: "Both sisters have husbands already. I was at their wedding myself. They say that both sisters cheat on them. Each sister with the other's husband. The husbands are grown together. Who knows how the tragedy will end."

"I guess they could divorce and then remarry, each one with her lover." I was being pulled into the tale.

"We both had the same bright idea. I gave them exactly that advice, but the sisters didn't want to listen. What will we get from divorcing and remarrying? they said. We'll just lose—both our husbands and our lovers."

The curtain dropped. The concert continued in our plates.

A soup was served. William explained it to me.

"'Nest of blue swallows,' that's what the soup is called. A poetic name. People climb trees, steal nests of blue swallows, and turn them into this soup, which smells like Chanel perfume. Apart from the rare taste it's also very healthy for the heart. They even say that it prevents heart attacks. No surprise there. All life is a continual process of transformation. I was in the slaughterhouses of Chicago—do you know what they do there with the millions of eyes of butchered cattle? They are turned into expensive ladies' stockings."

"I was in the slaughterhouses of Chicago as well"—I tried to show off for William—"but I didn't see anything like that. You know why? Because I felt like I had to throw up."

"The time will come when they'll turn ladies' stockings back into cows' eyes." William brought to his lips a spoonful of blue swallows' nest.

"My apologies for changing the subject, which is very interesting"—I got bolder—"but is your encyclopedia of modern world literature already out?"

"Oh, right," William recollected. "If you stay here for two weeks longer you can take a copy with you. You are very well represented, but I have to tell you the truth: the encyclopedia is just my hobby. Everybody has their eccentricities, which make them more or less normal. My passion is politics. I was already a politician in the womb. And to be a politician in these parts you need a lot of talent, no less than a Hemingway or a Picasso."

After finishing up his plate of blue swallows' nest, he pointed out a sign that ran the length of the stage: "You know what that says? I'll translate for you. 'Revolvers, hand grenades, and bombs are forbidden. Our dear guests are kindly requested to please leave these items in the coat check.' So that's an illustration of how easy it is to be a politician in this city now."

IV

The next moment his smile fled into the deep wrinkles of his forehead like a white mouse. He pleasantly greeted a fat man at a table next to ours.

"The Minister of Culture," my host winked at me with Asian irony, "or at least that's what he's called. That's the title he was given. One fine day someone said to him, 'Hey, loser, starting today you're our Minister of Culture.' Did he have a choice? That's what he became. We are victims of illusion. Idiots blare all sorts of stupidity in our ears, and we of little courage nod our heads.

"Who is a great artist? The one who's called that. A true artist doesn't know his true worth at all. But the poor bastard who's called Minister of Culture has no luck. You see the beautiful lady at the table with her fan? A young widow. Ten days ago the boys in the jungle shot her husband—the general."

His smile stretched to his ears: "And see what a dish he ordered. The bastard. He knows very well that the current liberal government forbade this delicacy. The widow of the murdered general will enjoy herself tonight."

I turned my head and improved my observation post.

Forward came the maître d'—the Chinese Napoleon—and behind him two Filipinos in leopard-skin uniforms, carrying through the empty aisle between the occupied tables a square cage made of intersecting bars.

They carried the cage by two brass handles, like a heavy suitcase. When they put it down on the table where the Minister of Culture and his lady were sitting, only then did I notice that something was sticking out from the cage's cover, through a circular hole—the confused head of a monkey in a shaggy hairy mask.

And perhaps this was no monkey head but a wild coconut? I saw such hairy coconuts once upon a time in Zululand. But there's no reason to delude myself. Amid the coconut's flowing hair I glimpsed moist, trembling blinks. They seared themselves into my memory, they pleaded for mercy, the head rotated helplessly as in a crucible, unable to duck back into the cage—but by the same token he could not yank his hands and feet out of the cage either.

The culture minister was still flirting with the widow, the cage with the monkey still at his right. Apparently he was finishing up a spicy story. The widow hid coquettishly behind her red fan and teased him, like someone provoking a bull with a red cloth. Now the culture minister took a long, special mallet and leveled a powerful, practiced whack at the monkey's brain.

There was a sobbing. Like the cry of a disabled child. And the head's moist blinking turned inward from cosmic terror. But the culture minister saw and heard nothing. He was hungry and (in my imagination) already full from the widow, but now he took from a dish a little pile of cooked rice, pressed it together with heavy ringed fingers, dipped the rice into the split-open brain of the monkey, salted and peppered the warm matter, tossed it into his mouth, and washed it down with a tall glass of something.

An orchestra hurried up and drowned out the crying.

"I see you're tired. Drank too much hummingbird wine." William tried to shake me free of the nightmare. "So let's go. It's getting too crowded here. The X-ray-eyed men are coming out. You see that guy at the entrance with the half-burned face, like the fur of a dead mouse? They call him Zuzupa Kandali. The opium dealers are scared of him; they tremble before him. So let's go. I'll take you back to the hotel. Don't forget tomorrow: the banquet in your honor in my personal villa."

V

I was in a daze when I got to the hotel. I barely had time to peel off my dirty clothes. The iron headboard of the bed, and the bars at my feet, gravitated toward each other and grew together over my body. The bed became my cage. My head stuck out through a brass ring in the top. I couldn't pull my body out and couldn't drag my head back inside.

The door slowly opened: William. The cigar in his mouth half-smoked, just the cold, dead ash attached by a spiderweb thread, like a glimmer of sun on the top of a damp tree when the sun itself has passed on beyond the day. In William's hand: a silver hammer. One William becoming another. A third. The room now full with Williams, all with the same face. All of them with the same cigar in their mouths, the cold ash hanging by a spider thread. In the hand of every one: a silver hammer.

I heard the pounding of a thought inside me: It can't be, can it, that a plural is so like a singular? Every particle of dust, every atom has its own face. And perhaps I was surrounded by mirrors here, like at the barber's?

I wanted to scream. But it doesn't matter what I wanted. My tongue was a wet rock. The monkey wanted to scream too, and she could only sob like a developmentally delayed child.

All the Williams approached the cage. Came closer and closer to me. Each one raised the hammer and dealt me a blow to the brain. At that blow, the dangling ash fell off the cigars. I felt like handfuls of rice were being dipped into me. The Williams would soon devour my soul.

"Run away!" I begged my soul. "As fast as you can!"

"Where to?" She showed her teeth, scared. "Where can I run to if I want to stay in my body?"

"Hide in my heel. The cannibals will not reach you there."

When I woke up, as if rising from the dead, it was already quite late in the day. The cage had turned back into a bed. A mosquito was standing on my forehead and pounding with a little hammer. Besides the one on my forehead, a whole troop of mosquitoes were fiddling away with silken ruthlessness. The room was full of blueish, airborne ash.

"Thanks and praise to you, Creator, who separated dream and reality," I prayed.

And the same power that had yanked me out of the airplane and brought me to the foreign city catapulted me back to the airport.

VI

"Even if I have to wait an entire day, I will happily wait at the aerodrome," I said to myself on the way there. But I got lucky—or maybe it wasn't luck, but thanks to the one who planned the whole adventure: I arrived at the aerodrome at the same time as yesterday. And just like yesterday, an airplane landed right away, and half an hour later it was off again eagling through the dry seascape to the place where I must land, where my friends are already worried and tired of waiting.

What happened to me? Why did I run away all of a sudden? Why am I insulting William and not coming to the banquet in my honor? Who is directing the show here?

I felt a tear in my throat and swallowed it. I felt a lot better. Did the tear perceive what my eyes didn't see? Yes, the tear had revealed to me, as in a vision, the reason why I fled. Should I call William, tell him, and ask for forgiveness over the phone? I wouldn't be capable of explaining my strange behavior, so I decided to write him a letter.

And since I had never before written such a letter to anybody, I remember its contents word for word, as one remembers a face, and I quote it in full here for the reader, so that he too can remember—until he forgets:

> To the very strange William Buk,
> I write these words at the aerodrome. I'm flying away from here soon. I am running away into the air, if one can use that expression.
> Neither of us is to blame that I didn't come to the banquet

(Zuzupa Kandali was probably there too!) and made you a laugh-ingstock in the eyes of the city president and the fantastic elite.

Let me tell you briefly the reason for my unfriendly response to your favor.

When we sat in the restaurant while your culture minister broke open the monkey's skull, my glance trembled over your face for just a moment. Do you know that you smiled then too, show-ing your canines? In that smile, I think, I suddenly understood that you and no other are my true murderer.

Don't worry. You did not hang or shoot me. Just the opposite; you were very humane to me and demonstrated generous friend-ship. Without you I would have had the same fate here as the monkey. But if we had met each other in Auschwitz—you have undoubtedly read about such a locale in the modern world—you would have certainly been my murderer. My intuition doesn't deceive me.

I know it's not your fault. You were never in Auschwitz and we never met there. It's fair that you should still become prime minister, and if the boys in the jungle don't do away with you, you will live out your years in honor, and they'll make a nice funeral for you and erect a granite monument. But even then you will not stop being my murderer. And that is the reason why I had to flee from my esteemed murderer as fast as possible.

May we never meet again!

1970

THE TWIN

I

This happened in the Aladdin Cafeteria on the steep hills of the Old Jaffa seashore. This cafeteria with the intense blue dome, blue like laundry bluing, old-fashioned glass windows set in narrow frames, steps made of marble excavated out of the very earth, which belonged to another time and another building, descending now a couple of stories into the depths of the mountain to a glassed-in terrace cut into its curved face.

I allow myself betimes to disappear down there away from my table, from my work, from ghosts and people, particularly during the day, when the cafeteria is nearly empty and no one keeps me from weaving the sea's weeping into my silence.

From here, the sea's edge, the prophet Jonah fled to Tarshish . . .

II

I'm in the Aladdin again today. It's a spitefully humid day. The sea air is limp. It floats face up on the small, shattered waves, and the gap in the air over the sea is the color of the inside of a mother-of-pearl shell.

A locust hatches in weather like this.

I have an idea, which progresses to a vision: the waves opposite me are not waves but the grandchildren of the whale that swallowed Jonah.

And as I chat with those darling grandchildren, the terrace suddenly turns into a glass whale. An evil darkness descends over the sea, slashing it to pieces with a glowing diamond. Galloping rain over the waves' battlefield. Extinguished, the light of midday with its candelabrum of matte milk overhead and its candelabrum below.

This all happens so hastily that the white waterbirds can't finish composing their letters, and they too are trapped among the slats of rain.

However, according to the clock it's now noon, and in the glass belly of the whale there are only a few guests: a drowsing old man with a newspaper in his drowsy hands; a snuggling couple like two thick branches of one, let's say, tree of love; a woman with a black veil over her face; and me, the witness to all this. Nevertheless, the cafeteria manager takes such pity that he orders the lights turned on. The bulbs manage but a blink and like freshly decapitated snake heads go out with a hissing of tongues.

On the outside of the windowpanes, which chatter like teeth, a cloud floats by, earth that has made its way up into heaven, a fiery plow in its breast. I see its reflection: the woman with the black veil is sitting at my table right now. The storm slapped the glass whale and slid the woman over to me, together with the chair.

Six digits carved into her left arm, ending with a one and a three.

III

Thirteen. The number is relevant to me. My birthdate ends in a one and a three. The house where I was born was also stamped with a thirteen. Later, that same number found its way to all my abodes, inns, and hotels, and it snuck, masked, into all sorts of figures and numbers that bear some relation to my wanderings over the earth. Occasionally it divided like an amoeba and doubled. Here it supposedly disappeared—say kaddish for it—and there a new transformation. And always just at the right time. It would be easier to rid myself of my own shadow than to separate from this enchanted partner. On the other hand, why should I try freeing myself? It wouldn't be any better . . .

"No, it wouldn't be any better," the woman barges into my thoughts, the black veil on her face: one cloud on top of the other, glowing tiger spots along the edges. "It won't be any better and it won't be any worse, it's just exactly as you wrote:

" 'I have tasted no other life

And don't know if terror is more delectable—' "

"Who are you?" I grab her wrist where the six digits are carved in with the one and the three at the end, and both palms wrestle, each trying to bend back the other. Our breaths struggle as our hands wrestle. The woman's breath is accompanied by a warm tongue, salty and sweet together. The dazzle of a shattered mirror infiltrates.

"Who am I?" Her face furrows behind the veil. "A good question. I've asked that of the One and Only for years, and may he forgive me, but it's like I'm talking to a wall. Possibly there's an answer on the other side of the wall, but my head and heart are already burdened from sitting. And you, so impatient, want to know who I am."

And suddenly the veiled woman bursts out laughing, the firestones of her laughter rolling down into my throat. "In any case I will tell you who I am. The One and Only has already forgotten who I am, but for me, his creation, the memory still flickers. Thus mark my words: I sought you out, and found this cafeteria by the sea, just to tell you who I am."

I can still feel her vanished laughter rolling in my throat. But now the laughter is mixed with the crying of the sea and the rain. "Do you remember the name Myron Marcuse? You *must* remember, because Myron Marcuse was your neighbor. You lived at 13 Vilkomir, and him—across the street. If not him, you should remember his daughters, who the street called The Little Twins, though each one of them was anointed with a different name and a different soul. The younger one was named Hodesl and the older one, born all of 13 minutes earlier, Grunye. And that, then, is me—Grunye, the older sister.

"I am Grunye, but I'm not sure. Until our premature adolescence we were as alike as two tears from the same eye. Ribbons were braided into our hair, Hodes a blue one and me a red one, so that people wouldn't mix us up. In high school we used to prank the boys—when Hodes had a rendezvous on a moonlit night, it was me, Grunye, who came, and vice versa. Only rarely did a suitor figure out that he was courting the other one. Most times we both ruined the game. Outsmarting or fooling the boys got to be a habit for us, second nature. But when the game got too serious, we stopped the acting—it could even go so far that someone in love with Hodes might want to commit suicide because of her sister.

"On the other hand, our souls were different, so no one had to braid any ribbons into them. Hodes was a born violinist. At six, like Mozart, she gave a concert with the city philharmonic orchestra. Someone said then that Hodes had put a white handkerchief on her shoulder because her violin was crying. Her music teacher quipped that instead of red blood cells, red violins coursed in her arteries. In my blood—the music of revolution. I would have stabbed out my own eyes if it would have made things brighter for my neighbors. What good is abstract brightness when you're blind yourself? I wasn't grown up enough for such an elementary idea. While I was handing in the last exam on graduating the Realgymnasium, I was caught in an iron net. I was accused of doing away with a provocateur on Belmont, that fir-covered mountain that Napoleon named, and where we teenagers carried on love affairs.

"Myron Marcuse was our stepfather. After the tragedy with our father—he was cut to pieces under a train—he married our mother more for our sake than for his own. During the day, Myron Marcuse was a goldsmith, and at night a thinker, a philosopher. He carried around a theory that the reason for all tragedies, individual and societal, is jealousy, and when you're jealous you're capable of anything. If *Homo sapiens* were cured of the disease called jealousy, they would turn into angels on the Earth. For years he performed psychophysical experiments on goats, dogs, snakes, wrens, and two baby monkeys, which he had bought off a Roma. Our courtyard looked like a zoo. Finally he extracted a kind of serum, which he called antijelin, which was also the name of the brochure about his theory that he published in three languages: Yiddish, Hebrew, and Polish.

"When Chaim Nachman Bialik visited our city, Myron Marcuse sent his brochure in to him and requested an audience. The poet received him in the Palace Hotel, where he was staying, and chatted with him for a few hours. Myron Marcuse later related that Bialik was impressed by his theory. He expected that when Bialik returned home to the Land of Israel he would be the messenger for Marcuse's teaching. He'd give speeches to make people inject antijelin into Jews and Arabs alike, creating peace between them. First though, he'd inject himself with antijelin so he wouldn't be jealous of the young hotshot poets."

IV

In the glass whale, the runaway clouds turn paler. A buzzing meteor—a flea. The channel of the sea floor, like an inside-out sleeve, is turned right-side out again. Grunye pauses in front of the rain. If it cried it out, the rain would feel better. As she puts a cigarette into her mouth, a bolt of lightning comes along and does her the favor of giving her a light.

Dull, sulfurous circles—wedding rings for dead brides—approach and are left hanging on my eyelids. The odor and taste of homebrewed Passover mead sticks to my palate.

The black veil disappears, and a veil of drunken smoke weaves itself over Grunye's face. The spun material gets thinner and thinner, turning into wrinkles.

She is silent. But now the cigarette is about to wink out into nothing and, sated with its ash, she continues: "His antijelin didn't manage to redeem humanity, but it did redeem him. While flogging the Jews into the ghetto with his whip, Myron Marcuse injected himself with a considerable dose of the godly serum and was redeemed from jealousy for eternity. Our mother needed no antijelin. She was jealous of no one but the dead. The Almighty had let her into their kingdom.

"Hodesl was a famous violin player. My sister played on the strings and me on the chains. In the death camp the strings became chains as well. Here we became alike again, Hodesl like me and me like Hodesl, like two tears from the same eye. The few who remembered us in the camp from our childhood and youth crowned us with the title The Little Twins, as a sign that the world is still the world and what it used to be.

"Everyone in the camp was little twins. The crematoria turned us not just into little twins but into hundreduplets and thousanduplets; one could not distinguish between a man and a woman, a child and an old man; everybody wore the same clothing and everyone's head was shaved, and every skeleton, as you know, has the same smile—but even so only Hodesl and I were called the twins.

"Not just our faces or bodies but our souls too, Hodesl's and mine, were twinned in the camp, if not like twin tears then like twin sparks from the crematorium. If we had girl secrets, ambition secrets, love secrets, we shared them like we shared crumbs of bread and shards of bone. Subconsciously we probably wanted to hide our secrets with each other. Secrets want to survive too, they want to live long enough to be revealed. When one of us is saved, the other's secrets should be saved too.

"Now I am coming to the most important part of my story, the reason I sought you out and found you and the reason why you are, if not a whole, then at least a half twin.

"We were really close neighbors. We grew up on the same street, and the same sleet bathed our hair. The same swallow skipped and sang from my roof to yours. You used to come over to our house, giving me your improper looks. I didn't get anywhere by flirting with you. I was too earthbound. It happened that you came into the workshop to listen to Myron Marcuse bang his hammer or to chat with him about his antijelin. I didn't have the guts to barge in. But a hammer banged away in you, and its echo resounded with the hammer that beat in my sister. No, you never mixed up the two of us.

"Among the secrets that Hodesl hid within me was the secret of the two hammers.

"You still don't understand why I looked for and found you? I was left with one passion: to wander across the world and kiss her memorial clouds. Maybe her image was preserved somewhere? Maybe there's someone alive who heard her play? Maybe a heart that trembled with hers still trembles? I didn't go to Paris because of the Louvre; I carry a Louvre in myself where an insane God hung his paintings. I flew to Paris to lay a bouquet of roses on the grave of a music teacher of Hodesl's."

V

"Music. I have no other name for it. Human is also a name for all humans. Just like Albert Einstein was born, Siegfried Hoch was too. Siegfried Hoch, commandant of the camp, had already tasted all human and animal pleasures, like the chef-de-cuisine in a hotel tastes every guest's prepared dishes. Only an orchestra was missing for his New Year's. So he gave a speech to the numbered skeletons: if there were any musicians in his kingdom, he would hire them for at least a year.

"Musicians appeared quickly. Famous musicians from Poland, Hungary, Austria, Holland. For them, Siegfried Hoch broke open the storehouses of plunder, and under fingers thin as strings and pale chewed lips, he saw cellos, violins, clarinets, and flutes come to life.

"Hodesl didn't want to reveal her artistic profession because she didn't want to be separated from me and had no wish to become only a half twin, and also because she didn't want to play for the Angel of Death. Like a mother, I insisted she join the orchestra. Maybe Hodesl could save herself this way.

"It was New Year's Eve, 1944. Siegfried Hoch sat on a podium, bundled up in a puffy white fur coat and a fur hat pulled over his bitten-off left ear (done by a Warsaw girl whom he drove into the gas chambers), peeling oranges and stuffing his mouth with them, tossing the peels into a basket.

"In front of him was the gymnastics court, and in the middle of it was a gallows from which the air hung in a noose, with its blue tongue sticking out. With the gallows and black, twinkling snow in the background, like blackbirds between earth and heaven, the musicians, barefoot and winnowed by biting frost, played Beethoven's 'Eroica.' The conductor, a maestro from the Vienna Philharmonic, tossed his long, flowing sleeves and tried to grab the baton like a drowning man grabs at a straw.

"The ensemble, with Hodesl playing first violin, tore open the purple heavens. The audience curled out of the smokestack with ashen faces. When the maestro bowed, moans of applause were heard. The commandant was also clearly moved. He piled up a big stack of orange peels and tossed it at the musicians.

"Even before the orange peels managed to glimmer into the snow, the musicians—like eagles with broken wings—swooped down to snap up the gift. The conductor of the Vienna Philharmonic, the baton between his frozen fingers, displayed a virtuosic nimbleness in hurling himself at the delicacy.

"And Hodesl? She alone stayed frozen on the gymnastics court with her violin clutched to her heart. She was too embarrassed by the ashen faces, the violin, and the 'Eroica' to kneel before the white fur coat and its orange peels.

"At the moment that separated those two non-Jewish years, the old and the new, the commandant wobbled into our block and called out Hodesl's number. I was the first to jump up from the wooden bed and stand at attention. Both of us then, Hodesl and I, were twins in the camp. I prayed that my sister with perfect hearing would go deaf, become deafened by a dream. The commandant had already led me out of the block and to the gymnastics court, where the gallows looked like its own shadow either falling forward or standing still. My breath melted the ice air, and setting a pace in that direction was easier.

"My prayer was not heard. The other half twin raced after the first—Hodesl showed the commandant her bare arm and the true, carved numbers. They shone like stars.

"The stars still shine in them. The numbers of my Hodesl were extinguished forever."

VI

Grunye lights a fresh cigarette from the last spark of the previous one. This time, it seems, with a specific intention: to weave a curtain of smoke between us.

Why doesn't she want the sea to foam in its darkness? Why is she scared of a splinter of sun?

I want to ask her this. I have a lot of other questions. But my words go out like so many stars embedded in Hodesl's arm. Once again the taste and scent of old-time, homey Passover mead sticks to my palate: "I told you one passion remained for me, wandering around the world and kissing the little clouds of Hodesl's memory. Cuddling up to those who loved my sister. Truth be told this is my second and probably last passion. After the so-called liberation, I had no other desire than to follow the traces of Siegfried Hoch. There is no corner of the earth where I didn't lay my traps for him.

"When the commandant disappeared in his puffy white fur coat, the camp inmates looked like gasping fish on the bottom of a pond where the water had run out of the sluices. Taking in the fresh air was not enough to live, to feel one's own wounds and enjoy their harm. To live one had to breathe death. A magnetic needle showed me where I should travel. The first station the magnetic needle showed me as my destination was our hometown. I found the gold that Myron Marcuse had buried under the cherry tree in our garden. It was in a box of gopherwood, together with several ampules of antijelin and his brochure with the same name. The roots of the cherry tree held out the box with their cut-up fingers, as if they had sucked the color and the energy of the cherries from the buried gold.

"Do you remember the name Zvulik Podval? His father was Tzole the chimneysweep. They lived near the pump next to the first brick factory. When I was in jail due to the business with the provocateur, Zvulik was my partner and my neighbor. The same Zvulik tracked down the commandant's wife in Linz, became her so-called lover, and sent me copies of her husband's letters and their addresses.

"It's a big world, but America is bigger—that's the naive saying of my grandmother's that stuck in my memory. So I've searched through the world and America both; I've learned Burmese and looked for the commandant in a Buddhist temple in Burma; I looked for him in Mozambique among the ivory sellers; I learned how to play the part of a belly dancer, wanting to dazzle him in a Baghdad cabaret. I can speak Arabic, Turkish, Portuguese, and Spanish. I understand the languages of the indigenous inhabitants of the Americas.

"We have both changed our faces many times. Our shapes. He disguised himself as a Don Ricardo Alvarez, and me as a Doña Teresa. I lay in wait for him in the jungles along the Amazon and in the Galapagos Islands in the quiet ocean; I looked for him in the Ecuador capital, Quito, and in the Andes and at the Cayambe and Chimborazo volcanoes, where an eagle can lift a young cow in its talons.

"For how many years do you think our worldwide game of cat and mouse went on? Thirteen? But all thirteen years I was the cat and he was the mouse. I made a fatal error, relying on his bitten off left ear as a distinguishing mark. But not every

Cain is fated to brag about his mark. If someone can be fitted with a fake soul, why can't someone fit themselves with a fake ear?

"Now you can hear how the international game of cat and mouse reached its finale. I was wandering in Quito at that time. A couple of months ago my mouse had become a bat. Zvulik Podval let me know from Linz that Madam Hoch was moving to Peru.

"When switching countries, and most of the time when moving cities, I always used to take a plane. It's cleaner in the air than on the ground. Now taking a train appealed to me. I needed to meet someone. In the middle of the night the train stopped at a small station. When I got off and went into the terminal to get something to drink, a barefoot Indian took a statuette out of his chest pocket and offered it to me for sale.

"I recognized it immediately. Its eyes, like blue drops of venom on needle tips, were not at all altered. His left ear was bitten off, and the stitches that held his artificial ear together were obvious. He only lacked the white puffy fur coat and the fur hat to become the camp commandant once more. I realized right away: Siegfried Hoch had been turned into a tsantsa.

"Do you know what a tsantsa is? In the jungles at the foot of the Andes Mountains there lives an Indian tribe called the Jivaro. The Jivaro are men of war and men of revenge. When they capture their enemies, mere suspects who hide in the jungles, or policemen, they cut off their heads, drop them into kettles full of secret juices, herbs, and rocks, and boil them until the heads are shrunken to the size of a fist. The hair, wrinkles, freckles, and moustaches are still there. That kind of head is called a tsantsa. The trade in tsantsas is definitely forbidden—yet the opium trade is forbidden too! Modern man likes the unusual, the forbidden, and tourists pay high prices for such shrunken heads. A tsantsa without a pedigree is cheaper. A tsantsa from a hangman is much more expensive. I was told that family members paid $10,000 for the tsantsa of a minister."

VII

The whale with a rainbow tail swims into Old Jaffa. The sea tried without success to break the chains and escape from shore. It surrendered to a cosmic field marshal. The storm flees too on its violin-string legs.

Here is the old man. The newspaper is still stuck to his glasses. He read it before in his dream, and now, on waking, the news is—old.

The branched-together couple splits sweetly apart, but the unseen roots are attracted to the same well.

And Grunye? Still veiled, only the 13 on her bare arm is illuminated by a pink ray of sunlight.

Fiery clouds reveal themselves on the horizon, and behind them a round, small sun swings over the water.

Suddenly, Grunye gets up from the table, and the black veil is ripped asunder by a mourner's tear.

"He's peeling oranges again, the merciful one, and he's throwing the peels into the snow, at the musicians. Hodesl will not bow, Hodesl will not bow!"

1973

THE FIRST WEDDING IN THE CITY

I

Then the city was transformed into a sunset.

The tombstones of the two cemeteries, the old and the new, were miraculously saved, hidden under the leafpiles of the surrounding maples or under the discolored, hoarsely crackling snow; these tombstones big and small, overgrown, covered over or sunken, look like hands of the drowning. The people are drowning, have already drowned in boiling maelstroms, and only their hands, their thin fingers, seek rescue, still have some sort of connection with everything pillaged aboveground. They search, touch emptiness, they seek the strawlike sun at the end of summer. Something to hold on to.

It was the first end of summer after the sunset, the first wedding in the city since generations upon generations.

II

Roytl convinced Dondele, her match, to celebrate their wedding, spend the night, and make their home in the noble brick house where she was born. On the other side of the Viliya, where the street ends, she loved to sit facing the mountain in companionable silence for hours, while wagons of clay departed for the brick factories along the river and a wind played at the foot of the mountain with water lilies in a pond, tangled like hair.

Although Dondele was born on the same street and was, like Roytl, branded in his very soul with that place, he somewhat resented the prospect of drinking their happiest night in that noble brick house facing the clay mountain, where no one else lived anymore.

Dondele would rather have had the chuppah in a forest of fir trees where blue canvas strung between the thickly grown branches was woven with golden threads and the song of birds. But he remembered that the aged fir trees also own a portion of the sunset.

III

Dondele was a chimneysweep. An important profession, almost entirely Jewish, and mostly passed down in that city from one generation to the next. Fathers taught the profession to their boys when they were still children, at the same time as the alphabet. Only one boy in each family was anointed with the soot. The other boys could be blacksmiths, carpenters, raft makers, or brickmakers in the brick factories. There was even a chimneysweep by the name of Meirem who taught his daughter because his wife didn't grant him any sons.

The dogmatism of letting only some offspring inherit chimneysweeping came from the fact that the profession is not so base as one might think. It is full of secrets and its own oral tradition. Walled up in the attics, and most of all, sealed between the bricks of the chimeys, there are treasures that the world has not yet seen. The crown of King Sobiecki is preserved there too. The diamonds of that crown and others shine from the chimneys in the dark autumn nights. The problem is that these jewels are very similar to sparks or bolts of lightning, so you have to be a real professional not to be fooled.

Most inhabitants of the city, Jews and non-Jews alike, looked down on the chimneysweeps as oppressed people. In reality, the chimneysweeps were on top, but even so, they didn't look down on those below.

The author of this story now lives in a city whose roofs are mostly without attics or chimneys. If there's no chimney there's no clay or limestone oven, no happy fire, no birchwood giving off a rainbow with its flame, no poker or oven broom, and no special cover with a little knob for closing the chimney. And over the roof there's no smoke, gray ladder to the stars.

Since there are no more chimneys and their treasures shining from inside, there are also no more homeschooled chimneysweeps.

IV

Dondele was 16 when he entered into the captivity of the seven-streets ghetto, together with his mother. He walked with a bucket shaped like a half moon on his back, and with a rope, lead weight, and a broom; and she, Asne, carried a book of women's prayers under her arm, imbued with tears and spice, full of sweet prayers that God enjoys.

In captivity, Asne stuck into the décolleté of her dress the carefully saved silver pin that her groom, who a little later was Dondele's father, gave her as a present when they got engaged.

The silver pin was a mnemonic that helped Asne remember that she was not anybody else.

When they started kidnapping old men and women, Dondele walled her up in a chimney in the passageway. When he later rescued her, Asne was black and shrunken like a cinder. He barely recognized her. After a few days, he had to wall her in there again because they started chasing after kids; his mother had started to look like a child.

Although there was no such prayer in the women's prayerbook, Asne prayed in captivity with these words: darling God, show favor by allowing me to live long enough to die in my own bed.

Her own bed was far away, was the point of the prayer.

By contrast, Dondele was alive and wanted to keep living so as not to die. He wanted to live both for his mother's sake and for himself. He wanted to live for his own sake.

V

Since the city's new rulers had moved into the brick houses and buildings of the previous inhabitants, the chimneys overhead had gotten stuffed with soot from lack of cleaning. Here and there roofs caught on fire, so the rulers had no choice but to seek out in the ghetto-of-seven-streets the last remaining chimneysweeps, giving them permits to move freely about the city to clean out its chimneys. But the chimneysweeps had to spend the night in captivity with their brothers.

Dondele was among the few who set out into the city in the early hours with bucket and broom, fluttering till sunset over the sun-baked roofs and their copper-colored shingles. The shingles, pockmarked and cracked, looked from a distance like pottery shards laid over the city's dead eyes.

While clambering over the roofs and attics, Dondele noted all the hidden chambers and hideouts and the different types of passageways between attics. He also made it over to his former neighbors, the brickmakers, getting food that he smuggled into captivity in the bottom of his bucket.

Asne smiled for the first time in that age of slaughter. That happened when Dondele returned from the city in the evening and pulled out from the soot in his bucket a fresh white cheese. Her smile was moist, barely sparkling, like a drop of autumnal dew on a spiderweb in the garden. Asne noticed right away, however, that the white cheese smuggled out for her by her son was covered in black fingerprints, and her smile melted away.

If Dondele's bucket had a tongue, what stories it could have told! It would have told those stories better. For example, how Dondele stole weapons while cleaning out the barracks and smuggled them into captivity in the same bucket; or how the guards at the gate searched the bucket and laughed at the crazy man who brought gray ash into the ghetto for his dinner. The stupid guards didn't realize that it wasn't ash but gunpowder.

The weapons and the gunpowder were not smuggled in for him. He delivered them to his friend Zvulik Podval, for the hotblooded boys and girls.

A blacksmith hammers through a winter night in the ghetto of the seven streets. Red sparks are hanging in empty space, and the shadows are frozen to the snow.

The roofs with their chimneys sticking out—like a forest covered by snow.

Dondele is wandering in this forest, and in the pail on his back is a child. He found the little baby in a ruined basement. Dondele has to save the child, hide it in the city. He knows that Fedke the brickmaker is a good person who won't kick him out.

The moon swings over the roofs in a sled hauled by a silver horse. Dondele jumps into its sled; the moon is kind and won't throw him out. They're about to take the sled across the abyss, but what's that ringing in the pail? A bullet from a night hunter splinters the cry of the bell into quicksilver shards.

Dondele falls into the abyss and onto a pile of snow. The horse with its empty sled vanishes into the forest.

When the ghetto and all those imprisoned within began to sink, Dondele managed to get his mother out.

He carried her on his back from one attic to another, through side alleys, back passageways, and orchards with overgrown apple and pear trees. Orphaned cats wailed from branches, longing for their vanished owners.

Dondele, with his mother on his back, swam across the Viliya and slipped into the brickworks called Faive Peker's Brick Factory.

There, in the tottering building, where bricks used to be baked in the kiln when Faive Peker lived; there, under the oven whose fire had been snuffed out, Dondele built a hiding place for his mother.

He cleverly rigged it up with the knowledge and eagerness of his neighbor, Fedke, the brickmaker, to whom Dondele had taught the art of catching doves. Fedke helped Dondele bring his mother's bed into the hideout. Not, God forbid, so that Asne, as she had said, would be lucky enough to die in her own bed. He did it so that she would be able to live.

VI

In the hideout in the brickworks, Asne realized that in the panicked flight from the ghetto of the seven streets she had forgotten, or didn't manage to take with her, her women's prayer book. While her son returned to the maw of the beast to bring back the tear-stained pages for his mother, the beast at that very moment slammed shut the teeth that had been lying in wait for him, and Dondele was left inside. Without heaven or earth.

The magic pail lost its magic, no more broom dunked in soot, no more rope tossing dreams between roofs.

First, Dondele thought he had fallen through a chimney. Something like that had happened before: a chimneysweep had a glass of something on the roof and *bam!*, headfirst into the chimney darkness. If that's what had happened, he couldn't comprehend why falling was taking forever.

He's not falling. He's riding. Under him, the wheels turn like mice on a carousel. The carousel stops, the mice become two-legged, and they slide him into an earthen sleeve.

His head is assaulted by the odor of death, and all the shattered mirrors from the city's attics splinter dazzlingly in his mind. But the splinters go out soon, and only their stabbing glass is left in his mind.

The thought runs through him: now he's in a grave together with the sun. Both are dead, the sun and him. He's just a little livelier in death so he can pick up the odor of the sun.

"Where am I?" His voice escapes from him like an echo.

Yiddish words sober him up. "Young man, where you are is hell."

Dondele grabs his ears. He thinks they are trying to humiliate him. "Since when do they speak Yiddish in hell?"

Another voice, the color of ash, answers: "Since Frankenstein has been king of the pits."

VII

Is it day or night? Two strong arms pick Dondele up, pull him out of the earthen sleeve, bring him outside. They are heavy, the two arms, like he was carrying a yoke bearing two buckets of lead. They bring him into a blacksmith's forge. A skeleton with bronze ribs shackles his legs in chains. The chains are loose and dangle down to the ground, so he can drag them. The chains must clank when he walks; that's what Frankenstein, the king of the trenches, ordered.

Congratulations. The chains are clanking. Now he knows the earthen sleeve is a deep grotto; this is his home from now on. Dondele realizes his mistake. The sun with whom he was earlier devoured is no sun; it's the glimmer of a pyre, a pyramid of burning people. Their limbs are birds of fire that keep rising from the earth. That man was right. Young fellow, where you are is hell.

That's how Dondele became a burner of corpses, partner to the others.

Those others were both the same people and different ones, but all had shackles on their legs.

Dondele remembers uncovering a grave and finding a mezuzah next to the corpse. He took it out and showed it to a friend in the chain gang who had studied in a yeshiva. That friend didn't sleep a single night, pondering over and over again if the mezuzah was still fit to use. By dawn he had reached his verdict—it's not— and beat the mezuzah into the doorpost where one descends into the grotto.

Someone else, while burning dead bodies, recognized his child. "I'm the happiest of all the dead!" he cried out, jumping into the fire with the child in his arms.

Among the burners of corpses was also a jokester who quipped bitterly, "Hey, I wonder what novel they're publishing in the *Forward* these days?"

At night, the burners dug a tunnel in the grotto to escape. Kostya worked out the plan. He quickly recognized Dondele for what he was, and the young chimneysweep became his right-hand man. They chiseled and dug out the tunnel with pieces of glass, wooden spoons, with their teeth and nails. Later they dug up an arrow, an ax, and a knife, which the victims had taken on their final path. They piled the dug-out dirt under planks in a nearby well.

The tunnel was almost ready. It just about reached to the fir trees on the other side of the fence. Kostya and Dondele had already selected the night and time to make their escape. But when they were digging the last few feet they hit a huge rock, a stumbling block.

Kostya wanted to give up. Dondele had a fit of desperation. But something happened then just when he had accepted his chains and his arrival at hell. A form approached him in the grotto and murmured face to face: "Dondele, do you recognize me?"

The question startled him. Of course he knows everyone here, but the voice was more familiar than the face.

The form took his hand and brought it under its clothing to its beating heart: "I'll tell you, if you still don't recognize me."

Dondele's fingers were imbued with a warm memory; he relived his first boyhood joy, trembling soft like a newborn dove.

"You? No . . ."

"Yes, it's me, Roytl, from long ago. I have a different name here. Besides my savior, no one here knows that I'm a girl. If Frankenstein knew, I'd long since be in heaven. He himself shot at me, a body burner picked me up on his pitchfork and brought me to the fire, but I must have trembled or cried for my mother, so he shoveled me into a trench and covered me with ash. He brought me over here and hid me that evening. In the meantime, someone else has died, so I'm acting in their place. The numbers have to match up.

"Dondele, I didn't want you to recognize me. I was embarrassed. I asked myself, why throw sparks on these wounds? But I had to reveal the secret now. I have to tell you: you've gotten weak. You and Kostya and the others are scared of a rock. Don't give up! You have to start digging again tonight. I'll help. Be ready with Roytl—or it'll get deadly."

Both were in deep silence, like inside a seashell. Their tears had not yet been roused like the resurrected dead.

"Dondele, I said before, I'm the Roytl from long ago, but I'm also the one from today. I have two faces."

Roytl tore herself away and lifted her head. A burning wind unrolled across the grotto. Its reflection illuminated him.

Dondele saw in front of him a face with two faces. It reminded him of an apple, half smooth and pink, with a dewy smile, and half peeled and eaten up.

He fell to both faces and kissed them both.

VIII

Dondele was closely followed by Roytl, Kostya by Dondele. That same night the body burners, with all their might and lack of might, kept digging. Roytl turned into fire, as if the fire that had burned half her face came to ask for her forgiveness, atoning for its sins with its fiery might. The dead floated into the tunnel from the pyre and helped drill. The rock began to fragment and completely shattered. A stream of heavenly air penetrated the hell of the forest behind the fence.

Chains clanked. Mines exploded. Electric wolves howled. The corpse burners raced to the stars. Some of them fell. Among the escapees were Dondele and Roytl. They carried Kostya with them. A mine took his foot off . . .

IX

The Green Bridge lay in the Viliya, exploded. A moldy green eagle of iron with its bill in the river, motionless wings spread out.

The hidden rose up in the just-liberated city. They rose from caverns and wells, from under shit and stalls.

Partisans in sheepskin coats like storks in their nests, forest dwellers, soldiers, avengers with gunpowder-scorched faces, traveling to and fro over the Viliya, from the city into the periphery and back, on boats, ferries, and tied-together logs. Impatient boys became their own boats, jumping into the river, where the rushing water set their muscles in motion and their arms rowing.

Dondele and Roytl walked into the city with a regiment of partisans from the Rudnicki Forest. It was deep cornstalk summer. A column of blue rose right up from the ground to the first little cloud.

Dondele took off his boots at a well and didn't put them on again. They had been on a German's feet before, and like a partisan Dondele had trudged in them through the swamp. Now, rushing to the brickworks and the walled-in shelter where his mother was, he had to take them off and wash his feet in the well.

Dondele stopped barefoot at the exploded Green Bridge with its head dipped in the water. He neither wanted to swim across the river under the power of his own arms and legs nor with a boat or a ferry. He felt again an attraction to the art of roof wandering, pulling himself over dangling gutters. He lifted himself like an acrobat over the iron eagle's wings, tiptoed to the bridgehead, jumped over the knife-edge currents between the sunken railings, and then found himself on the other side, where the periphery of the city is.

On the other shore, sitting near the church, the same beggar woman whom he remembered from his childhood. She hadn't changed at all, the same film over her eyes like eggshells. The same brass plate at her crossed legs. He used to throw a coin into the plate when walking by. Now he wants to toss in a whole handful, but he doesn't have more than a single coin left on him. He doesn't throw it—he bends down and lays it in the plate.

People are moving around here and there, but the street is empty. You can feel and see its emptiness. Is this a street or an attic? It seems to Dondele that the street is a long attic, with shattered mirrors bleeding out its many faces.

The door to Fedke the brickworker's shack is nailed shut with white pegs. Dondele breaks open a shutter and gets inside. An ax is lying on the floor. Next to the ax, in the dust—the sun, shattered. Fedke had struggled here with someone.

Dondele climbs up the ladder to the dovecote. He still knows dove language, so the doves will tell him what happened with Fedke, they'll answer him with their cooing.

He doesn't find anything in the dovecote besides bones, fluff, and scattered peas. But after he climbs down the ladder, a grizzled old man approaches him and pantomimes a noose around his neck.

"Fedke's gone. Hanged."

Emptiness rises from a weed-choked hill and chases, whips Dondele with a slender, scalding whip. Flogs him into the brickworks, which is empty too. The young and old bricks have turned into clay.

Pupils sway to and fro in the darkness of the wobbling building where bricks were once fired. His mother's hideout is masked, no suspicious signs. This is how everything looked when he bade farewell to her.

He slides out the hunks of clay from the nearby oven. Shakes out a couple of dozen bricks. He lifts up a cover with his shoulder and jumps down right into the hideout. He smells a familiar odor—the smell of the corpse burners. A slant of sulfur comes in between two bricks. Here is his mother lying under a sheet in her own bed. Her prayer was fulfilled. Let me live long enough to die . . .

X

The first wedding in the city was not celebrated in the noble brick house opposite the mountain, where Roytl was born, nor in a forest of fir trees, in that end of summer when the city was transformed into a sunset.

This is what happened. When Roytl entered her old home in the noble brick house before her wedding, she saw bent over a hot bowl of borscht none other than the king of the pits, Frankenstein.

Hurriedly, with a scream, Roytl dashed back through the wide-open door of the noble brick house like one possessed, falling into Dondele's arms at the threshold.

Truth be told, Dondele took it as a good sign that Roytl still retained the ability to be terrified.

The author of this story, a relative of the married couple, was a witness: the first wedding in the city for generations upon generations took place up top on the mountain that rains had washed clean. The stars tossed gold as their wedding present, and Roytl, fluttering underneath, was purer and more beautiful than the stars.

1974

MESSIAH'S DIARY

I

The pillar of fire advanced and the foe melted before it like lead—vanquished.

The pillar of cloud entered through the Lions' Gate in the wall around the Old City. It burned with a bright white sobbing fire. It burned both over the earth and in its bowels.

Now the pillar of cloud itself turned bright white, and the column of people between it and the copper-colored pillar of fire in front foamed over with white spray like boiling milk.

Is this the local color?

Is this the meaning of the verse: a land oozing with milk and honey?

Suddenly the sound of a shofar collapsed the boiling pillar of people between the two other pillars. Young and old, barefoot, naked and clothed, from their fire-consumed exile, lame, blind, and pregnant women, women with babies on their heads—all thirstily dropped to their knees before a wall with square stones, different from all other stones on Earth, sealing their lips to them. Their own lips and those of their forefathers and foremothers, the dust of whose bones is a desert between earth and heaven.

Given that the children of man wept with joy, cried, and keened like the possessed, so moved were they by the merit of kissing and biting the anointed stones—their din should have deafened eardrums. But it was all a still-small voice like inside a seashell, and one could hear the breathing of the square stones.

The stones woke from the touch of the lips, and silently they wept together with the children of men.

II

I was also with and among the human children of my clan. My skin—white dust of the collapsed pillar—was submerged in square waves.

Later, when the sun swallowed the pillar of fire, the stones turned into human faces. Bunches of serrated grasses and gray-haired herbs grew and split off between the faces, like frost plants on windowpanes from the past. A drop of blood sparkled on one of the herbs.

Maybe this was the Shamir worm, which concealed itself here after carving the stones for the Sanctuary and awakened together with them?

I didn't manage to finish the thought, for someone knocked on my shoulder as if it were a door—secret tappings to let me know someone needed to be let in.

"Sir, promises have to be kept. All these years I have remembered our handshake. And now I'm here. Greetings to you."

I didn't have to turn my head to be able to swear that it was him. His voice was a paintbrush that quickly and masterfully painted a picture of an old acquaintance. When I turned around I was not surprised. I wavered only a little bit. Should I extend a hand at his greeting or not?

To mollify my wavering and ease the trial, he stuck out his hand, pulling mine to his magnetically.

His fingers were dry, small-boned, like the remnants of a fish after a feast.

We stood opposite each other now. Time was traveling in reverse for me, like a train travels backward to switch tracks.

Covered with thick dust from the pillar of cloud, I found one thing hard to understand: Was the man naked or enveloped in dusty garments? But his face hadn't changed even a bit, the same pitch-black, curled sideburns surrounding the pale, garlic-colored skin, the same eyes with the pupils of a funeral horse, almost without whites; the same swollen lips, and in the lower lip, fresh tooth marks.

"Promises have to be kept. Decades are irrelevant here," he boomed out from a shattered depth, and I remembered that a long time ago his voice also sounded like an echo. "Do you recognize me? Don't be shy. Tell me."

His familiar tone stunned me for a moment. The last time we saw each other he was probably double my age, so he had the right to be familiar with me, and I, out of respect, had spoken more formally to him. But now the proportion of years is all inverted. I am probably double his age and have full moral right to speak informally to him as well.

"Do I recognize you—what kind of a question is that? I don't know if you'll believe me, but I recognize you more than myself. Someone who's changed not even a little bit! It's no wonder—time has no relevance to you. To tell the truth, I don't know what they call you now, but you used to be called the yeshiva student with three eyes, because on the other side of your skull, in the back of your head—that's what people said—you had a third eye that saw much farther than the two eyes in front (and those also saw more than others). But you confided in me that your true name is Yonte, Yonte the Palm Reader."

"The memory of a beehive!" He took a couple of steps backward, and in the billowing dust his footprints stood out like an X-ray negative. "Though why did you say that I *had* a third eye? If you have something once, it's a gift forever."

Yonte turned quickly, removed from his skull his headcovering, which was more like a bird's nest of straw and feathers than a hat or a yarmulke, and growled out in his echo: "Here's the third eye in the back of my head, round and rolling like a tear. Aim your gaze in its direction—"

I did what Yonte ordered: I aimed and penetrated my gaze into the open ring of his skull.

"My friend, what do you see?"

"I see a star being born, and its trembling blue born at the same time."

III

When Yonte lifted his headcovering, all of the square stones merged into a well-like darkness. The white foaming dust had spread all over, as if dynamite had blown up a mountain of limestone nearby, becoming well-like in its turn. Only the drop of blood or the worm flamed even more explosively red than the herb plants, and it traded secret signals with the newly born star.

Over the frieze on the wall, on the background of the ancient menorah silver, three doves revealed themselves opposite us, colored pink with the last spot of sun.

The crown of doves lifted for a moment, polishing the three pairs of wings, and it stayed hovering over the wall without the least trembling, immobile.

IV

Yonte took me under his arm.

"Let's get away from the crowds. It wouldn't do for anyone to recognize me here. I appeared only for you."

It wasn't easy to swim against the oncoming stream of shadows, which the night had freed from their sluices.

With the power of this world and the other world, using all sorts of clever tricks, we managed to untangle ourselves from unseen and yet real arms, legs, bones, rows of bodies, entering into a ruin on a path that rose to a height under the young star. It was the star at whose birth I was present.

We sat down on the ground and rested our heads against pieces of roof beams and bricks from the ruined building. A dull yellow glimmer was visible through the ruin's holes, and it looked like dunes were wandering nearby. Now what had earlier escaped my sight became obvious: my Yonte was not alone. He was accompanied by a cane of bone. The cane lay down at his feet with the loyalty of a seeing-eye dog.

Yonte began again, and his voice echoed with the color and rustle of the sandy glimmer floating past the ruin: "You probably thought I wouldn't keep my word; a spirit has no spirit, as a French philosopher once dared to quip. I do come from the world of truth, but everything I said in the world of lies I do fulfill."

I tried to keep up appearances. "Why do you suspect me of something for no reason? I waited for your arrival for several days. A solemn handshake is nothing to sneeze at. If it were my fate—I wouldn't betray you either. I remember our first meeting, I was sixteen years old—"

"Seventeen!" My colleague from the next world sneezed and I quietly said, "Gesundheit."

"I also have a bit of a memory. Maybe only a bit; I don't remember what I have forgotten. What did I want to say? Right, I have a request for you. Don't call me Yonte anymore. Instead call me what my father of blessed memory called me, the name of my grandfather, may he rest in peace, Yomtov. If you like you can add a 'Reb' to it. Why should I deny it? It's a yom tov to see you alive. You refrained from resurrection like those who continuously stream this way. Apologies for those minor footnotes. So go ahead, keep telling your story."

"Yes, really seventeen! They envied the wrinkle in my forehead. How young I was then! More than young—youth itself! I could have given them a whole town full of old people, and I still would have stayed young.

"It was in Jerusalem of Lithuania, the end of summer. And the summer was just as old as my youth. On the clayey banks of the Viliya, where I lived, there was also a cherry orchard where I loved to air out my thoughts. The garden wasn't mine. An orchard grower had rented it for ten years. They called him Munke Poyterile. A weird name, but that's what he was called. They said that his bride had died under the chuppah, and he promised himself he'd never remarry. The orchard grower was good to me. My climbing over the fence into his cherry orchard didn't bother him. He even later decided to give me a key to the gate. He worried I would rip my pants. It didn't make him fret either when I snacked on his cherries.

"In one of those late-summer evenings I went into Munke Poyterile's garden and just burst out crying, for my own good, to make it easier on my heart.

"I lay down in the sweet grass under a cherry branch. On the banks of the clayey shore the Viliya plashed. Its waves were not water but wine. They must have gone up into the garden and intoxicated me. So I dreamed this picture:

"I'm lying in the grass in the same garden under a cherry branch. A needle is growing out of my heart, and a dancer, as light and airy as a waterbird, is dancing on the needle. Her small, playful feet skip across the needle and don't get cut. I see her body reflected in the needle, and my eyes are turned to it. If I were to say or write 'beauty' or 'beautiful,' that would be a distant shadow of that dancer, whose movements were reflected in the needle. As soon as I tried to touch her, though, the dancer and the needle vanished together.

"I became melancholic. The garden wilted overnight, though even then it blew out fiery cherries, like a bellows blowing up and out barely glowing embers. I laid my hand on my heart, on the left side, there where the needle grew, and I said to my disappointed fingers: 'Children, it won't help, you *must* touch the dancer, or else . . .'

"Though I spent my days then in libraries, studied Spinoza, and was full of his intellectual love, melancholy did not stop sucking at me like a leech. Spinoza wasn't able to solve the dream and help touch the dancer dancing on a needle. But Munke Poyterile the orchard grower noticed, better than did my folks at home, that something was the matter with me, and I was sputtering like a candle. The same Munke Poyterile told me of a palm reader in town who they called 'the yeshiva student with three eyes.' He reads dreams like people read letters in Yiddish, and the wrinkles and signs in a person's paw are—to him—like paths through a dense fir forest. Go to him, Munke advised me, the three-eyed yeshiva student will read out your fate and treat you.

"I'll get to the point: Munke gave me your address, and I left to see you. You lived in the passageway. Near the gate there was a little store selling rusted hardware, and a scythe was stuck into the threshold. You lived in a building whose plaster was falling off in chunks, a black roof beam holding up its ribs. You had to be an acrobat to get up to your attic apartment. The wooden stairs had no railings.

"I remember your shattered mirror with the green stains like leaves of water lilies. A samovar whistled under the mirror, as if there were frost outside, though the summer had not yet packed its green suitcases. The table was straining under *seforim* in gilded leather. Near them lay open a book in Latin with a drawing of a hand cut through with lines, and between those lines—numbers. You wore a cape of gold spiderwebs and a red velvet yarmulke."

"That's all true," my companion agreed, nodding his sharp chin and feeling his yarmulke to make sure it was still perched on his skull. "That's all true except for one small error. The samovar didn't whistle. It was cold."

"You probably remember better, so let that be. My point is to recall the main thing: I barely managed to open my mouth when you shared with me the news that my name is Avrom. Thereafter you engaged in a close reading of my trembling right hand and gave me a brotherly slap on the back: It's enough to see a dancer on a needle, you want to touch her too? Don't be a know-it-all, you think a person can touch a soul? Let her dance. And make sure to stay true and love the dancer whose mirror dance you were lucky enough to see in the needle that grew out of your heart. You both will continue to dream and dance together, but no one will be able to separate you . . .

"Let's be frank: the solution was more obscure to me than the dream. But your personality and your scanning the furrow of my brow with your third eye stabbed me no less than did the needle that grew from my heart. It was the healing poison that burned away my melancholy.

"Before I left you—descending by the wooden steps into the abyss, which was more dangerous than coming up into your attic—I placed a coin on the table, as one does after visiting a doctor, a gold coin, because that's all I had. But you threw it out the shattered window. 'Let it roll for luck.'"

V

The pale yellow, sandy light that poured past the pits of the ruins now made its way inside with a diagonal slice, like rain slanted by a sudden wind. Yonte, or let's call him Reb Yomtov like he requested, picked up the staff of bone that was resting at his feet and started writing with it in the dusty air—first one line and then another, with the flexible grace of a conductor. But instead of a musician's downbeat, I heard his familiar echo: "Your golden coin has rolled for many years through many streets, and unfortunately it has landed on the wrong side. My companion," Reb Yomtov put the staff down again at his feet, "*you're* the one that told me about our first meeting. *I'll* tell you about the second one:

"It was in the same place that your golden coin had rolled away to, losing its powers. Ignorant people call that place hell. An empty cliché. An empty container. Compared to the hell we both lived in on earth, the real hell is a true Garden of Eden. I remember how people fought over a piece of horsemeat, which the inhabitants thought up a name for: Equinia. I remember a mother whose screaming child was torn away from her, turning the trees gray with fear. I remember a boy who called out to his friend, 'Drink eau de cologne, you'll be bath soap!' I remember how a passerby who was called to a minyan raised a fist against himself: 'How can you daven if Hitler has become God's partner?' I remember how the goyim hung a sign on the city slaughterhouse: Ghetto. And I remember the rulers of Jerusalem of Lithuania playing chess with pieces carved out of Jewbones.

"Why tell everything I remember? What I want to tell you is something else. A person musn't be popular, neither in hell nor heaven. The goat leading the flock is the first to the slaughtering knife. Just think how many people in the city knew about the three-eyed yeshiva student. A few dozen, that was it. But as soon as the seven streets became seven traps I had to hide, brother, not just from the exterminators but also from our own. Thousands of hands assaulted me, demanding I read what was written on them. I remember one fascinating character, a pharmacist. Before I read his fate, he wanted to pay me with a dose of potassium cyanide. 'I don't care about living,' he said, 'only about surviving.' There was even someone there without arms who dangled his empty sleeve in my direction.

"I saw yellow Stars of David on the palms of most captives. About that I kept my bitter silence. Lies aren't my strength. In some rare people the Stars of David were blue like cornflowers. I wasn't afraid of telling them the truth: you won't just live, you'll survive.

"My companion, I knew that you were to be found in the same place your gold coin rolled off to. I followed your doings from a distance. I also knew that we would meet. And it happened: you dropped into a basement on 6 Shavel Street to bury manuscripts, and I was buried there, too. Wait, when did that happen?"

"Erev Rosh-Hashone!" I shouted out, getting a twinge in my heart for not saying

it quietly.

"Yes, *Erev Rosh-Hashone*. Your memory's as reliable as a Swiss watch, but don't yell like that; I'm not deaf." Reb Yomtov gave a little cough. "We sensed each other in that basement. We celebrated the anniversary of our second meeting right here. I helped you bury the manuscripts with a spade. Here's another sign if you want: you read a work of yours to me by heart. You were telling the stars how the children of men are acting out on the Earth. I still remember a dozen lines, and if your work had more rhymes I'd remember more. While you were reciting, we both heard the so-called Angel of Death galloping up overhead.

"It's nothing new for little birds to be chirping away in my gray matter. But since the time of my birth I had never heard such a thing as you babbled to me then: if one of us should survive, the other must bring him a greeting from the next world.

"Let me tell you a secret: I had never in my whole life spent as many tears as shot out of me at those words. A thread of light wove its way into the basement from somewhere. Before we completed the agreement and gave each other a solemn handshake, I saw on your palm a small blue Star of David. Then it became quite clear to me which of us would bring the other a greeting from the next world.

"It's true, I dared both worlds and assumed a superhuman risk. But that's just my nature. When I agree to something, it's with joy and my whole heart. You are a witness of my clear conscience."

VI

Reb Yomtov suddenly got up and assumed the aspect of a ruffled eagle. The staff of bone jumped to its master by itself. Half walking and half soaring, he approached the doorway of the ruin. The yellow, sandy light was extinguished on his dust-covered face. Dawn started coming up through the holes and cracks.

"Reb Yomtov," I loped after him, high up, the exalted son of the same city I came from, "Now it's our third meeting and it could be the last one. Who are you bringing me a greeting from, who? Did you see my mom and dad, my sister? Give me a sign that you come from those parts."

A couple of steps from the exit, Reb Yomtov stopped, extracted something from his chest pocket, and gave me a rolled up megillah: "I know you like loose pages of manuscripts. Old folios, ancient scrolls. So I brought from those parts several parchments from the Messiah's diary. If you can read them, you will discover many secrets. Including the secret of that dancer who danced on a needle. Don't ask how and in which cavern I found the diary. Who knows if I would have been able to keep my word if it weren't the time of the resurrection of the dead. The coin flipped onto the lucky side."

"As long as you weren't late." Cold mallets began pounding in my temples. "Such a treasure must not remain rolled up and concealed." I couldn't control myself. Right there in the ruin, I tried to unroll the Messiah's diary to find out the secrets of death and life.

A piece of parchment broke off. Its writing, to the extent I understand such matters, was like the script of the scrolls discovered at the Dead Sea. Should I keep unrolling? The treasure could crumble into fragments between my fingers. It also would not be so simple to read and understand the script. The only thing I could do would be to go to an archaeologist. But would he believe the story about the solemn handshake? Would he believe where, and from whereabouts, I was brought this scroll? How it came into my possession and who the author is? Above all, I was mostly tortured by a question: May someone else, a stranger, read the secrets that were confided to me alone?

A bright white dust again floated in the air and fell once more onto the anointed stones. Half walking, half soaring, Reb Yomtov made his way away from me to a dewy height opposite the ruin. Again, like yesterday, he doffed his headcovering, more like a nest of straw and feathers than a hat or a yarmulke, and I glimpsed in the back of his head his third eye—through the open circle of that third eye a star shone. It was the morning star.

1973

Where the Stars Spend the Night

LUPUS

I

After the hammered copper door was locked and bolted seven times, I hid like a treasure at my very heartbeat the clever key with indented snake's teeth, placing it in the vest pocket of the lining of my red velvet blouse.

They should give a medal for such genius: Who am I hiding the key from? If the thief is outside, he can't get the key out from inside, and if the thief is inside, why and wherefore would I hide the key in such a tiny pocket?

Though I live on the highest floor of the highest wall in the city, and more and more often, rather than people, my guests are retinues of drunken clouds seen through the open window, like Rubens' warm-bodied pictures; though there's no ladder in the city that can reach my window, not even at the firefighters' station, out of hypersecurity and from fear of an evil cosmic eye I closed the inside shutters and hung them with uncompromising brocade portieres.

All of this so that nothing and no one can disturb me in my chemical and alchemical experiments to transform an orphaned shadow into its formerly living owner.

II

The dented, polished lamp that I acquired for a trifle in the bustling flea market of Old Jaffa, its fuel old-time kerosene, its odor a greeting from the bowels of the earth, is more fitting for my character than electricity, that golem. Electricity is electrified wires and the electric chair. Since there's already such a chair, it could very well be that electric beds and electric brides and grooms will become popular, and electric children will be born and die.

My loved ones are astonished that I avoid pressing electric buttons. If I ever do, my nostrils stand on end—they detect the odor of burning human flesh.

On the other hand I have as tender a feeling toward the old-fashioned lamp as I would for a living creature. The kerosene lamp is my first critic. To it I read my compositions, freshly extracted from the smelting oven with tongs, and based on its expression, its flame, I know clearly and definitely which of my creations should be sent straight to hell and which to heaven. From time to time I ask it for some advice, a solution to a puzzle. Through the opening in the hood, its burning tongue, like a poppy in the wind, nods yes or shakes no, more helpful than a colleague in solving a psychological conundrum. Occasionally the lamp hiccups with unclear, fragmented sounds, as if a dying philosopher were uttering his last confession, and then I finally comprehend: the lamp is speaking to me with a language of other worlds.

Who knows where the lamp was hanging before and whose wisdom it inherited? I would give up my right to many other faces if I could see the face of its previous master. Now the lamp hangs with its concave glass on a chain of copper tears over my writing desk, tracing out overhead, on the ceiling's parchment, a mildly radiant circle. This is the magic nocturne in my office, protected with books, suspended between heaven and earth.

III

It was so quiet between heaven and earth, you could hear the dead breathe.

It must happen tonight. Every wave must reach a shore once in life. The orphaned shadow has reached sufficient chemical ripeness for me to completely convert it into its former living host. It's good I took mercy on him; otherwise, wild animals would have ripped him to shreds and I would barely have found his black skeleton. I already breathed a warm dream into him mouth to mouth. His limbs begin to move. From the flickering darkness his ribs phosphoresce. I recognize the rib from whose clay a sculptor kneaded Eve. The awakening shadow perceives my thoughts. A smile begins to play over his soon-to-be face. When a swallow lowers its breast and slices into the water, a drowsy ripple begins to send its rings outward in a river in just this way. Look—the mirror begins to ferment a living being, and I hear human speech.

"Why must you sacrifice a dream to create *ex nihilo*? Don't tell me that it's according to the shadow's wishes that you yoke him to veins? Who cares about his former host? White funeral shrouds aren't the only ones that don't have pockets—black don't have them either. That child of resurrection will pay you back with resounding curses!"

"Who are you and how did you break into my private chambers?" I get up from the chair, ready to have at my guest with my dagger, a letter opener.

"You've brilliantly detected my intention," the figure utters throatily with obvious enjoyment. "That's why I appeared, so that you could do me the favor of unenlivening me with that dagger. Instead of turning a shadow into a human being, there's a human being right here in front of you: turn him into a shadow! It's easier and more worthwhile. I am not capable of doing that myself. I was already on fire, but tears put me out; I jumped into water, but that attempt was all wet. May one have a seat and smoke a pipe?"

"Have a seat, burn in hell, and have a smoke," I want to growl, but I'm curious to see what we'll cook up at this meeting.

I start playing the role of a generous host: "An uninvited guest is a guest too. You can certainly sit and smoke a pipe." I turn up the wick on the lamp over my desk so I can better take the measure of this character.

"I'll keep it short—pleased to meet you. I ain't no meat stew," the guest rhymes mischievously and sits with legs crossed, not on the other side of the desk but on my side, so close that I could touch his face with a single hand motion: a ball of dried-out moss between two fireflies.

He puffs. A smoke dancer bubbles out from his pipe. As her legs wiggle in a pirouette over my skull, the thought occurs to me that there's only one chair in this office, and I'm the one saddled up for eternity. It's clear in the dark that my guest is seated. In midair.

IV

Whatever, I think. Let him sit. Let him hang. As long as the shadow will forgive my keeping him waiting for his resurrection. Meanwhile, my uninvited guest is talking to me: "Truth be told, I thought you'd recognize me right away because I have the privilege of being the object of your hatred. You still don't recognize me? A terrible thing! A person doesn't remember when they were born, doesn't remember when they died—what do they remember? Enough with hints, then! My name is Lupus.

My mom and dad actually gave me the name Velvl—Wolf—and that's what they called me, but later, among the non-Jewish students, I was gentiled into Lupus."

"Not just a Lupus, but a Lupus dealing in potassium cyanide." I confirm his pedigree. "You don't need to go through the whole song and dance of how you stole your way into my place: instead of locking the hammered copper door and hiding the key in my undershirt, I should have locked another door altogether. Now I am under your control."

"And I'm in yours," the firefly says with precision among the dried-out moss. "Since you already know that I'm Lupus, the potassium cyanide salesman, and through which door I'm entering into your domain, I can lay my cards on the table."

Apart from the chair that I'm straddling, there's no other chair in this office as far as I know. But it's illogical to argue with logic: I see and hear Lupus slide closer and closer to me, using the wooden leg of the nonactual chair to knock the dried-out tobacco from his pipe. A tiny spark jumps out of the pipe and with a stinging burn is extinguished on the tip of my tongue. Lupus packs the pipe and blows out a new smoke dancer: "My strength and weakness are due to the fact that I have never in my whole life felt sure of anything. But this time is different from all the times before that were jerry-rigged together. I give you my full consent to de-life me. I'll produce this in black and white and sign it. I will also add a codicil that you will remain my only heir."

My tongue is burned, but the words don't give in—they rebel. "Lupus, my guest, before I accept or reject your request, there's another entire scroll that we must unroll. If your hands are trembling, don't be shy, admit it. I'll unroll it myself. I have a good memory because I'm too weak to forget. I see your mossy bangs nodding in agreement. You're ceding me the honor. Thanks. Now I'm unrolling the old scroll."

. . . One winter night was set aside for us from all the past and future nights. Together with us, the winter night is fenced off with electric shovels. But while the supposedly loyal winter night will soon disappear with the dawn, the shovels will feed the hungry shovels of the earth with—us.

Wrapped in snow shirts, we lie in a frosty furnace. No one is cold. The child, frozen to the mother's nipple, obviously wasn't cold. The stars smile, happy that they're not taken out and shot.

Suddenly—a movement of purple bones; a redeemer is revealed carrying a bag of potassium cyanide! He's wrapped in a snow shirt, too, and his breath's like a sharpened knife.

The stars smile, happy they are not taken out and shot. But us, the chosen stars on earth, do not envy those above. We only envy the lucky among us, those born with a silver spoon in their mouth, who have hidden on them a jewel or ring and who, only with their magic while still living, cajole a portion of death out of the hands of the potassium cyanide seller.

Ten-branched ice candelabra are extended: "Have mercy, a little bit, a crumb—"

"So as not to be ashamed at dazzling dawn—"

"Good man, just for my birdie—"

"I played chess with your father—"

"Lupus, save me from life; I'll marry you in the next world—"

But Lupus doesn't give away his merchandise for free. There's a price, and the price is going up and up. Less and less potassium cyanide, more and more jewels. There's Lupus, looking like a he-goat who tore a wolf to shreds!

V

The third smoke dancer is curling out of his pipe. She is black as all hell and wears a shimmering cord around her hips. She's beating time with castanets—or maybe that's my temples?

Lupus hears my thoughts and interrupts them: "You unrolled a real megillah. Everything we saw now is real like your scorched tongue. My soul would have long since broken off me, but it's hammered in with long nails. Nevertheless, you didn't see everything: Who was the first to take potassium cyanide on that winter night? Me—Lupus! A stronger poison gurgled in my ears, though, mocking this one. So only then did I become the potassium cyanide dealer, to convince others that death is weak as a lamb and the venom in the veins is stronger. That was the last comfort. My friend, you seek the sense? As soon as you find the sense you'll lose your senses."

"Why didn't you give the poison away to the poor, the have nots, instead of only letting it be purchased with a jewel?"

"I didn't want the holy rings, those jewels, to end up in the hangman's pocket. Later I hurled them over the fence of the shovels into the abyss."

"In such a frosty furnace, Lupus, how did you get potassium cyanide?"

"I extracted it from my father's pharmacy, concealing it on my body throughout all my struggles. My father redeemed the poison right at the beginning. The potassium cyanide was even stronger then than the red poison in the veins."

"And who was the woman who asked you to save her from life?"

"Emalia, a student. My lover. My God. But God is too far away to cheat."

"Lupus, I believe your commentary to the megillah. I saw a lot but didn't really perceive everything. Both of us are strange mistakes from that winter night. But the sense of my staying alive cannot be denied life. If you were the object of my hatred before, that hatred has now evaporated like the potassium cyanide of that winter night. Let's drink a toast! To unlife is not in my artistic power."

VI

I left to get some slivovitz and two glasses. When I came back Lupus wasn't there. But on the margin of my manuscript, steam rose from his quivering letters: "I thought you were smarter. You'll understand me better and bring closer your meeting with Emalia. I'll make a real toast there."

The wick of the lamp drank up the last drops of kerosene, and the night sun on the parchment-colored roof beams burned out into a circle of ash. But another wick, just lit and submerged in kerosene, shone a mild good morning with the brilliance of a diamond through the cracks in the shutters between night and day.

1975

WHERE THE STARS SPEND THE NIGHT

We are both silent in the small park that has finished its summer, me and the sunset. In reality, our silence on the wobbly bench had just started and the sunset is already heading out. Just wait, my friend, what's the rush? You really find it more pleasant to sink in the sea? The sharks will dismember you and corals will build a metropolis on your golden skeleton.

I let my teeth sink into its cosmic flesh. I want to hold it back. Let our silence at least finish its first chapter. But instead of holding it back and saving it from sinking into the sea, I bite off the tip of my tongue and it gets hard for me to keep silent.

Dangling sparks fall from the almond trees. A bird with a crown of mourning and pupil-colored feathers returns from a funeral. Now I'm again with someone. In place of the sunset, a woman appears from the purple avenue and gets comfortable next to me on the bench. "Someone born young and old," my bitten tongue chatters in me. "Someone born young and old."

"Volodye, what are you doing here?"

I'm Volodye like I'm the king of Portugal. But how do I know who I am? I remember a poet's lightning flash: "I—am someone else." And I nod my head, like the bird who returned from a funeral and is swinging on a branch opposite me. "Yes, my darling, you guessed right."

"You're alive? Amazing! How can you live if your one and only soul is no longer in your head?" She speaks silently into my left ear with the tickling of a silken stalk.

"I've been living like this since my birth and maybe even longer and no one has threatened to walk out yet. True, I have never seen it, my soul, but nevertheless I could swear that it's buried somewhere deep inside, where no sophisticated soul-thief could steal it."

"Don't, don't!" Her unfamiliar fingers, smelling of cinnamon, seal my lips.

"Don't you dare swear. The Almighty won't forgive such a backwards oath, so false. You didn't see your soul. But I did."

"Where and how did you see it?" I blow little puffs of air between her cinnamon fingers, which reminds me of playing harmonica when I was a kid.

"You might even ask what my name is." She takes pity and frees my lips.

"Don't take offense, but I'm asking now. My memory has begun to limp lately, like a horse who lost a shoe."

"Lily, Blond Lily. A name and a woman that you shouldn't have forgotten." She lays her head on my knees, with her face turned up for me to recognize.

I could have sworn that I was seeing that face for the first time. The name was also unfamiliar to me. Even in the half darkness of the park, its lamps extinguished, it was easy for me to convince myself that she's as blond as a crow. It's enough to have energy for the truth. Do I have to have energy for lies as well? Nevertheless I am completely silent. My curiosity is glimmering—a lighthouse for lost thoughts. I shake my head again, agreeably. "I remember, Lily, I remember."

"Thank God, as long as your memory isn't like a horse. And now, Volodye, you'll hear how and where I found the soul, and what happened to me and both of us."

Fine, let it be Volodye, let it be Beet Dye for all I care, it's obvious Lily is mixing me up with someone else. I'll enjoy the exchange. Nevertheless it's somewhat difficult for me to understand how my very own face, a secret manuscript on aged parchment, could be replaced. Did an art forger imitate my portrait in living flesh?

And perhaps the blond Lily is not in her right mind? If she's not in her right mind, her mind is right. The bird's shadow sings more beautifully than the bird.

"Lilinke, start with the when. When my soul revealed itself to you, the where will become clearer."

Her tousled head leaps off my knees and straightens up like a spring that's been let free. Lily snuggles up to my shoulder and embraces me. Her legs hang off the bench, dangling like a little person's.

"I didn't thread time onto a string. I can't count its pearls, what there are of them. I only remember that this happened when the city turned into a black clock with the people set out like numbers around a giant circle. A fiery hand went around the people-numbers in the circle and cut, cut them down.

"Death wasn't lucky for us in the city, so both of us fled into the forest and its frozen depths. The hand from the black clock was cutting there too; we fled into its subconscious, that is to say, into its overgrown swamps where the fiery clock only showed its reflection."

"Lily, that's enough lecturing to me in your silence. I remember as if it were yesterday, as if it were tomorrow. We both sunk into separate holes in the swamp and our bodies could not reach each other. Only our hands, red and full of desire, reached across to each other, one day after another . . ."

"Volodye, let me finish. Hunger sucked out both of our skeletons and we just couldn't get full. We ate poisonous weeds and tadpoles. Then one night, a bridal gown rustled over the swamps, they began to freeze; I saw your soul swim out from your mouth and approach mine. It shone light blue like a sapphire, the size and shape of a dove's egg. You know, darling, that the hunger was chirping, a mouth has big eyes—so I ate it up."

"Thank you, Lily, you did a good job, otherwise it would have sunk for all eternity. I would like to make pilgrimage to those swamps. Where are they, in what location can I find them?"

"I'll give you a sign. It's where the stars spend the night."

1975

BACKGROUND AND CHASM

I

Someone told the story silently and their friend took notes:

"I committed suicide twice, or as the language purists say—committed self-murder. I didn't succeed the second time. I know deep inside you're making fun of me—'He's got a screw loose. He succeeded the first time?' I'm going to tell you straight out, friend, the first suicide I only committed in myself, and that was the true suicide, the one and only till this very day. By the time of the second suicide I was satiated from death, from the first one.

"A single moment is as old as time. In that blink of an eye, or gaze of the soul, I became a fanatic believer, believed with perfect faith in a continued life after death, couldn't believe that the Creator could be so generous and leave me at rest after my unrest had quieted down.

"I'll tell you the story of both of my suicides, their background and chasm. Let it be carved into the black marble of my memory, or the white marble of a piece of paper."

II

The high school where we both went and fell in love with the same girl—Miriam was her name, remember? I mean the high school on Rudnicki Street, where on the sandy courtyard, spotted with living freckles, grew a single tree. Around the tree a carousel of shadows revolved, and we both, like two horses, turned round and round Miriam. The sun was free then too, ownerless, lighting its rays on fire even on the Sabbath.

The devil take it, I can't remember what fruits that tree bore during the daytime. But I remember that at night dazzling green fruits hung from its sighing branches: prowling cats in love.

III

A person's life can occasionally seem unnatural, but every so-called death, even the one that one's own bold will takes hold of, is always natural.

I chose that naturalness as a refuge, so that I would not fall into the purple gloves of my hangman while still alive.

It was the start of night. A rain slaughtered itself with bent daggers, but from its open throat splashed water, just water.

The high school we both went to—surrounded by machine guns. My hangman only looked at his watch and said a prayer to his noose for the rain to stop dripping, the day to dawn clear blue, transparent till the very depths of heaven. His ready noose should find me in all hidden dimensions, even where there's no sign of my breathing, and tie itself cleverly under my chin like a silken cravat.

You can't keep any words, but you should keep your word! So I promised myself that the next day would not see him take me alive.

Don't stop me thinking, I said to my thoughts, that because of you I might lose the anointed crown of my death! But they revolted against me, rearing up on their hind legs as if wolves were baring their teeth at them. Full of wrath, I overpowered them with both fists and raced through the driving rain to outrun my life. That's how I ran all the way to our half-ruined building where we went to high school once upon a time.

The building was overflowing with captives, its doors under guard and wired shut.

In my heavy soldier's boots I climbed onto a gutter. I heard water sluice down the gutter with a noisy racket, wishing to die on contact with the ground. Its stream reminded me of the strumming of a drunken musician. Now I'm up on the roof, flesh and blood in chimney shape, twinned with a brick chimney.

IV

Why was I obsessed with committing suicide from only this building, definitely not any other one? You can ask the director of this theatrical production.

The driving rain kept rolling with its crooked daggers; the water didn't stop splashing from its open throat.

Then, my friend, I so deeply experienced my first so-called uncompleted suicide that I was scared of nothing and no one except the generosity of my creator, being able to rise up from the dead after my unliving. I thought my way to the strange idea that so-called death lasts an entire human life, and when the person is extinguished, their death begins its rebirth. There in the rainstorm on the roof I also remembered a line from a poem, I can't remember whose:

"There's a bird in the blood, the nest is far away, away . . ."

The longer I spent thinking, the thinner the air spread out over the city, like a sieve sifting the rain. Where heaven started, in its plowed-up clumps, gold stalks were lighting on fire.

People with helmets began appearing near the machine guns around the building. Faithful servants of the machine guns.

I detached myself from the chimney and slid over to the roof ledge. Down there is the ideal spot to hurl myself. The pavement is a good guarantee that I'll shatter into bits in the blink of an eye, along with all my drowsing worries, which to date haven't been able to make it out of their crater.

For the last time I breathe in the fresh post-rain September air, where summer spices hover barely clothed in fog, and with a wide-open eye that cuts through my whole clouded body, I jump. No—my wide-open eye jumps down first, and it sees what the director of the show had the idea to arrange: a garbage can!

And though I know that the only place where no one dies, or rarely dies, is a cemetery, I still felt in my chest a bitter insult, not so much for my sake as for my mother's. Is that why she gave birth to me, so that I would croak in a garbage can? Everyone who wished her mazel tov then would be reckoned as liars, liars for all eternity.

Having quickly convinced myself that the dybbuk burbling in my guts was correct, I quietly dragged myself on hands and knees to the front of the building. Down there was the entrance to the classrooms.

I don't think up anything else. To think up something is to stop thinking! You can convince someone that a piece of glass is a diamond. But my truth is the real thing, and you need no loupe to see it.

When I had dragged myself to the front of the building, I decided to jump off headfirst, like a good swimmer off a boulder into the sea. My soul, I thought, isn't mine, so I need to redeem it with one good blow to the brain. And if there's some concern about the other parts of my chosen body, let someone else worry about them.

The someone else wasn't someone else, though, but the stage manager or director of the show. When I took a step back to hurl myself forward, all of a sudden he changed the scenery, and on the high school's sandy courtyard there appeared the same single tree around which, in our tender youth, we circled on the shadow carousel as we tried to reach Miriam. The amazing thing about the show is that we all—me and you and Miriam—actually chased each other around that tree. My ear was even pricked by the song of its birds. So instead of losing myself, I became two people in one—thirteen years younger and thirteen years older, both.

V

From the rain that split the heavens, nothing was left on the roof but an orphaned reflection. With the same smile the sun dries cattle drainage and a dream's tear.

Wailing issued from the building. Someone was using tongs to pull nails out of crushed heaps of living bodies.

I still had time to throw a farewell glance at the tree, to measure how high the mercury meniscus of my insanity was rising now. One hundred degrees, two hundred, maybe a thousand. I no longer remember how many degrees it got to. But I remember quite clearly how you and I kept turning in the shadow carousel around that single tree, and those shooting at us couldn't even penetrate the mirror blue between the branches.

Now I felt another sort of strength in myself. I was surer than sure that I was destined to play a mystical role in this production whether I wanted to or not. Who is the author, who is the director, and who pulled back the bloody curtain? I don't know, but I have to play my role until the end of the last act. Till the curtain rolls down like a megillah and the dead applaud.

VI

My friend, we are now at the last act.

Be patient and sit through the end of the show.

The same bullets that were dazzled and struck by blindness when aimed at me and Miriam are now all-seeing, slicing across the roof with fiery scythes. I have skipped and jumped among the scythes like a shackled horse over a meadow; where the building faces the other side of the street, the Aryan side, I hurled myself down without fear or final confession.

What do you think happened just a minute later? My director prepared the show and set it in motion with dramatic effects.

Having hurled myself from the roof, I was riding on my hangman's shoulders. I already mentioned that I was wearing heavy soldier boots. The boots had horseshoes forged into them. Iron boots. Without meaning to, I broke my hangman's neck. By the time his echo came back down to earth, it didn't have anyone to reach.

I traveled—farther and farther and farther away. I probably became invisible.

I'm old now. Not in years. My wrinkles are anchored inside. But, friend of my youth, I swear with my last silence, if there is such a thing, that me and you and Miriam are still revolving on the shadow carousel around that single tree.

Both of us now know that Miriam didn't love either of us. She harbored a smoldering fire for a cripple—a mathematician. Muni Zalkind was his name. Miriam sacrificed herself for him later, and both of them were devoured by the same furnace.

Miriam was the most beautiful girl in town! Her hair breathed the last scent of my youth's springtime. I was crazy for her eyebrows, like wings of an eagle that tore out my heart.

Did Miriam fall in love with the cripple out of pity? Is pity a more powerful magnet than a body's muscles?

This question too needs to be asked of the director of this show.

1977

FAITHFUL NEEDLES

I

On the anniversary of the death of their father, who the world called Monske the Tailor, the two younger sisters, Tzertl and Tzirele, got together at the home of their older sister Tilye in her isolated, corroded tower by the sea.

Tilye, the older of the three sisters, or one could say the oldest, even the most lively, has made her residence in that seaside tower since the drowning of her happiness.

That happened at the sputtering out of her girlhood, when the first gray hair appeared in the shattered mirror, an uninvited relative.

That happened in the very old time, when she had emigrated here from her home in Lithuania, a time that people now call before the flood.

Tilye immigrated here together with the shattered mirror.

How Tilye found out the day or night of her father's extermination is a riddle for this story's author or eyewitness. Not even two stones together, or two people, remained from that location in Lithuania. If anyone was left she was scared to meet them. The two younger sisters, Tzertl and Tzirele, whom the enemy exiled to a city of slaughter together with their father, didn't know or didn't want to relate additional details.

The author or eyewitness of this story tends to the belief that he himself, Monske the Tailor, whispered to his older daughter when the day or the night of his death anniversary might be.

II

The two sisters Tzertl and Tzirele appeared in the vault of the tower. One could have taken them for two gray, disheveled seagulls. Tilye kissed them hello. From her expression it was clear that their lips and cheeks were quite salty.

A tall wax *yortsayt* candle was melting in a niche of bricks kneaded with straw and growing together into each other. Sunset's inheritance.

"Don't forget, children, you are at home," she said, smiling at her guests in a motherly way. Tilye remembered how in the tailor's house they also liked to call her younger sisters "children." A smile slid off her aged face like onionskin.

Behind a barred window the sea polished its waves. Some distance away, at the horizon's horizon, a burning hand was drowning without having anything or anyone to grab on to.

"Children, you must be hungry; let's eat dinner." She helped her sisters get settled on the old-fashioned, much-used chairs facing each other across the table. "I've made a dish you haven't tasted in a long time. Potatoes in their jackets."

But Tzertl and Tzirele winked to each other mischievously. For some reason they sat down on the same side of the table, next to each other.

When the jackets were taken off, the potatoes let off steam like wolves in the forest. Tzertl gobbled them up like she was hungry as all get-out. "Tilynke, you were an artist and have stayed one. I haven't tasted anything this delicious for decades."

Tzirele barely touched her plate. "Since I've been hungry, I'm always full."

Tilye also barely touched her food. Her appetite had left while she was preparing the festive meal. She let wine gurgle into three goblets and, bowing to her sisters, took a long draught from hers, sucking it dry.

III

Whether it was real drunkenness or drunkenness from the *yortsayt* candle, Tilye woke up scared that the sisters might have stolen her dream from her. Her clever eyes examined them from across the room.

"Children, today is the anniversary of our father's death. I called you here, darlings, from a great distance to give him respect and to share memories. It's true that we are three sisters, but we didn't have three fathers. Let's show him our love."

Tzertl fluttered with a rustle of silk. "He loved to make people laugh and to play jokes, Dad did. I was only a little girl then, but I remember a coach stopping in front of our gate, and then the deranged son of Pan Gintilo, the landholder of Kalvarija, came into our house. He looked like pale weeds from a cellar. Pan Gintilo sent his so-called prize so that Dad could make him a suit. Dad squinted at him with one eye, took his measure, and told him to lie on the ground with hands and hooves spread out. When he did that, Dad outlined him with a piece of chalk. That's how he took his measurements for the suit."

Tzirele gave a half laugh but regretted the second half.

"When Dad's needle finished the suit, it perfectly fitted the son's bulk. The old landholder from Kalvarija, Gintilo, came down later to our place both to pay Dad and to thank him."

A smile slipped off of Tilye's face again.

"Of course, both of you were still little pipsqueaks then, so you don't know why the old landowner came down to thank Dad himself. Gintilo suspected his wife of having a lover behind his back. Dad gave him a magic charm: take a frog's tongue and put it under his wife's left breast while she's sleeping. She'll blurt out everything. That's what happened."

The three sisters became more sisterly. Tzertl and Tzirele remembered their goblets of wine, lifting them to their salty lips. They wanted to say lechayim but were embarrassed.

Tzertele blushed from the first sip of wine. Her goblet turned in front of Tilye in a maelstrom of silence. A molten shimmer sparkled from the inside.

"Who remembers how Monske the Tailor, our dad, became a matchmaker who paired off and clothed orphan boys and girls to get them to the wedding canopy?"

"Me!" shouted Tzirele boldly. "I even remember that at one of those parties Dad put on a top hat and served up rhymes for the parents and the bride and groom. Yes, he liked to make people have fun, but why didn't he get *us* married? After all, we're orphan girls!"

Tilye banged on the table with the bony tines of her fingers.

"Tzirele, come on, you ran away with the college student with the pointy white hat; what argument can you have with Dad? And you, Tzertl, put all your eggs in one basket—but the eggs broke. Am I any better? I had to disappear quick as a wink, otherwise I would have rotted in jail. The needles were dearer to him than his daughters."

Here all three sisters burst out crying, as if the needles that Tilye had mentioned were stabbing them in the heart. The weeping of the oldest sister was humanlike, but that of the younger sisters engaged in call-and-response with the salty music of the sea, which kept getting closer and farther from the tower, farther and closer.

Tzertl was the first to calm down, shaking the foam from her eyelids.

"But later, when we found each other in the city of slaughter, Tzirele and I were as faithful to him as his very own needles. Even more. We hid our dad in an attic for a whole winter, warming his legs with our breath. It didn't help. They were paralyzed."

Tzirele clicked her tongue. "Let's add that even while hidden in the attic and paralyzed, Dad was the type to make people laugh. Which people? His neighbors, who were hiding in the attic too. Dad was only bothered that he couldn't laugh aloud, raucously, so that the merriment could really get into the ears of the ones he was playing to."

Tzertl bent over the table, and her outspread wings embraced Tilye's shoulders.

"With his joyful mood in his hiding place he also cheered up his faithful needles so that they wouldn't rust, God forbid. I have to tell the truth, though. The very last time I saw our dad, he was so pale that you could imagine burial shrouds glowing underneath his skin."

IV

The flame of the *yortsayt* candle leapt up to double its height. It was actually about to drown, but then it struggled against the waves of wax and overcame them to swim out overhead.

A whistle was heard. Tilye also jumped up to double her height. Who's whistling? Is that an approaching ship? No, the blue teapot in the kitchen was boiling, and she forgot about it. In its whistling language it's reminding her—"Ready! We can drink tea."

The tea glasses are full of golden water. Lemon sails leaning on their surface.

Another smile, left too long on the flame, slid off Tilye's face. "Drink, children; I kept a few lumps of prewar sugar for you, the kind that isn't available anymore. They're hard as granite; you have to have teeth like a mouse's, strong teeth. It's all because our dad liked to drink tea with a lump of sugar."

"Hot!" Tzertl acted like she had burned her tongue.

"Cold!" Tzirele made a face as if someone had made up something ugly about her.

Tilye now swam toward them with her eyes, like a detective. "The farther you run away from a cemetery, the closer you are to someone else. One of you started to tell about the last time, and what happened with Dad—afterward?"

They heard something like a wave approaching a shore. Tzertl's lips were covered in foam.

"Dad made me swear to leave him in the attic hideout. He said the faithful needles would protect him."

"True, true," sang out Tzirele with the same voice. "Dad made me swear too, to leave him in the attic and save myself. True. But I didn't hear that faithful needles would save him. Tilye, I know what you're hiding in your thoughts. You want to ask us if we always followed what Dad asked. Tilye, for your information, no! Yes, I escaped through the sewers, swallowed all manner of growing things, but I did not follow what Dad made us swear. I wandered back to the city of slaughter, to our paralyzed father. See this red dent in my forehead? On the journey back a bullet kissed me. Tzertl wanted to return to the attic as well, but the crying of a baby, her child, didn't let her."

V

The two sisters, now aflutter, started to pack up for their return. Time to go home.

Tilye warmly embraced them like a mother. Tzertl and Tzirele seemed like two wings that had been consumed by fire but were now grown back.

"Don't hurry off, children. I have good news for you. Dad is alive. He's with us. Sitting in his old chair just like at the head of the table at home."

The two sisters, with Tilye between them and all clasped together, see it very clearly. Sitting in a chair at the head of a table, illuminated by the *yortsayt* candle, is a small, thorny plant. Monske the Tailor.

Among the thorn stalks his face is like a leaf.
Stuck in his shirt are numerous burning needles, like buds.
Here is Dad's finger crowned with a thimble.
Here the green measuring tape on his neck.

And the father, who the world called Monske the Tailor, laughs out loud, raucously, from the thorny plant.
When he finishes laughing, this is what he says.
"Everything is true, daughters, as I live."

1977

THE HUNCHBACK

This happened and kept happening when the sieve of that autumn night sifted the "who shall live and who shall die" down into the alleyways. "Who shall live," for a day and maybe less. "Who shall die," for an eternity and maybe less.

Draped over the alleys is the starry sieve. An unseen hand is shaking it. The children of man, piled up with dippers, fall in sighing silence. Sifted guiltlessly through an empty, inverted sky.

Prayers drill through here and there. The glare of their words—frozen, bathed in tears.

A fragmented voice, like a stone talking in its sleep, hides in my ear, seeking a savior from its hideout.

"Brother dear, how do you go insane?"

It was Khemeh the Hunchback. The only hunchback left in our kingdom.

When did we become acquainted? Oh, I remember: when we swam among thousands into the stony veins of the alleys.

His majestic hunchback attracted me. It looked like he was carrying his tombstone on his back.

Only his shape was hunched. I was convinced right away that form and content are no twins in this case but rather a perfect singleton.

His name attracted me: Khemeh. Where did they cook up such a curious name?

At our first hurried exchange in the stony veins of the alleyways, in answer to my question whether he was born here, a local, he hissed out without hesitation: "I'm a refugee from another planet."

Although I was already used to his demonic paradoxes and his sayings that cut to the bone (I had written them down on loose leaves of paper and then had locked them in the storehouse between heaven and earth, but I lost the key to it later),

I was still taken aback by his question in the star-studded sieve of that autumn night. "How do you go insane?"

I rubbed his hunchback for good luck. "Why are you asking that?"

Khemeh turned around and butted me with the point of his hunchback, like a ram using its horn. "Till now I believed with perfect faith that everything before my eyes is an illusion, a dream. For example, when I saw a dog guarding a pair of kids' shoes in its teeth, running around to find a barefoot child to put them on, or if I saw a cherry tree hanging on a gallows, or a shadow waking up unable to find its owner, I had a negatory incantation for all of that. 'A dream. A dream. A dream.' Now, at this late hour, I have lost the power of denial, and I see blood dripping from the dream."

A blue, aged man holding over his head a Torah scroll in a wrapping of pure sparks broke through the crowd. There were those who believed that the old man would save the Torah. There were also those who thought the Torah would save the old man. Believing or thinking this way, everything kept sifting through the starry night sieve.

Khemeh shrank. His hunchback, like a tombstone, started to sink. With the fringed tufts of his rags he looked like a thousand-year-old feathered owl. His pupils became glowing rings. "Every end is a beginning. Now it's my big beginning. But it all depends on you. You must dub me insane. With the power of insanity I will make the enemy insane and we'll all save ourselves. A snake can't poison itself with its own venom."

A thought turned over in me. Only the impossible still had some sense. I laid my hands on his matted hair and dubbed him insane.

Shining, thus anointed, Khemeh extracted from his bosom a shofar and blew on it such a growl that it was as if all remaining breaths of the slaughtered were blowing with him.

The starry sieve of the autumn night suddenly collapsed; the enforcers of the city really did go out of their minds, biting each other's throats in two.

1977

LEGEND OF TIME

I

The chain of people over the city's bare bridge was really a chain of people. Not a metaphor or a symbol.

The chain of people was forged with freely dangling rings placed around the swollen legs of the captives, so they could walk one behind the other in wooden clogs over the bridge.

The round freedom of the rings was the captives' only freedom.

In a helmet of swamp green his excellency the Angel of Death marched in front of the chain of people. It looked like he, the Angel of Death, was the only living number one in the city that had fragmented into shards, and behind him—a line of clanking zeroes.

The chain of people traveled there and back. At dawn, from captivity to the pits, and in evening, when the slaughterhouse of the sunset started roaring, from the pits back to captivity to bed down for the night.

I can only breathe out a few sparks in my preserved ember-language about what the captives managed to do. They exhumed the city inhabitants from their graves, erecting from their dead bodies, like bricks, a fiery pyramid.

II

In that chain of people lived a boy whose name was Me. That's what he called himself and that's what his fellow captives called him. The only one who called him by his digits was the Angel of Death.

But the little boy didn't approve of numbers. The Maker fashioned the world and all its creation with words, not with numbers. He only had to count to the number seven.

Though the little boy was fated to erect the fiery pyramid with bricks of dead bodies, he did not blaspheme anyone and did not envy any of the human children on the earth. He wouldn't have exchanged his Me for anyone's You.

When one of the captives, out of desperation, would babble that they'd like to die—so that they wouldn't die—the young boy would give that person a tender slap on the back.

"And I would like to live, so that I won't live."

Truth be told, he wanted to add something and clarify the obscure thought, but a shattered laugh flew out of him like a falling star.

Another time he swallowed his own words before they saw the light of day.

"A person is, after all, a person. It's easier for one of us to turn into an animal than for an animal to turn into a person."

When the words turned upside down inside him, he comforted himself for their sake.

"Let's say it more reliably and faithfully. You can never know what a person is not."

III

It was the beginning of summer. The snow was melting on the surrounding mountains, like the leaking whites of eyes.

The young boy dug in the bony earth and found a pair of tefillin wrapped around a skull and an arm. He unwrapped the tefillin and took them away, and in the evening, before the chain of people assembled, he put them on and marched in them over the bridge of the fragmented city, as if he were bound in chains.

He certainly knew that at the gate of captivity the captives are hand-searched like bags of flour.

The Angel of Death with his helmet of swamp green appeared at the gate right away, and his right-hand man, a fresh type with a scorched face, weighed and patted down everybody.

The young boy felt his fingers sniffing their way under his left sleeve and sensing the four-sided eye as they patted him down under his hat.

But instead of tearing off his tefillin and beating him, or even worse, the creature with the scorched face did nothing to him. It only pulled the boy's hat down lower so that the Angel of Death at the gate would not notice. The creature with the burned face also put its hands on the young boy's shoulders, as if to bless him.

IV

That night two white doves flew out of the lining of the tefillin, and he, too, the young boy, turned white and winged. He flew out of captivity and followed the doves over the city's towers and roofs. From up high they looked like illuminated tombstones.

The doves brought him to a faraway country, and there they flew back into the tefillin. The young boy, in whom time had multiplied, was listening to their prayerful cooing.

Only later, when the straps of the tefillin grew into his flesh like the roots of oak trees, did the creature with the scorched face appear to him in a vision, telling him, in a whisper like the swinging of a branch, who had worn the tefillin before him.

1977

THE BOOT AND THE CROWN

1

Trofim Kopelko doesn't like tears. He has a saying that tears are ladies' buttons; they have no point for a real man.

He would hang tears, if such a gallows existed.

But his left leg, made of wood that he himself whittled, delicately shaped from a young, oozing fir tree, weeps a few tears of honeyed sap from time to time.

Trofim Kopelko doesn't like those tears either. He dumps his pipe ash on them. But the sap tears are set on fire by the hot ash. Burning tears please him even less than the extinguished variety.

Nevertheless, Trofim Kopelko found a way to deal with his tears. It was like this. Kim, the commander of the partisan brigade, remembered him, dubbing him the executioner of the forest court. Trofim Kopelko had the honor of submerging his victims in the swamp with his left, wooden leg. Like the frozen snakes, the sap tears of his wooden leg also froze.

In the Narocz woods they relate that Trofim Kopelko's people, dressed in the enemy's uniform, had recently lain in wait for partisans. When the partisans fell into their clutches, his buddies chopped the forest dwellers into pieces.

But Trofim Kopelko was cunning. When the Germans were no longer wearing the iron trousers, Kopelko changed his spots. He stretched out his leg to his Tatar adjutant, who removed his boot. Trofim Kopelko felt around inside for a long time, as if searching for his luck, and drew out from the inner lining a sweat-stained medal testifying to his heroism in the war with Finland.

With the polished-up medal on his Berlin uniform, he eliminated his blond advisers in the blink of an eye.

From then on, appropriately armed and accomplished in action, Trofim Kopelko became a man of renown in the area.

One autumn dawn, while he was slashing deeper into the Narocz woods, a landmine exploded under his left leg, which, together with its boot, flew up to hang like a dead raven in the crown of a birch tree.

His faithful men, who had stayed in service to their favorite, swore later that Trofim Kopelko nearly bit his pipe clean through from the pain, but his wolflike eyes stayed as dry as gunpowder—as his adjutant, the little Tatar, pleaded: "My dear man, saw off my left leg and put it on, it's yours."

He clenched the pipe with his teeth and spat out sidelong at the little Tatar: "*Nye nada.*"

II

The little Tatar in the sheepskin coat is still a valued attendant of Trofim Kopelko's. Together they ride, together they lift a glass, giving each other a light for their choleric pipes.

The little Tatar also built a bath for them both in the wood. A kind of dirt house over a spring of fresh water, colder than ice. A bucket of spring water on glowing stones and it's good and steamy like at home. The little Tatar smacks him all over his limbs and parts with the broom, even on his wooden leg, which Trofim Kopelko doesn't remove for a moment.

His hairy body of clouds throws off bolts of lightning.

Great Kopelko is as red as a crab.

Then the little Tatar lifts him onto his shoulder, naked, and throws him outside, rolling him over in the snow.

The tips of Trofim Kopelko's copper-colored mustache hanging below his chin are the scales of justice. The sins of spies and traitors are weighed on their scales. Yes, the eye over the scales is the watchful eye of the commander, but Commander Kim is generous, very generous. The mustache of Trofim Kopelko swings to and fro, to and fro.

III

The frozen sun warmed itself up. Its own red ash blew on its sparks, scattering them over the snow.

A green hand, growing out of the earth, pulled a green thread through the needles of the evergreens.

A lonely stork, like a violin bow without a violin, traveled straight over the woods.

Then he rose, Trofim Kopelko, and shone in his full glory.

He galloped through tumultuous forests, and behind him, his faithful bloodhound with a tinder-red tongue hanging out, the little Tatar.

Both rode slowly on the way back. Behind them were the most beautiful girls of the forest, hands tied, dragged along on ropes by the riders, nearly unrecognizable: Katya, Lyubotshka, Halinka, the lovers of the section commanders, commissioners, and other courageous officers.

Trofim Kopelko looked like Caesar and the little Tatar—like the little Tatar.

IV

On one of those days in the beginning of spring, two young horses started neighing near Miastro Lake among the branches concealing my division's earthen house.

With its flexible steel, the horses' laughter hurled the newly frozen stillness with a splash into emptiness.

I woke up opposite a crucified face with three burning pupils. The third pupil was the fire of a pipe. "My name is Trofim Kopelko," the night messenger introduced himself. "Commander Kim ordered me to bring you to the staff."

What was this game for, if we knew each other? Why is he being catty, if it's more natural for him to be like a dog? That's what I'm thinking, but I don't ask any questions. I grab my fur coat, load a bullet into the chamber, and walk out of the earthen house into the frozen stillness, following the tracks of a boot on a wooden leg.

My friends' suspicion accompanies me from the earthen house outside. The breath of their stares fanned the sparks in my spine.

When we're both saddled up, me behind him, Trofim Kopelko says to the little Tatar, "Get the horses drunk to make them move faster, but don't forget to leave some for us three, too."

The little Tatar unties a flask of moonshine from the saddle strap of his stallion and tips it into the wide-open mouths of both horses, first ours and then his.

They feel spring burning in their guts, and the horses, whipping themselves with their tails, lap up the wooded miles with their lusty gallop. The little Tatar gets out in front of our panting horse and gives a light to a waiting pipe.

Single gunshots ripple into empty space, like echoes of nearby wolves.

The last tufted snows, like frightened rabbits, slip off the branches of fir trees.

Our drunk stallion rears up on his hind legs, and we are transformed into a marble monument.

Trofim Kopelko searches the forest with his nostrils. "That's enemy fire. I recognize it from its echo. A defeated army is nearing our positions. We must gallop to the other side of the Miastro before the sun cuts into the ice!"

The little Tatar rides farther into the wood in a zigzag. It looks as if he wants to gather up the gunshots. He catches up with us on the lake, over exploding ice.

The dawn, a purple demon, swings on a branch at the horizon.

V

Trofim Kopelko leads me into the commander's dirt house. The quiet in the earthen room was a secret map. Spring isn't just overhead, partnered with the sun, but also underneath, in the earth's veins. The smell of rain seeps out from the inside of the dirt house among the branches.

A warm, trustworthy hand closes on mine. I immediately notice that the commander of the brigade has been transformed. The wrinkles on his young face are older than the face itself. His beard, too, as yellow as a freshly hatched chick, is too mild for his sharp wrinkles.

"If you're curious why I called you so urgently, here it is. I received a radio telegram from the partisan headquarters in Moscow saying I should send you there. Get ready. Tomorrow, you'll be escorted to an airfield of ours by three armored partisans. An airplane will land there and you'll fly over the front. I have to warn you that all the roads are full of danger, but if you're lucky you'll have a mind in your heels."

"And some in my head." I'm playing it real cool.

"No, the main thing is to have a mind in your heels." The commander's being stubborn. "If you're walking over a minefield, how would your head know where the mine is waiting? The true partisan drops his soul into his heels."

While Kim's talking I feel a glowing in my heels. My life depends on them.

Trofim Kopelko lurches in. The thought occurs to me that his wooden leg is whiter than his conscience. He confides something into the commander's ear.

"Just the girls!" Kim shouts out furiously and signs a piece of crumpled-up paper. "And don't let anyone come in. Nobody."

Kim comes closer. His voice gets closer and conspiratorial. "You heard me: girls. The roots' secrets are whispered by the branches. Let me explain the riddle to you. Convinced that we are stronger than their armies, and that forests are their generals' graveyard, the German scum thought up a clever trick to defeat the partisans with one shot. They took girls, each more beautiful than the last, infected them with syphilis, instructed them carefully, and let them loose, the foxes, into the forest, to infect our best, bloodiest young men. I won't deny it. They were quite successful in this devilish game. Most of the girls are now trembling in our net. I signed their sentence earlier."

He had barely managed to get up off his chair before he was following in his shadow's footsteps. "I'm not thinking of the girls. Let the swamp choke on them. I'm thinking of my sick comrades, division commanders, heroes. I'm keeping them in a dirt house under guard, but I can't drag it out much longer. I can't let them free either. We are preparing to meet the enemy's defeated army. The horns of an impaled bull are stronger than him. Trofim Kopelko believes that the sentence for the gentlemen should be the same as the girls'. No standing on ceremony. But the issue is different now. I'm sending you over the front. When you fly over it and get to headquarters, tell them the whole story of the sick young men exactly as it is, and let them make the judgment about what to do."

They don't even see their last sunset.

The little Tatar leads them out one by one from their captivity, blindfolded with their stockings.

Katya, Lyubotshka, Halinka: each one holding on to a branch, and the little Tatar leading them.

He's leading them out of captivity to the trees, dried out and stripped of bark, the deadwood. Only one reigns there: Trofim Kopelko.

Little shots make sounds. Like laughter.

With the flat, anvil-like underside of his wooden leg, Trofim Kopelko knocks out a pane in the thin, green, frozen swamp window, and with the same leg he lowers the girls into the swampy, shattered heaven.

VI

Krasnogur, Maligin, and Leibele Blat—my chaperones and protectors for tomorrow.

Krasnogur is busying himself with a horse-drawn sled, Maligin's bent over a map, Leibele Blat is cleaning a machine gun.

Trofim Kopelko is being hospitable. I and my chaperones will spend the night in his dirt house. The little Tatar made dinner for us.

I'm the last one at the campfire.

The campfire is struggling with a wet fir branch.

The fir defends itself with its bitter smoke, but fiery teeth rip its muscles and veins to shreds.

The partisans are already asleep in the dirt house. Someone is still playing the harmonica, but he drifts off to sleep while playing.

I lie down on a pallet of straw and pull my fur coat over my head.

My last night in the Narocz woods.

Tomorrow at this time I will either be or not be in the middle of a minefield wandering my way toward the partisan airfield. Kim is right: if you're lucky, you have your mind in your heels.

Suddenly: Can a dream explode? Is a dream a minefield? There is a thundering report inside of me, near me, and in front of my awakened dream. A white crucible in whirling rings.

No, it's not inside of me. It's in my neighbor, Trofim Kopelko. The little Tatar is standing over him, carrying a revolver, and from it a smoky tongue points at the lord of the swamps. Those who were recently his friends and attendants jump with the sweet joy of revenge on the man who was shot dead, disassembling him like ants dismembering a dead insect.

One runs off with Kopelko's wooden leg and hurls it into the hungry campfire.

Another, with Kopelko's shirt. Standing opposite the freshly painted moon, letting it shine through the shirt to see if it's worth his while. The moon is weirdly red; warm drops drip from it onto an isle of snow.

Again I see a face crucified by three burning pupils. The third is the fire of a pipe.

The little Tatar curses as he pulls off Trofim Kopelko's only boot and then doesn't know what to do with it. Let him fly to the devil, to his fellow boot on the crown of the birch tree!

He pins on his own heart his commander's order of bravery.

1977

THE VISION OVER THE RIVER

I saw a vision over my hometown's river decades after the incident.

The spring that was raging over the barely breathing earth wasn't like any spring that had ever sprung.

At the start of day it snorts with its dark, searching nostrils, blowing over the layer of ice covering the river, and the tangled ice is sharpened down to a glowing, blue, shattered mirror.

The raging spring sees then very clearly that it is not like its face.

There's a thundering and a clanging in the river, and a black fire of rolling waters leaps out from its caverns.

As in a dream of white bears shot from the sky, ice floes are tumbling. Floes over floes.

The black fire of floe-choked waters is now over the shores—toward the nearby villages.

Cocks are crowing now in those nearby villages.

They are crowing to their angel, the sole star.

Lords are waiting in their huts like leeches full of blood.

Their axes rest above them on the arboreal walls, and the finger of sunrise extracts their last drops.

Gallop of floe-choked waters, devouring the huts outward and inside.

Only the roosters are innocently torn from the earth, and they hang there in midair, gravitating toward their angel.

When the floes retreat from the battlefield, they stay a while in a grove of fir trees not far from the former huts.

There, they spade out of the yellow earth a frozen wedding with bride, groom, and musicians.

From the fir grove a hand with a glass of red wine is also excavated.

The floes lift the wedding onto their shoulders and float off with the domain of the rushing stream.

A chuppah is woven with threads of sunlight over the river.

The bride smiles behind her veil, like the first leaf of spring from the veiled earth.

But who are the musicians playing for?

1977

GLIKELE

1

I got her letter first. Not in handwriting but in heartwriting, the kind you see only on the accordion paper of an electrocardiogram. Violet tics of little bolts of lightning, portending nearby uninvited thunder.

I wasn't able to decipher the mysteries of her letter—and here she was herself, talkative and real, the same purple tremblings of her letter carved into her silver face.

Is this my first love, Glikele? Glikele with the red hair, nine years old?

Her braids were woven from ash, and the spindles in her hair were rusted.

But there's a voice remembered like the taste of childhood, a voice whose flavor didn't change.

"I don't know how to begin," she began. "You think I'm someone else, but it's not true. Every person is more like someone else than themselves, but I'm like myself. The spitting image of gall. I don't know how to begin, just like I don't know my age before I was born. So I'll be silent without mercy and let my tongue free. Tongue-tongue, play out my world lost to fate, or I'll murder someone."

When Glikele let her tongue free, her homegrown voice caressed my ear with the same violin sound as long ago. Her eyes, I thought, were also the same as when she was a young girl. Green clocks that glow in the dark. The woman is right, of course; she's like herself. The spitting image of gall. But something's grinding in my temples—why is the same one someone else?

"Your best friend is the one you meet in your dream; he'll always warn you and never sell you out." Glikele, or her tongue, fed those thoughts to me. "And that dream friend confidentially ordered me, as soon as the war against me began, to take along my father's cleaver no matter where I would find myself wandering. I was already carrying around a living cleaver, a warm one, underneath my heart, but that's what I did and so protected my warm one with that cold cleaver."

"Remember, Glikele, when we were kids, I whittled a stick for you in the forest with your father's cleaver."

"My memory is my jewel. But hear what happened next. From under a heavy blanket of the dead we fled Ponar, the three of us, me and my two cleavers. It was a winter night, but I didn't feel bare naked.

"Where to? Wherever I'll walk to, I won't make it to Glikeleville. But just walking, running that way, breathlessly, urged me onward. The snow didn't make any sound underneath because I was barefoot. When I turned around, my footsteps became shining stairs, I don't know to whom. Do you think Elijah the Prophet can disguise himself as a farmer woman?"

"If he can disguise himself as a beggar or a magician, he can disguise himself as a farmer woman."

"As we both live, I think the same thing. The ninety-year-old Papusza was Elijah the Prophet. She hid me in her hut, in the chicken cage on top of her oven, so that the gobbling and crowing of the birds would drown out the cries of the boy I gave birth to.

"Have you ever met a day in black shrouds? I have! I got infected with typhus, and it was dangerous for my child to stay any longer. Do you think Elijah the Prophet can catch typhus?"

"I don't know."

Glikele grabbed me under the arm. "Let's take a walk in that neighborhood."

While we both headed to the door, our heads floating in that hanging mirror, I sensed that my very existence, truly, was in that mirror—on the inside.

II

Her arm under mine, like a squirrel on a branch, we headed over to that neighborhood together.

When Glikele came to my house, the ripe summer would bloom with colors and scents, and the sun would cool its muscles in the river. Now the river lies in a casket under a heavy cover of ice; a light gray snow is falling from the sky's unextinguished fire.

Out of that light gray snow appears a solitary hut with a chimney shaped like a boot. An old woman, bent over, is limping toward it with a bundle of sticks. At her side is a dog whose barking yearns for something, scratching away at the dirt underneath with its paws.

"Glikele, that's where you gave birth." I point at the hut. "I see your thoughts just like I see the willows next to us. Just like I can feel the willows, I can feel your thoughts."

"Can you chop them down and saw them up too?"

"No, that I can't do. Or maybe it's more correct to say I don't want to."

"If that's the case, my tongue is pointless; you can see my thoughts already."

"Glikele, you wanted to say earlier that you left the kid there."

"True."

"Sick with typhus, burning and smoking like a torch, you ran away to the other side of the green lake. You rigged yourself a place in a fir tree, and the mother fir mercifully warmed you up under her bark. Later you had a guest: a mother wolf. You sucked her warm milk, and the milk was a cure for you."

"Instead of my child breastfeeding, I did. Do you think that mother wolf is still alive?"

"No, Glikele, that mother wolf long since departed for the next world. The same one who aimed bullets at you shot her to death. But then you sprang down from the fir tree and cut short his breath with your cleaver."

"So I'll light a candle for the soul of the mother wolf."

III

The closer we got to the hut, the more it distanced itself. Threaded on silver, the barking of the dog scattered over the snow, woof by woof. A marble fortress appeared in front of us. We were forbidden from going any farther.

On the way back through the light gray snow, the neighborhood got summery again.

At stars-out we came to the lively city. Young couples, like eagles with unfurled wings, were out for prey—their own bodies.

Glikele stopped at a fountain where a dancing water nymph was tearing her clothes off. "Now do you see my thoughts, too?"

"You want me to show you which one is your son among the people in love."

"I've been looking for him ever since I lost him. And every time I've found him, I'm doused with boiling lead. It's someone else."

Glikele lifted herself abruptly up off the ground and away from me, falling on her knees in front of a shaggy youth kissing a girl in the middle of the street. "Papusza, Papusza," Glikele sobbed while kneeling down, so her son would remember something.

The young man unclasped the girl from his arms, lifted Glikele from the ground, and caressed her braids spun from old ash.

Now I was the one taking Glikele under my arm. She was light, as if the earth under her had lost its gravitational pull. Her green clocks started phosphorescing: "He's someone else again. How long will he be someone else?"

1977

THE BEGGAR WITH THE BLUE GLASSES

I

You see a beggar, a walking bundle of rags. Either the beggar's hand is like a seashell thrust out by the sea onto dry land, without an ear to hear its cry, or it's a crippled beggar betrayed by his legs, which left him for someone else; and you walk past him with thoughts like magnets polarized in the opposite direction.

It doesn't occur to you to get acquainted. You aren't curious enough to ask his name and whether he was born to a mother. Whether his mother was a girl once.

But something happens. While you're walking by the beggar, an idea chases you like a pony, like a lightning bolt dashing after a cloud. You want to pluck loose your past sins. So you come to a stop and let a drop of metal fall in front of the beggar. Your conscience is relieved. That's it. Away you go. No word. No smile.

Why should I lie? I've rarely smiled at a beggar myself. Even rarely smiled back, like I do with a skeleton. So it went on like that, as long and as short as it did, till the angel who guarded my pen decided I should write this story.

And shaped before me there was a beggar with blue glasses.

II

The guy in blue glasses appeared on the corner of my narrow street, next to the mailbox colored sunset-red that I have fed for years now with my letters to my friends and unfriends, like it's a living creature. It's possible he was standing here before and begging then too, but suddenly I really saw him. It's quite a distance from seeing to perceiving.

This is how it happened:

I hurried out into the street at dawn, carrying with me a letter, still warm, for the red mailbox. The city was still empty, without the steam of people. Two birds sang each other awake.

As I held the envelope at the rusted mouth of the mailbox, I heard a voice in Yiddish. "A donation for an inanimate object and not for a beggar?"

That's when I saw him for the first time, like a tree appearing out of the fog.

Besides his blue glasses, my memory took note of his small beard, like a radish just pulled out of the ground.

What does the blueness of his glasses recall? Blue fragments of glass found in childhood that make you happy like no treasure can.

Let the mailbox stay hungry today, I decided. I was happy that the beggar's argument provided a reason. I had written the letter too excitedly, with a boyish, unchecked jealousy. And if the iron golem had indeed devoured the letter, God forbid, I would have looked for a match to light it on fire inside.

I tore the letter and the envelope into shreds, and my jealousy was shredded up in me too. But instead of my thanking the guy with the blue glasses, a needle jumped out of my tongue and stabbed him with a sharp word. "You're at work so early?"

A bony smile shone: "Only the dead have it easy. If the living knew who I was they'd come to me all the way from Honolulu."

"So let's imagine I come from Honolulu. But let's get acquainted first." I stuck out a hand. "What I go by is—"

"You don't offer your hand to a hangman or a beggar, and if you do, there should be a coin in it." The bony smile shone again.

Just my luck. My pockets were empty. The guy in the blue glasses took pity on me. "An honest person will visit me at home to return a debt. Here's my card."

The city was taking on motion. Bricks poured down from the walls and became people hurrying along. Cars were shuffled like playing cards. The sunrise ascended to the seventh heaven.

The day after and the one after that I did not perceive the beggar with the blue glasses next to the mailbox. I was beginning to think it had been a dream, a nightmare. But then I felt his calling card in my pocket:

HORACY ADELKIND

PHILOSOPHER AND WISE MAN

With the street and the house number. That same evening I went to pay him a visit.

III

No, it wasn't a made-up address; my suspicions were for naught. He himself, the philosopher and wise man, invited me into his room with a knightly bow. He looked a little different here, wearing a cape and boots, a yarmulke woven with silver threads on the tip of his skull. His blue glasses were on a side table on top of a stack of paper, illuminated by a hanging lantern.

"I'm no longer a beggar, so we can shake hands," he said, smacking his lips. "So let's be casual. I don't like to speak formally. Yiddish is a beautiful language, but all praise to the Holy Tongue in which one always speaks in the second person—with beggars as with princes."

He brought me a rocking chair. "Cognac or a glass of wisdom?"

"Make it a glass of wisdom, a strong one." The rocking chair teetered underneath me. "Before the glass burns my ear, I have a question. Why the comedy? Dressing up as a beggar?"

"One glass of wisdom isn't enough for you." He crouched in a rocking chair opposite me. "Every human being is born with a mask: their skin is that mask. Even so, they put on more masks to disguise the first ones. If I hadn't disguised myself as a beggar, I would have really been a beggar."

"Where's the logic in that?"

"Logic plus logic is demagogic! You with a question like that. Everything is habit. You're an eagle if you just get used to it. If a person were born with seven legs, you and I would seem to him like desperate cripples. Man is not a cosmic animal, as my colleague Schopenhauer teaches, but a cosmic person, as Horacy Adelkind teaches. And the cosmic human being, which I am the classic example of, must change their skin-mask—and not just on his face. He has to change so death won't find him. If such things are comedy for you, that's a personal tragedy. Let's shuffle the cards again: if I hadn't begged, your pupils would have deleted me from existence, and you would have actually put your letter in the mailbox. Do you know what would have happened then?"

"I would have eaten myself alive."

"You both would have died of hunger from such a dish—you and her."

IV

Both rocking chairs and us inside—like the two ends of a ship—we rocked over sighing waves. The former beggar with the blue glasses, and the current philosopher and wise man Horacy Adelkind, splashed with the rudder.

"Since you know the secret of my disguise, I'll tell you the secret of my self-revelation. You owe me a debt that's more than the sum of all the coins I have gathered. Here's your debt: to be my heir! I, the cosmic person, have no one left on our small planet. My near and nearest have left for the galaxies. My only friend is quite a different creature. I am so lonely that I recently asked a psychiatrist to make me sick with schizophrenia, to split my personality so I wouldn't be so lonely."

"Did it help?"

"Yeah, I got twice as lonely."

"That's what you want me to be the heir of?"

"Not that. I want you to be the heir of my wisdom, my aphorisms. I've written seventy thousand pages."

"And what do you want me to do with them, for instance?"

"Publish them in seven hundred leather-bound, gilded volumes."

"Before I assume this sweet burden, I want to have the merit of hearing some of these aphorisms."

"Here's one:
We understood each other well,
The gorilla and me.
Unfasten these bars,
She said,
Then we can chat.

Another:
A single moment is as old as time.

A third:
You're too far away for us to get closer,
Too close for us to get distance.

A fourth:

> 'One of you will not betray me,'
> Jesus said to his disciples.
> And that one was—himself.

A fifth:

> Tears are sparkling eye words.

A sixth:

> Men are created in plural,
> Women—in singular.

A seventh:

> Silly painter,
> Don't complain to the tree
> That it grows and blossoms
> Realistically.

An eighth:

> I'm a boarder
> In my own body.
> I pay rent
> With my tears.
> When I don't have anything to pay with
> The owner will evict me
> Into the cold and rain.

A ninth:

> Too soon got to be too late.

A tenth:

> I'm not less than anyone
> But less than myself.
> For myself I'm just a little one
> Who's barely cut his teeth."

V

With the nimbleness of a kitten, Horacy Adelkind got up, took the hanging lantern off its hook, and shone it on the loaded shelves. "Dear heir! My writings are hovering on these walls. Mazel tov. They are now transferred to your authority. My past is my future."

Barely a knock on the door.

His voice was hoarse: "It's my only friend. This is the time he comes by. I already hinted that my only friend is quite a different creature. He's a worm. A hoary gray worm brings his thoughts here, and I write them down. The writer Słowacki, he says, was an angel's secretary, and I, Horacy Adelkind, am a worm's secretary. Do you want me to introduce you?"

I blocked his path. "Another time. Enough for today. Is there a back door?"

Horacy Adelkind lifted his lamp over me and pulled at my sleeve. "Yes, there is. There is. And you'll take a gift from me. My blue glasses. You'll be able to disguise yourself as a beggar and be a cosmic person."

1978

CUT LIPS

Youth is a tree. The tree of youth, my shining tree, shakes off its summer garments to rustle even more youthfully than last year.

These words were murmured across cut-up lips by a man of many years, spoken to quite a young woman who had just emerged from a summer fog.

The man of many years, the wise man and the idiot with the dust of a furnace on a lock of his hair—gnarled like a thorn—mumbled out these words not in front of the woman's entire form but at her hand, while falling with his cut-up lips to her merciful fingers to relive the taste of his youth.

The man of many years then felt, not just in cut-up lips or frostbitten mouth but also in the gnarled roots of his tangled lock of hair, as clear as fire, the sweet taste of rough raspberries and the smell of flowing sap in the forest with overgrown branches where those raspberries grow.

Then he experienced something rare. Where his soul is ending, a new one starting, and where the new one ends, death doing its dying.

A moment and a half later, when the young woman had freed her smiling hand from his lips, that same death had stopped dying in him.

The man of many years, with his tear's magnifying glass, looked deep into the secrets of one single finger of hers that was higher than the others, and he again murmured from his cut-up lips: "The tree of youth reaches even past your shadow from last year. You are not fated to taste its heavenly wine. I could swear that your true face is the tiny, wet face of this finger here. Its little face is furrowed out with many small pits. The half moon at your finger's horizon will never again rise to warm my bones.

"You're a wave that swallowed a human being.

"Your furrows are older than my fear, older than the both of us.

"You are older than the old lady, four feet tall, dressed in black silk fastened by needles, feeding the merciful, compassionate doves with peas at the city museum."

1978

THE HEAVENLY COIN

I

Why do they need money in heaven? Who is forging silver coins in the upper worlds? What can you buy there with those coins—stars, clouds on the moon?

Those were the sort of thoughts and questions, a few but not a great many, that buzzed through my brain when my rebbe Shloyme-Leyb first showed me the *alef-beys* wearing his snow-covered fur coat, and an angel tossed down a silver coin for me and my honor right onto the siddur, letters shimmering on the first page like black stars.

I can pronounce them fluently with my mouth but not with my eyes.

Among all the questions that I ask in my inner ear is certainly not whether that silver coin was meant for me, and whether the angel who gave it was real. Shloyme-Leyb wouldn't lie. Wait, I can convince myself. Little wings, secretly shining, are growing out of the coin, a sign and an indication of who they belong to.

I protect the coin in the warm nest of my fingers, in my left hand. A sweet pleasure diffusing through my limbs. The heavenly wings are trembling and making themselves at home. There's no way in heck I'm going to let them go today into the beet-red sunset.

II

Shloyme-Leyb is a neighbor of mine in the next hut over, near the Irtysh River. A pity to think of how we both got here, this Siberian ground, this Siberian snow. To be true, I did hear something about my parents and remember their fragmented words: war, wandering . . . But I was thinking that if the sun was going to wander along with me, it wouldn't be so terrible.

In our hut I also heard that life or time has for quite a while been divided into parts that they call here "years." By that reckoning I'm cut into five equal parts. When I'm cut into a hundred parts I'll be exactly a hundred years old.

Shloyme-Leyb is tall, with a black face. His black, glowing eyes are the same color as the skin on his face. His thick facial hair is the same color as his skin. When he goes walking he strides along in high snow boots that go up to his knees and that squeak out—no, play the song of a living path between the huts, there on the sparkling snow. I could crawl into one of his boots and fit there, to get warm.

I found out the reason why I was studying the *alef-beys* with Black Shloyme-Leyb and not with my father, renowned throughout this area as pious, intelligent, and a scholar: my father is sick with typhus, and a sleigh stole him away from our hut.

III

The heavenly coin is beating in the nest of my fingers in sync with my heart beneath my fur coat, and I run to Shloyme-Leyb the next day and ask the rebbe to show me those wonderful letters from the *alef-beys*. Now—I've realized—each letter isn't just separate; they thread together in words.

I was too nervous, for an entire day, to unfasten my fingers and enjoy my coin. I couldn't allow my sinful glance to take pleasure in an angel's gift. Who knows when the evil eye might put in an appearance? After all, an angel wouldn't give me a second coin anytime soon. Nevertheless, every once in a while I lifted my head to look up at the roof beams while bent over my siddur.

Shloyme-Leyb nudges me. "Boy, the siddur is down there."

"Up there, I think," I answer right back.

"What do you mean, up there? What are you looking for in the ceiling beams?"

"The crack. There must be a crack in the roof."

"What crack? There aren't any cracks up there. What's gotten into your head?"

"If there's no crack, then the question is—how did the coin fall down to me?"

Shloyme-Leyb is completely astonished by my question. His dark face acquires a round furrow, like the water in our deep well when the chain lowers the bucket into it and swishes the liquid's mirror all to pieces. Having put Shloyme-Leyb to the test, I was sorry for him and tried to rescue him. "I've got it! I saw a little bird in the coin; it flew in through the chimney."

IV

How long will I keep the silver secret captive? I have to protect it from regular eyes, but from my own? I won't give myself an evil eye.

The day is hammered out of snow and cutting sun, but frost is king. If you spit into its kingdom, a splinter of ice will fall to the ground. I don't do that, though, because a glowing *alef-beys* is spread out on the snowy plains near the huts, and there the tall, windblown Shloyme-Leyb moves his diamond pointer to and fro.

The birch trees stand pale and naked at the frozen Irtysh, without a stitch on their ribs. The Kyrgyz set up a campfire here recently, and the birch trees cheered up, issuing warm breath. Now the campfire is also frozen, and the birch trees are barely breathing to themselves, like the Irtysh's waves under ice. But me, in my fur coat and hood and with my silver secret in the nest of my fingers, I'm not scared at all of the frost and its whips.

Among those birch trees at the frozen Irtysh that are set apart from the huts and people, I awaken the coin from its heavenly slumber and reveal it to God's world. Its little wings tremble in happiness. They shimmer and sparkle in the hammered clarity.

Now a strange question steals into me. Then another. What's the difference between heavenly and earthly money? I'm curious: What can I buy at the market with this coin?

I have an answer right away for the second question. I won't give up the coin even in return for the entire market.

I'll give it up only for a treatment for my father, so he can get well.

I kiss my heavenly money and put it in my pocket.

V

Ever since I kissed the silver coin, I've been frightened and distracted by its sharp, pungent odor. Goodness, where did I smell that smell; have I been in heaven before?

There's a crying inside me and the tears are mine. They melt the birch trees in the window, but the clouds hiding the moon don't know anything.

Who should I ask? Who can I confide in? Daddy is far away; a sleigh stole him. Mom isn't here either; she followed him along the blade tracks in the snow. Should I ask my friend Changuri, the Kyrgyz? He'll laugh at me with a yellow laughter, yellow as salted butter. I don't have a choice; I won't be shy, and I'll ask Shloyme-Leyb.

My studying is different today than yesterday or the day before. I don't look up at the ceiling anymore and don't seek out a crack. Let my rebbe remember that my coin flew through the chimney. I bend even closer to him and his pointer. But I no longer hear his chesty voice or see the letters. Now I'm only studying with my nostrils.

"What are you sniffing at?" Shloyme-Leyb's shadow brushes over me.

"My silver coin. The smell—"

"Silly, don't you know that I bring kerosene to all the huts? Let's keep learning."

To this very day, whether we're studying or not, a glowing *alef-beys* is spread out on the snowy plains near the huts, and there the tall, windblown Shloyme-Leyb is moving his diamond pointer to and fro.

1977

The Prophecy of the Inner Eye

THE ARTIST

The artist even enjoyed Death. And what about Death? Yes, he was jealous of the artist.

There are silkworms and silk-people. Since the silk-person had not ceased weaving his art, the thousand-eyed Angel of Death didn't stop competing: "Let's see who's more talented!"

With a snowy, purple fire, he froze a terrified birch forest that was embracing a lake. He didn't want to freeze the lake yet—just bound its banks with shimmering silver.

The condemned built his fortresses among shattered, mirrorlike birch trees.

The earth is a marble hunchback. Axes and shovels strike it, breaking off fingers like icicles. If a captive falls, either the hungry attack him, or—but the "or" is not so simple. The human children aren't able to dig graves into the ground. Wolf eyes jump out at every blow to the disobedient marble hunchback, as if the thousand-eyed one were crouched under every ax and spade.

What do the human children do? They saw off slabs of ice next to the lake, cutting out a bed to lie on, putting the dead inside, and then putting on top—another slab of ice, to lock in eternity. Then they launch the crystal sarcophagi onto the waters of the lake.

The sarcophagi float. The sun, frozen, can't melt them open. The frozen sun is itself a burning person in ice. Its bony rays cut through the crystal graves, and the living recognize their loved ones from a distance.

It happens that the dead meet. Two sarcophagi, of a man and a woman, collide, melting the ice with the power of their lips.

At night, by the light of the single star, which makes a lighthouse for the floating sarcophagi, the artist draws on snow with black charcoal. While sketching, he feels his heart float into his fingers. In glowing ecstasy, he depicts that vision on the snow.

1953

HANUKKAH CANDLES

A couple hundred people who had all been born with the same face; we lay like a many-eyed creature within a ball of limbs, standing on the icy bridge leading to the Lukiszki Prison.

The square was a terrible, four-sided mirror framed in brick buildings with barred windows. Where the buildings came together over the square's jagged corners, there rose up guards in proud helmets who directed lightning water jets from rubber hoses, demonic gullets, at us, over us, the people who had been born.

If they're firefighters, who's on fire? No one's on fire. Everyone is freezing. The ringing swords of the water jets dance over our naked bodies.

The captives now understand that the firefighters want to freeze them. A volcano once toyed with the people of Pompeii in exactly that way. When the chosen guests come to the exhibit, they'll enjoy the frozen sculptures.

A woman with a child at her breast was immediately frozen. Her breath on the child's breath—a smoky, diamond dove suspended in midair over a broken egg.

Here's a musician with a violin under his chin. The strings extend from his fiery beard. Sounds cover him (snow and ice). His violin slowly stops: a ship among ice floes.

I hear fragmented voices.

"Why isn't the snow cyanide?"

"I tell you, brother, that the creator is jealous of us."

"It's Hanukkah tonight, the fifth candle!"

A voice or a heavenly echo?

Half-frozen pupils, where tears are laughing at other tears, saw the bars to pieces and move into the marble air. They seek and find the heavenly echo.

Five burning fingers, which a Jew had lit from his own hand, five Hanukkah candles, are lifted as five tongues over the ice sculptures, melting their iciness, burning the firefighters and the barred walls.

1953

THE HAPPIEST

There was an exceptional crop that fall. Old ravens, older than the old city, hadn't seen anything like it since their birth. In the gardens and orchards near the Viliya, sunflowers and cucumbers, apples and pears were sprinkled with Hebrew letters. A dewy Hebrew alphabet appeared on the childlike hands of weeds that grew from the gashed earth. Where my home used to be—after my home had rolled up to heaven in a fiery chariot beyond time—Mother Earth had been transformed into a meadow made out of stray leaves of holy books.

I had just been resurrected. Hungry. Hungry to live. Newly born. With clay lips, I fell to a piece of fruit. The fruit was like amber at the fire. Its Hebrew letters were illuminated by sunlight from the inside.

I shouldn't say whether I bit into the fruit. I can say that I read its writing:

> After my death, if I were able
> to press my child to my breast
> I would be the happiest
> of all the dead
> who ever died on earth.

Since then I have been wandering over the world and unworld, wandering in myself, searching for, rummaging for the name of the unknown singer, seeking the happiest of all.

1979

A BLACK ANGEL WITH A PIN IN HIS HAND

I

His whole life he had been called Moyshe-Itzke, a familiar name, like you'd call a boy. The only people in whose memory he's still barely alive remember him by that name.

Moyshe-Itzke was born because he wanted to be born. That's what he told me. He then added confidentially that an entire collection of dark forces didn't want to let him shine, but his will was stronger. The anointed writer Moyshe-Itzke was born in order to live eternally.

"I'm going to stay the way I am," he said, assessing me superciliously, with the sort of face that would well up out of a shattered mirror. "Death isn't relevant to me; we belong to two different worlds. It's a pity that you won't be walking these streets in a thousand years. You'd recognize me in throngs of people. I won't change. Like a rock doesn't change."

He burst into hysterics, laughter like a dispersed mold, and kept going on like one possessed. "You say a rock can be overgrown with moss? Yes, my great soul will be overgrown with a beard. And you say that sparks sleep in the rock? They sing in my veins! The storm that can extinguish my sparks has not yet been born."

II

I had already had the luck to hear the song of his sparks. Most lines of his song were consumed by sparks. But poem-sparks and poem-fires erupted from it—the storm wasn't born that could put them out.

During our walks and talks on Castle Hill, I found out that he was a complete heretic when it came to recognizing authority. He only recognized the greatness of three human beings in all of world history and literature: Moses, Napoleon, and

Dostoyevsky. Everyone else were just *books*, not great people.

"There are billions of books! Show me someone alive!"

I tried to bargain with him, have him add just one poet to his three chosen ones. "What about Byron? Would you reject him?"

Moyshe-Itzke waved a hairy hand. "He too was lame at poetry."

In a summer evening of transparent amber, coming down off Castle Hill and making our way to the Viliya, I had the guts to knock off a little of Moyshe-Itzke's eternity. "The three of them, the greatest—Moses, Napoleon, and Dostoyevsky—they all died. So how can it be that you, Moyshe-Itzke, will live forever?"

His rusted brow furrowed—a bolt of lightning in a cloud at night. Under the skin of his face, a glowing spider web. With the voice of a lost echo he thundered out: "Someone can break through!"

III

He lived on Gitke Toybe's Alley in Meyerke's Courtyard, where Motke Chabad had lived.

His father had two trades: butcher and bootmaker. He butchered in winter and made boots in the summer. I don't know what he did the rest of the time. His father believed that one profession was enough for his refined son: bootmaking, and this he would teach him.

But Moyshe-Itzke's hot blood was attracted to the slaughterhouse. Where the condemned calves and oxen shriek and bellow; where the shochet plays the cello on their warm necks; where his father cuts out their double crowns, pulls off their purple boots.

As his bar mitzvah approached, the boy got restless, even more than before. He decided to pay the price of manhood by saving at least a few oxen from the cleaver.

It was during a murderous frost. Dawn. A single star hung over the slaughter-house. Moyshe-Itzke stole in through a narrow window.

A single ox, like the single star, stood tied to a pole, kicking with its hoof.

In the steam of the ox Moyshe-Itzke warmed his pierced ears.

A couple of sturdy young men appeared in the slaughterhouse with ropes and skinning knives. The shochet also appeared, bulkily attired in a fur coat and carrying a small case under his arm. His father happened to be observing the anniversary of his father's death and was delayed. As the shochet was unwrapping his fur coat, Moyshe-Itzke revealed himself from within the deadly shadow, with incredible swiftness leapt to the butcher's block where the shochet had put the case, grabbed the cleaver, and stuck it into a mound of sawdust.

The shochet was sure he had forgotten to put the cleaver in the case. The young butchers made themselves scarce, cursing. The single star, which had emerged in blood from an icicle, also vanished, taking within its inner eye the secrets of the earth.

Two were left inside: Moyshe-Itzke and the rescued ox.

In the meantime the sun had appeared in the slaughterhouse: the cleaver was wandering out of its hideaway and slashing into empty space.

Moyshe-Itzke drew close to the ox, stepped into the fenced-off portion between the poles to make his acquaintance. The boy's entire body was suffused by the sweetness of a good deed.

But who can understand an ox's sense of fairness? Instead of paying back his savior with a smile, with a heartfelt thank you, the ox first bent down low in front of him, then hoisted him up on one of his horns.

IV

All the details, images, and nuances relevant to the ox were confided in me years later by Moyshe-Itzke, when his poems were bellowing on the giant pages of the *Vilna Day* newspaper and the poet himself was inducted into the fellowship of Young Vilna.

From Moyshe-Itzke's hoarse, demonic voice, I realized then that the ox had hooked its horn into his mind too.

The horn overcame somebody.

Since Moyshe-Itzke bragged that he would live forever, that someone would break through, I was capable of believing for a while that the one who the horn stabbed in the slaughterhouse was Moyshe-Itzke's Angel of Death, which had already taken up a battle station in his mind.

As though he were a soldier in muddy trenches in an endless war, Moyshe-Itzke wandered among insane asylums and was given leave only during the ceasefires in his soul.

V

During one of those ceasefires, it was the day before Passover, on returning home to Gitke Toybe's Alley, to the crumbling wall where he lived on the ground floor in a single room with an antechamber, Moyshe-Itzke saw a dogcatcher in leather pants chase a dog across the street, lasso him with the noose attached to his pole, and drag him struggling in a semicircle through the mild blue spring evening to the wailing wagon close by.

Moyshe-Itzke's blood grew roused, crouched inside him at the ready, then shouted out like freed streams of spring flowing under the thin layer of cracked ice. It escaped from the reins of the arteries. Moyshe-Itzke's hands began to gallop after the dogcatcher in the leather pants.

"You have to give me back my dear dog right now, or I'll make a measuring tape out of your guts."

The dogcatcher in the leather pants had already managed to load the lassoed dog into the wailing wagon. "Try your story on someone else. That's not your dog."

Moyshe-Itzke bellowed hoarsely, "Hamlet, bear witness that I am your master." (That's what Moyshe-Itzke called him, because the dog's fate was suspended between to-be and not-to-be.)

The little, just-incarcerated dog stuck out between the iron bars of the wagon his face, which was covered by an adorable red glove, while behind him an orchestra of stray dogs was barking, yelping, and howling. He cried like a child, "Oy, oy, oy."

"Now do you believe me?" Moyshe-Itzke spat fire at the dogcatcher.

The dog hangman gave a brilliant smile like a splinter of glass in a garbage can. "You're both lying. But I'll give you a chance. You can redeem the piece of shit for no more than ten zlotys."

Ten zlotys. Where could he get his hands on that? With the few rubles that his father had tossed with a jingle into the pocket of his blue robe during a visit, Moyshe-Itzke had already acquired tobacco, a yellow copying pencil, and some paper to match wits with Byron and Dostoyevsky. He essentially had nothing left but a few pennies. It's an insult to the lips to haggle with a dogcatcher. It's the time and the place for action. Hamlet's fate hangs in the balance. As soon as the wagon starts off there won't be time for any appeal. There's only one way left: force! Beat up the nooseman and free the dog.

A double miracle occurred. From within the crowd surrounding the two men, a girl like the newly hatched spring approached, wearing a man's double-breasted jacket and a flowered blouse. She redeemed the dog from behind bars with her ten zlotys.

Her name was Yetl Gonkrey. The double miracle was that along with the dog she also redeemed Moyshe-Itzke's loneliness.

VI

After leaving for the institution alone and coming back as a group of three, they made the musty room in Gitke Toybe's Alley full of life.

The father with the two professions saw right away that he was superfluous and departed to make his lodgings with a relative, learning a third trade: playing and losing at cards with his friends the butchers.

Yetl was short, with yellow hair. If you like, blonde—a thread of freckles on her throat. Both of those smiles, on her face and her throat, teased each other and a third, Moyshe-Itzke. He liked to tell the story over and over again how Yetl first got into his head and then his heart. How her skin is misted over. And if her men's jacket had been buttoned over her flowered blouse at that first meeting, nothing would have happened.

Yetl was a kindergarten teacher. She worked with ease but lightly, since now she had someone to work for. Besides her own mouth, she had a second mouth to feed: Hamlet was sitting at the table now like a real person.

VII

The teacher was in love with Moyshe-Itzke, not just head over heels but also over her abilities. She believed him that he would live forever, that someone could break through. But she was miffed that it couldn't be both of them, only him. Moyshe-Itzke taught Yetl all about it and explained why he was the chosen one.

"When a person dies, Yetele, it's because the number of words God has set for him has run out. But the number of words set for me is without end."

Another time, he added: "You must know, Yetele, when a person dies all of a sudden, there's no one to talk to."

She also heard these words of comfort from him: "You shouldn't be embarrassed that you were born a girl. They'll still write about you in the papers."

When Moyshe-Itzke would read aloud a poem he had written to Yetl, or roar out a short story that consisted of one sentence a mile long, her cheeks would light up with colors of desire. So she also gladly accepted his philosophy of life. There was only one thing Yetl couldn't get used to—the way he would suddenly explode in laughter. When Moyshe-Itzke would roar out such laughter in the middle of everything, unasked for, unhinged, she would accompany him on the keys of her tears.

VIII

One fine day, the room in Gitke Toybe's Alley was enriched with a sewing machine from the Singer Corporation: a gift from Yetl for her chosen one. If he kneads the air with his legs for a couple of hours, she thought, his breathing will be made easier up above.

On another fine day, Yetl came home from kindergarten and walked into a cherry garden. What happened, did she get lost? No. Moyshe-Itzke had stripped the walls of dozens of layers of old wallpaper, and instead of writing on the walls with a pencil he was stitching out a new work in black thread with the Singer machine, line after line.

From behind the old, faded wallpaper appeared the earlier wallpaper, young, fresh, and fiery.

Since then, the walls in their room and the anteroom have assumed the colors of the four seasons.

IX

"You're my living treatment." Moyshe-Itzke caressed Yetl in a calm moment. "Since you're already me, I'll break through together with you. And that'll count as me breaking through by myself, since that's the only way it can be."

Yetl believed him.

"We're not going to break into eternity through some back door, oh no." He described to Yetl their personal end of days. "I met him on Butcher's Street yesterday; I stopped him and told him clearly and absolutely, 'We're not going to break into eternity through some back door.'"

"Who did you meet?" Yetl swept his thorny hair away from his rusty forehead, and it stabbed her finger.

"Stupid people call him Death. But he's really just a black angel with a pin in his hand!" Moyshe-Itzke burst out in his interrupting laughter.

Yetl told me about this episode when I was visiting her on a loud, end-of-summer day.

My memory was also enriched on that visit with three things that happened.

Yetl had gotten thinner in the three months since I had last seen her, since Moyshe-Itzke wished for her waist to be as slender as the waist of the Singer machine.

Moyshe-Itzke dreamed that a dentist extracted his molar. When he arose at dawn (Yetl was a witness) the tooth was missing. Now he's waiting for the doctor to show up and demand payment from his patient.

Hamlet became a sleepwalker. On moonlit nights one can clearly see a silver hand with a silver leash taking him for a walk over the city's crooked roofs and cornices. Then Hamlet crawls back into his doghouse, and the next day he doesn't remember anything.

The walls of the room turned blue during that visit. A blue sky, washed out with rain, with the golden tail of a rainbow.

Yetl put a bowl of hot beans on the table. Moyshe-Itzke unrolled a sewn scroll for me and read out a prediction: a prophecy that hunger will soon cease. People will eat each other.

While Moyshe-Itzke read his sewn lines, I felt the needle of the Singer machine dancing on my backbone.

X

Our last meeting was on the first ghetto night.

Barefoot, in only the fragments of a shirt, and with a scroll under his arm, he fluttered like an eagle dying in midflight over the paralyzed waves of human beings barely breathing on their transit through the alleyways.

A black angel with a pin in his hand, alone and protean, appeared in a blink out of the paneless heavens and gaping attics.

The night rolled out of time, which disappeared.

Moyshe-Itzke dropped down facing me, illuminated by his own blood. "Do you still think that someone can break through?"

He unrolled the scroll and pointed to a verse. "Child of man, I already broke through. I'm eternal now."

He broke out into his interrupting laughter.

The only laughter on the first ghetto night.

1980

PORTRAIT WITH A BLUE SWEATER

1

My mother knitted me a blue woolen sweater for Hanukkah, a beautiful new pull-over that went up to the neck. Warm and motherly, it was the only one like it in town. Coatless, I parade in it through the Hanukkah snow, which is already as high as I am—I want everyone to see it and die of jealousy. Or if not that, then at least demonstrate respect and esteem for the sweater and the person who's inside. Mainly, I want respect from those sorry excuses for writers who want to clip my wings before they've even had a chance to grow.

At that time, a number of years before the Second World War, I made the acquaintance of a young painter in the Jerusalem of Lithuania, who had recently immigrated here from Paris together with his wife, a teacher. The woman had gotten temporary work in a high school, and as for her husband: full time with brush and easel.

They settled into a room with clay walls and a glassed-in balcony, which was given the name atelier. Both of them fell in love again. Not as man and wife but with the old Jewish city on the banks of the Viliya, which they had heard about but never seen in person. Although the painter had studied and painted for a few years in Paris, where they moved from their poor Polish towns right after getting married, they had a really hard time of it there. What's more, the young painter's lungs were severely affected in Paris; the old city on the river in Lithuania sparkled from a distance, attracted them.

We first met at Rokhl Sutzkever's picture exhibition. We felt a closeness to each other by our second meeting when he took me up to his atelier to show me his pictures.

He was a master of silence. His speech, and it was barely that, was plagiarized from his silence. His painting, however, was talkative and original. Its originality and genuineness were revealed from under the paint, as if he had painted them over with other colors. Like a cloud painting over the sunset before a storm. Although the style of his painting was not startlingly new, someone of good taste encountering his paintings' secrets would soon taste their distinctiveness on his palate, like an experienced wine drinker could detect from the odor of the cork where the grapes were cultivated and the age of the wine in the bottle.

ll

Our third meeting and fellowship was at my house. He came in with a box of brushes, tubes, other paraphernalia of his, and a largish, stretched-out canvas.

It seemed obvious to me that my blue sweater had inspired him to paint me. And since a head with tousled locks, like a duck from a pond, is sticking out of it, that's even better.

Pine trees were already traced on the windowpanes. The sun won't saw them down so soon.

Although I was warm enough, I still asked my mother to warm up the attic. That means to heat up the clay wall-oven that served as divider in the attic between my room and hers. This oven was in my mother's room.

In my blue sweater, my back to the wall-oven, hands behind my back, I sat patiently on a stool and posed for the silent painter.

While painting my portrait he doesn't block the canvas with his face like other painters, which drives their curious models crazy. The canvas was positioned so that I could plainly see myself being reborn. The painter turns his head in my direction every once in a while, angles the fishing pole of his glances, adds a line, a nuance, the color of a dream over or under my skin, over or under my thoughts, and grants them eternity on his white canvas. He clearly doesn't realize that while he's painting me, he's also my model simultaneously. I'm painting him on a ray of sunlight hanging in midair.

While we're painting each other, a different sort of face is really what I see. Each eye of his hails from a different neighborhood. One eye's blue, like the detergent that Mother adds to the washing tub, and the second has a pupil of amber, an owl's gaze trapped inside.

We both finish painting our portraits with the last lit match of sunset.

III

Suddenly I decide to run away from home, leave the city, in the middle of a frosty night. Not like a shackled horse, though, but in a train. The train needs to run away, and I'll be inside. Where to? Warsaw!

And money? People you know in Warsaw to support you? Leaving your mother—isn't that criminal? Your dry thoughts lit quite a fire.

My questions and counter-questions were pointless.

I glimpse a bloody hand among the windowpane fir trees. It bars up my window. If I don't flee tomorrow, or the day after, it'll shut up the entire attic behind bars, and then it'll be too late.

My good mother, who's ready to give me her soul, has given me saved-up zlotys.

What's the reason for my sudden detachment from city and home? Who's at fault? You can blame the evil spirit who cruelly wove gray into my mother's head of hair. I can't take it. I challenged the evil spirit to a duel, but he didn't show. Now I'm going to look for him away from home until I find him. If I can't, I'll challenge myself to a duel.

IV

The railroad leviathan spits me out, clad in the motherly blue sweater, into the midst of the Polish capital.

Frosty violet dawn.

An iron hand on the top of a streetcar, like the hand of a drowning man clutching at a straw, grabs a dangling wire that runs and cuts through streets, showering gasping sparks.

I buy an *Express*, where "Rooms for a Night" are always found, and I pick an address completely randomly: Dzielna 27. Just my luck. Right opposite the local prison.

A Jew, coughing in long underwear and a dusty hat, leads me into a salon hung with heavy purple curtains—it's like four whole theaters are putting on productions at once.

"I read in the *Express* that I can get a room here."

"To spend the night."

"And to spend the day?"

"Young fella, just to spend the night."

"Can I see my room?"

The coughing Jew lifts the edge of a curtain and drags out a folding bed on wobbly springs. "Young fella, here's the room."

"And how much does it cost to sleep here?"

"It's not much for a Litvak. No more than five zlotys a month. But you have to pay in advance, advance."

I give him five zlotys, a considerable fraction of my capital, write my first name and last in a tattered register "for the police," leave my suitcase in the symbolic room, and walk through Warsaw to struggle with the evil spirit.

When I come back late at night to my prepaid room, at first I think I've gotten lost and ended up in a hospital. The salon is full of dense rows of folding beds, so I can barely make it through to my spot. The rows aren't empty; rather, they're overflowing with tough guys and gals. Swilling whiskey. Making out. Hollering. Between one holler and the other sounding like a hoarse pendulum, the nasty green cough of the Jew who rented me the symbolic room.

I see very clearly what kind of mess I've gotten myself into: people from the underworld and criminal butchers. They don't need any rooms to spend the day. They just need a place to spend the night with their hollering girls. My nostrils are assaulted by the odor of cow udders and ox guts. A calf bleats in a sack. Am I really going to spend my nights here for a whole month? I have no choice. It's prepaid.

V

I get used to the nighttime people little by little. I listen closely to their thieves' argot. I get drawn into their stories, like a suspenseful novel published in installments. When a writer with whom I've gotten acquainted offers to put me up on a freezing cold night, I make my apologies.

One night, the vacant rooms fill up with police and secret agents. The tough boys and girls don't get scared. Everyone's nice and friendly. The guy they're looking for (someone offed a collaborator) already made his exit. But they can handcuff his folding bed.

If it weren't for hunger, I wouldn't have to make money to eat. I'm working as a house painter's assistant, scraping walls. I scrape and the other guy paints. It leaves me enough time to read in the library and get to the Gensher cemetery, where I can listen eagerly to the oral masterpieces of the wailing women and the eulogizers. I meet actors, poets, world liberators.

I was also fated to have a short love affair. A blushing girl sits next to me in the Grosser Library and browses Tuwim's poetry with her eyelashes. We meet. Her name is Saltshe.

Before you know it, Saltshe tells me her dad wants to meet me. Of course, anyone who wants to see me can. She leads me by the hand—her hand is also blushing—down Dzika Street, through a courtyard festooned with icicles. On wobbly, slippery stairs, Saltshe brings me into a building where sewing machines are throbbing.

Her dad jumps out wearing a red shirt, carrying a big pair of scissors. The needles on him shine like sparks from a grindstone.

A good dad. But when I find out what his workshops produce—suits to dress up dead goyim in their coffins (that's why the fronts are elegant black and the backs white goatskin)—I quickly turn back through the avenue of black suits and giant fluttering ravens, slide back down the wobbly, slippery steps, and leave forever.

I would have stayed another month in my symbolic room, but a tragedy occurred. It's dawn, I finished my overnight, I want to get dressed. Oh, no, someone's stolen my sweater! Who will protect me in the unfriendly world? This blue sweater that was my only comfort survived in the portrait the young artist painted of me in my hometown.

Embarrassed, I traveled back.

VI

I come home. My panicked trip to Warsaw was for nothing. I did not conquer the evil spirit. In my absence, he wove new gray threads into my mother's head of hair.

Perhaps the evil spirit is nestled inside of me?

If that loss wasn't enough, here comes another: the painter and his wife have vanished together with the portrait. Did they flee to Warsaw to follow me, or did they run away to the ends of the earth?

Here's an important guest in my home in Tel Aviv. Marc Chagall is here, bringing a box of paints as a gift for my daughter.

We drink a toast. Tell stories. The fans of Chagall at the table are soaring, spirited.

I was also soaring over time, over skeletal days, and I told—probably better than I did here—the story of the blue woolen sweater that my mother knit me for Hanukkah, about the young painter, the portrait he painted of me, and the fate of the sweater that I can't stop yearning for.

Suddenly, a knock at the door. Believe it or not, the portrait of the blue sweater comes in and climbs up on the eastern wall, where his home is to this very day.

The only one who wasn't astonished was Marc Chagall. With a movement of his hand he pointed to the portrait and congratulated me with a Vitebsk smile: "If you truly long for something, you'll get everything you long for."

1985

THE GUNPOWDER BRIGADE

1

This happened in the upside-down time, when a swarm of locusts attacked my city. The locusts didn't just devour stalks and weeds but also young and old, babies and the aged. Besides flesh and bone, it was deadly important to the locust to saw off with its saw teeth the part of the human being one calls the soul.

This was the tastiest portion for the locust.

I was caught in my attic room by a messenger of the locusts on an early autumn dawn. He had just been a student in a white cap, a neighbor of mine, and now he had trapped me outside, alongside others who were also taken prisoner throughout the night, and we were driven through the streets, up and up into the mountains where the street ends.

Maple trees lining the street had already rained down their yellow patches.

At the end of the street, the line was driven ever onward between two mountains, one looming like a monster opposite the other.

The belly of one mountain had a belt of barbed wire and crossed iron bars. Its intestines were soon revealed: trenches and caverns, fortresses and embrasures that the previous ruler had prepared for the city's defense.

The line of people headed into the trenches.

Another messenger of the numberless locusts came out of a cavern wearing mouse-gray short pants and delivered a brief sermon to the arrestees. Since we had touched off a war to subjugate the world, we have to pay dearly for it now. The first installment: on our backs and shoulders, we'll carry stink bombs and gas bombs from the belly of this mountain to the mountain facing it.

II

The space between the mountains, which you once could have reached across with your hand, was now remarkably elongated under the load of the bombs. As if the earth had turned into dough that was rolled out to the horizon.

As luck would have it, thanks to his excellency, my fate, I was marching with the Gunpowder Brigade (the name someone gave our column) under a load of gas bombs. I was in the middle of the brigade, wending its way two abreast.

My partner was bowed low under the weight of his stink bombs. I sized him up with a sidelong glance in the midst of my autumn sweat: a face with a weedy overgrowth under the shadow of a straw hat—in memory of summer. Pince-nez on a cord around his left ear that was on my right side. With each step his pince-nez jumped like two people in love on a carousel (the grotesque image has stayed with me till this day). I momentarily freed my right hand from holding up the load on my head and pushed my partner's pince-nez onto his nose.

The Gunpowder Brigade walked and walked, yet it hadn't gotten any closer to its goal. With every step we took forward, the mountain opposite us retreated backward. I acquainted my partner with the demonic music of creaking bones. A fragmented conversation that was interrupted by panting began between us, in order to forget the desperate roles we were playing and the distance we must travel through the desert to the hoped-for mountain.

Dr. Horaci Dik, that was his name and title. A psychiatrist in a hospital for the insane.

III

We were both afraid to look in front of us. Dr. Horaci Dik was luckier than I was. His pince-nez was matted with a glue of dust and sweat, so in any case he couldn't see what he didn't want to see. I more and more had the desire to raise my leaden eyelids. My eyes had become alcoholics, dying for a chance to drink the strong, pure spirit of the air.

An explosion. One of the first in the ranks of the Gunpowder Brigade fell, carrying his burden. A fountain of brown smoke rose over the horizon's blue canvas. During the resulting, small unrest, my partner peeled off his ash-covered jacket. The explosion had given him the strength to keep walking.

Dr. Horaci Dik described his ancestry to me. He was a grandson of Aizik-Meyer Dik, author of hundreds of volumes of stories and novels.

It seemed unbelievable. I know something about the biography of Aizik-Meyer Dik, and his stories aren't unfamiliar to me. I tried to calculate when Aizik-Meyer Dik was born, got married, had kids, and died, and somehow the math didn't work out. Those doing research on the novelist had somehow never mentioned that there's a grandson of his in town.

"Maybe a relative? Or a great-grandson?" I tried to bargain down the esteemed doctor's pedigree.

My partner didn't budge. A grandson. He even remembered his grandfather's jokes and witticisms. When Horaci was a cheder boy and went by Hirshke, he heard a saying of his grandfather's: "We have to eat dirt, but we have no teeth."

A transparent smile hung on his face like spider webs in the sun.

Someone else in the Gunpowder Brigade collapsed, but his load didn't go off.

The mountain facing us got tired of sliding backward and stayed looming in the same place it had recently been.

The locusts' messenger in short pants rattled past our Gunpowder Brigade on a motorcycle. He shot over our heads and in between the walking partners.

When the baking oven of the sun dropped lower, to bake challahs out of our bodies for Shabbos, the same locusts' messenger already awaited us on the other mountain. He was standing like a scarecrow at the edge of a clay pit that for years had fed the brick factories in the area with wagonloads of clay.

Silence gurgled in the clay pit. Some of the Gunpowder Brigade were already drowsing there, purple sealing wax on their foreheads. It seemed like the clay pit had given birth to the dead. And there at the clay pit where we unloaded the bombs, the creature in short pants gave us an hour's rest.

IV

Now I could give my friend a real look over. I decided to research his family connection to Aizik-Meyer Dik some other time. (I believed in time.) Meanwhile, I ripped several strips from my shirt and used them to dress his wounds.

But Dr. Horaci Dik was miffed at me for doubting his grandson status.

My interest was piqued by his manner of speech: daytshmerish, Aizik-Meyer-ish, as if I were listening to A. M. Dik's story "Chaytzikl Himself" or "The People of

Durashitshok."

Out of curiosity, I asked him if he was a local. And if so, why his Yiddish sounded so old.

His answer was tangential. *"Ja, ja,* in *dieser* city, colleague, even the goy who ran the bathhouse spoke an amazing Yiddish."

My partner in walking and in fate was already speaking about the city in the past tense.

He came upon a sweet flower at the clay pit and refreshed himself with it.

I again decided to stop my investigations into ancestry. At the clay pit everyone's is the same.

Dr. Horaci Dik got more comfortable with me. He changed the subject, leaned on his elbow, and told me a story about an experience he'd had in the hospital for the insane: the doctor instituted a policy that the attendants shouldn't be taken from outside the hospital walls but from inside, from among the unraveled souls. Even more: there was a schizophrenic, a doctor who treated himself while treating the insane. The chief cook was also a hospital patient.

One fine day—as people are wont to say—Dr. Horaci Dik went into the kitchen just because. The door slammed shut behind him. The chief cook and his stewards tied him up; then the chief cook approached him with two long knives. "I'll slice you and cook you up. For once we'll have a delicious lunch."

His life was in the balance. But in that moment he remembered that the chief cook's insanity derived from the fact that a thief had stolen all the city's salt, and without salt food has no taste. Aizik-Meyer Dik's grandson shouted out, "Pani Hendeles,"—that was the chief cook's name—"what's the matter with you? Lunch will be completely salt-free and tasteless. Let me go, and I'll bring a handful of salt."

That's how Dr. Horaci Dik was saved.

His conclusion: only through acknowledging that an insane person is right is there a chance to escape his knives.

V

The locusts' messenger popped up again at the clay pit. Rest time was over. Now we have to follow the same order in reverse—bring the bombs back to where we got them, behind the barbed wire on the opposite mountain.

At this moment Dr. Horaci Dik lifted himself up like a bird, and I heard and saw his fiery speech before the locusts' messenger. "Since we, those captured together, set off a war to subjugate the world (according to what was said), and since it's not yet clear who will win this war, he could pay dearly if he were to brutalize us."

Though the doctor was not similar to the short David, nor the locusts' messenger to the armored Goliath, for all that the people of the Gunpowder Brigade played along in this life-and-death game.

Those sleeping in the clay pit with the purple sealing wax on their forehead pricked up their unliving ears.

The gas bombs and stink bombs, so it seems, also take a side in the unequal contest.

When Dr. Horaci Dik finished his speech, the locusts' messenger turned thin and black like a burned-out match.

He gestured to us. "You're free." He vanished without a breath.

But truly and historically we couldn't be free then because the pure air of the beginning of autumn was hanging on the gallows.

1985

AN ANSWER TO A LETTER

What a question—of course I remember! Your name is actually Munke, but the forest people, both Jews and non-Jews, called you Munke Poyterile. Beats the heck out of me where your nickname came from. All I know is, you were both joined at the hip. Wherever Munke was mentioned, Poyterile was too.

Is your current name, more assimilated to English, a translation of the previous one? I can't figure it out. In any case, you were and will remain Munke Poyterile, galloping continuously for decades in my memory. I see your shocks of hair shoot off red sparks, like your father's forge in Myadl, until it was devoured by its own fire.

Do you want another sign that you're continuously galloping through the forest of my memory? One night, when we were on our way to Misuni village (Hulka Hulevitsh and his gang ruled the roost there), you brought me a thrush you had slaughtered so that it could take the edge off my hunger. The gift wasn't so appetizing. "This bird is going to come back to life inside me and peck me to pieces!"

Now to the substance of your letter, Munke. You're about to die, and you want me to forgive you.

How do you know you're about to die? My friend, the poet Leizer Wolf, has a line: "We die daily in small doses." That's a genuine line. But it wouldn't be any less true for both of us if it said "big" instead of "small." I'm going to make an effort to grab the substance by the horns: you want me to forgive you.

You asked the same thing of me once before. Then, Munke, you were still living.

That was during our encounter that followed the liberation of those living in the ruins of my dead city.

You fell to one knee in front of me, leaning on your rifle. I was astonished. Such humility from Munke?

What happened for you to ask my forgiveness twice over? Let's recall.

In late fall 1943, when the devourer of seasons had already spread burning stained glass in the Narocz bogs, and the wind polished and sharpened the moon-like snows on the fir branches, Kim Zelenyak (the same one who cut the cord for that woman Lucy, who gave birth to a forest child) found a frozen Romani kid, barely alive, on the dog paths (that's what the hidden partisan trails were called), wrapped in curlicues of familiar-yet-unfamiliar writing. Since Kim was a frequent guest in my earthen hut, and he understood that my ancestry had some connection with that script, he brought what he found to my dirt house.

Right away they named the little Romani "Roma." That's what the Romani call themselves in the Romani language, so it's like naming a Yid "Yudl."

When Roma revived from his frozen state, like an ice-covered windowpane thawed by the sun, he related in sign and blood language how he fled naked and alone from the valley of slaughter near Kurenets, where he had been brought with a wagonload of other Romani. In that wagon, curled up next to his dead grandfather, were his three sisters. Their horse died there, standing in harness. Running away from that valley of slaughter, naked in a frosty night, he wrapped himself in these garments: sheets of parchment from a torn-up Torah scroll that was lying on the ground in Kurenets alleys as they breathed their last.

Perhaps you remember that I buried the parchment under the lonely birch tree next to the earthen hut and said kaddish. I wrote some lines on the bark. An arboreal tombstone.

Roma stayed in my earthen hut. Dr. Podolni extracted a bullet from his shoulder.

No one in the forest was as lonely as the little Romani. Even us Jews looked down on him. A little guy without a people. But the one who caressed him with her eyelashes and was always fetching him things was Lucy. The same Lucy for whom Kim Zelenyak bit off the cord last year when she gave birth to a forest child.

It's true; while you—as an intelligence officer—made your way into the enemy's maw and tore out his molar, Lucy spent her heedless time extracting the little Romani's loneliness. When you came back whole, bearing a number of victories, Roma was already back to normal. He had learned Yiddish, and I'd learned a bit of the Romani language from him. Lucy learned the Romani language even better than I did. When Roma shook up the woods with a song in his native tongue, the birds in the snow-covered nests joined in.

Munke, I don't know what battle played out in your blood when you came into the earthen hut and found Lucy playing with the Romani's shimmering forelock. I saw out of the corner of my eye that you weren't looking at things the way you had before. In the darkness of that earthen hut, your look had the glowing green stare of the hungry wolf you had recently tangled with.

After some time passed, Roma become part of the espionage unit. He happily left to avenge his three sisters and the innocent horse who died standing between the wagon shafts.

News arrived in March 1944 that an airplane would land in the Ushachy region to take me across the front. While you accompanied me there, I asked you to take care of the little Romani. It was of vital importance to me that he survive to see victory. You promised by all that was holy, though the word "holy" didn't grow in the forest.

When we met after the liberation of those living in the ruins of my dead city (we had been looking for each other!), you got down before me on one knee and asked my forgiveness: Roma had been torn apart limb from limb while skipping over a minefield.

Munke, you didn't sin against me at all. I don't have anything to forgive you for. Twice you showed me great fellowship in the forest: when I couldn't take off my boots because the ulcers in my feet were stuck to them, leading you to expertly cut them open to free my feet from the leather cages and even give me your own boots; and when you brought me a slaughtered thrush to take the edge off my hunger.

Munke Poyterile, all these years you haven't stopped galloping through the forests of my memory. When you stand before the heavenly court and they weigh your sins on one side of the scale and your good deeds on the other, the little Romani will jump on one of the scale's pans.

Then the lord of the scale will render judgment.

1985

THE WHITE CANE

1

Was my back now a door? I felt someone pound on my back during a steamy summer evening in Tel Aviv while I waited for the eye of the iron golem to flick from red to green so I could cross the street. In the midst of my *hamsin* confusion I wanted to answer "Come in." But my head turned to the one who was slapping, and I glimpsed a white cane held by a veined white hand that was like a continuation of the cane. An old man attached to the hand took shape, also white, with white hair, as if he were born from whiteness. His eyes—two pools of chalk with mother-of-pearl pupils. Mother-of-pearl whitepils.

"You don't recognize me, as if we exchanged our respective fates, you blind and me sighted. But that's not true. Me, the blind one, detected you with my nostrils. My nostrils replaced my eyes a long time ago. Lately, though, they've lost that sensitivity, and I can't fix them with spectacles. They are going out like fireflies. So I thought a white cane would split the darkness for me. But that's not the way it's going at all. An unknown foe blackened my cane. Proof—I cut the air with it when trying to cross the street, and it doesn't help. Instead I've been cut several times myself. Still, I had a spark in my nostrils: I sniffed you out."

"Who are you?" I took the figure under his arm, and when the iron golem blinked again in green I led him to the other side of the street. There I attempted to calm him. "Beat out with a stick the thought that your cane is black, sir. Truly, it's white-white—white like the milk you suckled from your mother's breast."

"Why are you using 'sir' with a friend of your youth? We didn't just grow up on the same street, we grew up in the same courtyard with the sole apple tree and the rusted pump, we both chased after bats and played soccer in a brick factory. We even played hide-and-go-seek with the same girl. Chvolkeh was her name. She would lift her calico dress up over her knees for an apple. And you wouldn't deny her a second apple either."

"Zundl!" I cried out, as if someone had rubbed a grater over my skin.

"Yes, Zundl. Horeh was my father's name, Horeh the Leech-Seller. I was, and have remained, his only child. My very name, Zundl, Sonny Boy, sticks out its black tongue at me, but Zundl's what you're calling me, friend. If I thought yesterday was today, a sunny snow would be falling on me."

"Where should I accompany you, Zundl? Oh, why am I chattering away? There'll be no accompanying you; we'll go to a bar where we'll drink a toast and have something to eat, and for dessert we'll make delectable conversation."

"But not too long," he responded throatily. "My old lady won't know what to think."

II

I took him to Jaffa and we went to Aladdin, the drinking establishment by the sea where I often hide from all sorts of annoying types—and where my pen favors me. Behind the window's glass armor plate, every wave, day and night, is a sunset, each trying to overtake the other and with diamond edges cut open the windows of the Aladdin. But the waves aren't strong enough.

The waiter knew the caprices of my taste buds. I signaled with my finger for two settings, and I requested a carafe of red wine.

I wanted to start with: How long has it been since we last saw each other? But the words were smarter than their owner and ignored my orders, so that the "see each other" didn't have a chance to hurt Zundl.

Zundl heard my thoughts as they appeared inside of me: "You wanted to ask how long it has been since we last saw each other, but you didn't want to put your boot in it. My good friend, your hesitation is unnecessary. I read your mind better than you read it, because you only read books and would have to go to school again to read your own mind, whereas I read the mind's living hieroglyphics. I'll tell you just *exactamundo* when we saw each other last, when the cloud of our ghetto issued its last thunder and we descended into the underground sewers of the city. We were lost down there. I spent 16 months of my life in the sewers. I didn't know that the red flag was fluttering aboveground over our graves. When I saw the sun I lost my eyesight."

I filled the glasses. "Lechayim, Zundl, to our meeting."

The glasses lit up and were extinguished.

"If I were to grumble until the seas go dry, I wouldn't manage to expel all of the experiences from my guts." His voice grew more comfortable. "But I have no complaints about my fate. Even blind, I reached the Land of Israel. I'm happy."

"I have grumbling to do too, but let's leave that to the sea. Our conversation today is obviously just a start. Let's turn to those young days of our youth."

"But make it short, otherwise my old lady won't know what to think."

"Tell me about your father, Horeh the Leech-Seller, as they called him. I won't ask about your mother because she died in childbirth. She died and you were born. I even thought once that a dead mother gave birth to you, and that's why there's an otherworldliness about you. Your father was a puzzle. Maybe I'm wrong with the 'was.' I apologize."

"You can say 'was' about my dad. Neighbors looked down on him. Dealing in leeches is not a Jewish profession. There's something not kosher about it. Selling hog bristles would be more kosher. Kids in the street used to be scared of him. 'There goes Horeh the Leech-Seller!'"

"Right, how did he end up in such a trade? They said that he had a leech factory on Soltanishok Street."

"Inherited from my grandfather. Grandpa's leeches were famous across Russia. Dad didn't want me to get involved in the business, in its leechy secrets. He wanted me to go to school, finish gymnasium, study astronomy."

"Why astronomy in particular? Maybe he thought the stars are leeches."

"You still like to kill a joke. Back then, when I was sighted and couldn't see what one needs and what one doesn't, I couldn't read my father's mind. I only remember that from time to time my father would climb on the roof at night and talk to the stars until dawn. I couldn't hear or understand what they answered him."

"There were also rumors about how your father remarried with a relative who lived in Luniniec, but she disappeared after the wedding night."

"It turned out that the relative in Luniniec was born with a tail. She used to buy jars of leeches from Dad. She always wore a stenciled dress down to her heels so her tail wouldn't show. It's no mere speculation. I saw the track of her tail in the snow. I was scared to tell Dad. Later, it was too late."

III

The burning sea waves curled up to the windows to eavesdrop on the secrets of our youth.

"Enough about the relative from Luniniec. Do me a favor and tell me about your father. Did you ever go to his leech factory on Soltanishok? How did he leech it all up there?"

"I'll tell you since you're curious. Of course I went. The whole factory, as you call it, was a piece of a field fenced off with rocks and clay. Shards of broken bottles were stuck crookedly into the clay up top. Two narrow brooks like sharpened swords chased each other in parallel in the fenced-off area. The brooks couldn't ever catch each other. At the site of their bloody conflict and struggle was a small well. Into that well my father inserted fresh eels, as thin as needles, that had just been hatched in a nearby hut. They reproduced and grew up in the well and soon began swimming against the current with full strength. Two types of leeches swam in the springs: red and black. The red were of a better vintage. And that's how they were raised in Dad's paradise. They used to come back to the well at night to sleep. The water of the brooks was so cold that I nearly froze a finger off in the middle of summer. Dad also dropped shredded herbs into the well; he kept them in a bag under his shirt."

"Who bought his merchandise?"

"Country doctors, wandering healers, quacks, and those who applied heating cups in the city baths. Without my father's leeches there wasn't any point to cupping with incisions. Horeh the Leech-Seller had a reputation. People used to order his merchandise from abroad."

Zundl raised his cane. "My old lady won't know what to think. She's jealous."

"I'll take you home in a taxi. Where do you live?"

He gave me an address in Kerem HaTeimanim—the Yemenite neighborhood.

"How did you get to be with the Yemenite Jews?"

"That's another story, not for now."

His face changed, its wine color reddening under the skin. It seemed like his blind eye sockets were twitching with twin red leeches.

The wine started singing through me too. Intoxicated my words. But I was sober enough to blame myself. Why did I keep prompting him to speak? Why bully a blind man? My cruel pen was guilty. Pour gold down its throat; it's still hungry.

When I had finished with my questions, Zundl bowed to me over the table and I felt his weedy hair on my face. "I will now reveal two secrets. The secret of my father's life and the secret of my father's dying. Horeh the Leech-Seller, as they called him, wasn't a simple person. He distributed to the poor what he earned from the factory on Soltanishok. His dream was to create a kind of leech that wouldn't just suck out the extra blood from a sick person and make him well—although that too of course—but also suck out the evil. A leech who could transform a villain into a tzadik. When that holy leech was about to be born, a devil who lives on a black star dropped onto the earth and appointed a monster villain to rule over all human children.

"Then Dad left for his Soltanishok springs, stripped butt naked, donned the royal garments of his leeches, which were swarming in the little well, stretched out on the ground, and let those who he had created and bred suck the life out of him."

So ended the dream told to me of the one called Horeh the Leech-Seller.

IV

We were the last ones left in the bar. When we stumbled out, the rays of the sunset that had been shaking the silence had turned into fragmented moons.

The night, a silvery fishnet pulled out of the sea, shimmered and dried in the warm wind's caresses.

A single firefly wrestled with a lantern. No luck: the lantern went out.

A taxi pulled up. Inside, we were both silent as it dropped Zundl off in Kerem HaTeimanim. It was a further installment of the silence that had lasted till today's encounter.

We said farewell at a door hanging on one hinge. He knocked on the door with his white cane, and again it seemed to me that he was knocking on my back.

When the door opened, a cat's paw was hanging on the doorknob.

The cat, with eagle eyes, jumped onto Zundl's shoulders and cuddled up to him. "I told you that my old lady wouldn't know what to think!"

1986

MY GRANDMOTHER'S LANGUAGE

I

As long as I've remembered my only grandmother, I've remembered that her grandmotherly nature was different from that of my friends' grandmothers. Their grandmothers were called just Grandma, and mine—Step-Grandma. No matter how many times my mother tried to get it into my head that when my real grandma had died my grandpa had married this one—making her my step-grandma—it didn't stick in my brain.

The way I understood it, someone found it necessary to impugn her ancestry—so my ancestry seemed to get a little shaky, too. If grandma is a step-grandma, then I'm a step-grandchild. I felt sorry for us both.

She lived all by herself next to the Wilenka River, in the neighborhood called Poplaves.

A friend of her father's used to send her packages from abroad and occasionally throw in a few dollars too.

The friend from abroad also used to send her old-fashioned bridal outfits, all of the same sugar color. These were snapped up by the young ladies on both banks of the Wilenka. Pranksters started the rumor that the young ladies were hurrying to get married just because of the fluttering, full-skirted dresses.

Her father's friend from abroad had a significant change in his fortunes, in a good way. Grandma started getting packages with capes, dazzlingly black with folds like the waves of the Wilenka at night in a storm; others that were silvery with mother-of-pearl scales; and some that, with their stately colors, would have made a rainbow pale in comparison.

But the ladies on both banks of the Wilenka couldn't understand merchandise like that. Customers for the capes had to be sought in the homes of the rich.

Ever since my grandma stopped being a step-grandma for me, and I crowned her Queen of All Bubbies on my street, I gave her some advice that only a smart-al-eck can think of. It happened while she was sorting and arranging the newly arrived capes in her little house—so many it made me dizzy: "Why should you suck up to the rich people when the fancy ladies will try on your capes only to say to themselves in the mirror, 'Too expensive'? Better to dress yourself up in another cape on Shabbos and yom tov, wear them to shul or when visiting a neighbor. Or put it on when visiting my mother, or me, to make our attic room more beautiful; then those same fancy ladies will run after you and offer enough for one silk cape to buy a silver samovar."

My cleverness got up her nose like snuff on Yom Kippur.

II

When Grandma first dropped in unannounced into our attic room near the Green Bridge—she was all dolled up in her cape outfit—people did run after her flabbergasted, mouths open. Whoever recognized my grandma was astonished. "See how a single piece of clothing can completely remake a person!" Those who didn't recognize her were astonished that a wealthy landlady would set foot in such a decrepit courtyard.

When Grandma came to our attic room and unwrapped the cape fastened around her neck with a hook, hanging her treasure over my outstretched arm, I saw very clearly that the cape sent from her father's friend had performed real magic: my former step-grandma had turned a lot younger. It didn't seem appropriate that the queen of the grandmas had gotten so much more youthful. Her black, swishy dress with the lacy collar and the bright red buttons, like rowanberries, on the wide cuffs—savagely cinched at the waist. You could embrace her with less than ten fingers.

I also noticed a hairpin with a diamond face sticking out of the braided bun on her white head of hair. The face was strangely like Grandma's face but considerably miniaturized, like a raindrop resembles the rain.

Maybe Grandma was back to being a step-grandma?

No, it was the same grandma, just with a different appearance. Whenever she starts talking, her manner of speech is one of a kind.

"Sophocles, you'll honor me with kibud-ov." ("Sophocles" meant "Sof-kol-sof," at long last, because the name of the tragic Greek philosopher had not yet reached the beringed ears of my grandma. And "kibud-ov," honoring one's father, was for her a synonym of "kibud-bobbe," honoring one's grandmother.)

"That doesn't play any royale for me." (For her that means: "doesn't play any role.")

She would always bring a treat, which in her language she called "lamdarine." It looked like melted glass. You had to break it up to taste it, smash it with a stone or a piece of metal. A splinter of that lamdarine recently almost took out an eye of the only old maid in our courtyard. They called her Shishke. Grandma compensated her with a gift of a wedding dress, the last one she had, and promised to look for a groom for the lady.

"Someone who's ordained as a rabon." (She meant rabbi.)

My grandmother was a master in making preserves from cranberries. And her tastiest dish was what she called "criminadl" (a side of beef pounded and softened with a bottle).

She only eats "half-silken bread."

And when it's mild and sunny outside, she calls it "a delicious dish of a day" in her grandmother's language.

III

On big summer days, the boys on my street used to spend hours catching "summerbirds"—that is, butterflies—in the brick factories next to the Viliya River. They caught them with all sorts of stratagems, in regular hats, top hats, in girls' stockings stretched out on metal hoops tied to a stick. The boys would bring home what they caught, stick pins through them, and dunk them in whiskey or rubbing alcohol so they'd be preserved for eternity under glass, gold and silver wings splayed.

May the angel of the butterflies bear witness that I never terrorized those miniature lives. I trembled with each victim and kept my distance from the violent boys.

It happened that Grandma came to our place once on the day before Rosh Hashanah so that we'd all get blessed. She was wrapped in a royal cape that seemed woven from the Milky Way. Instead of a lamdarine, this time she brought a bucket of honey.

Something probably happened then with her bun, or she was tricked by an evil eye. For just a second, Grandma took out her hairpin with the diamond face and tried to fix her bun. But I was sure that Grandma saw in me a spread-out butterfly, and like one of those violent boys she wanted to grab me, stab me with a pin, and dunk me in whiskey to make me live forever.

Grandma did smell of whiskey, it's true, because there were also distilleries near her house on the banks of the Wilenka. The air around the distilleries was so full of whiskey that you could get drunk just by inhaling.

Out of excitement or fear I gave a desperate scream, and as I screamed I sprang through the open window.

The window to the attic room was as high up as the cherry tree across the way. The last bunch of cherries had dropped off the tree with the earthquake the day before Rosh Hashanah.

I didn't break any bones, but my soul limped.

IV

I wasn't in a hurry to reveal to Grandma the secret behind my leap through the window. But a secret is a fish baited by a worm on a fishing pole.

Grandma got the secret out of me herself. She did that when she discovered that her hairpin with the diamond face had gone missing.

"That's a boy's kind of trick—taking a living hairpin and drowning it in the Wilenka."

"Howdya know I drowned it?"

"I have a friend, and she knows everything."

"If so, she should know why I had to get revenge on the hairpin!"

"My friend knows everything, but she doesn't tell me the reason why you got revenge on the hairpin. She only says that it will be recovered."

"Tell me, Granny, what's her name?"

"Her name is Madam Truleloo. She's a doctor."

"If you tell me the secret of your friend, I'll tell you the secret why I drowned the hairpin."

V

Grandma's friend Dr. Truleloo lives on Piromont, not far from the old field. Women are drawn to her with their sicknesses like ants with eggs in their mouths. To give her respect and not to demean her in comparison to male doctors, they call her Mister Doctor, or Herr Dr. Truleloo.

The landowner Vernihora also visits her in his open carriage. Calls her Madam. My grandma calls her: my friend.

Why my grandma didn't tell me about her mysterious friend some time ago, I'll never know.

I remember now that when accompanying my grandma home from the attic room, she always bade farewell to me near the Green Bridge and turned left toward the old field. I also remember the story told to me by my friend Lipe the Dove-catcher. When one of his ringdoves stopped on Dr. Truleloo's red chimney, a fiery hand reached out and pulled the dove inside. If it had just happened once, Lipe would have kept this to himself, but the fiery hand pulled his two ringdoves into the chimney.

While unraveling one detail after another from Grandma about her friend, I had to promise her that I wouldn't tell anyone about it, including my mother. "Where was your friend born, if she was really born?"

"In Baltermantz."

I'd never heard of such a town, but if Grandma said Baltermantz, I had to believe her. "Married, kids?"

"Plup plup plup." (That was her way of saying pull up, pull up, pull up, wait a bit, patience.)

"I'm plupping, Grandma."

"She had a husband in Baltermantz. A real intellectual. One fine night he disappeared. A year later they find out: the intellectual became a priest in Rome."

"Where?"

"Rome. It's a town. And then can you believe what happened? He missed his two beautiful daughters. He arrives in Baltermantz one winter night by sleigh and knocks on the door . . ."

"And?"

"Plup plup. The Angel of Death carries all disease but is healthy as a horse himself. When the intellectual was heading back through town on the sleigh, the Angel of Death waited for him in the form of a butcher, tested his cleaver on his neck that night to make sure it was kosher."

"And what happened with his two beautiful daughters?"

"Went blind."

VI

The peak of my eagerness to see this friend with my own eyes, not just Grandma's, came on a Friday when Grandma brought us fish, and while she prepared it, a hairpin glimmered out of its guts.

Grandma quickly stuck it into her bun. "You see? My friend comforted me, said that the hairpin would turn up soon. Now I understand that saying, 'You can't dam up the Viliya with a pin.' And if you don't have the guts to go on your own, I'm taking you to the doctor. She told me recently that something is not right with the boy." (That is, with me.) "The butterflies have to be driven out of him."

Before we left to see her, I managed to get out of Grandma the news that Dr. Truleloo learned doctoring from an envoy from the Land of Israel. Pharmacies here, including those in our town, happily accept prescriptions when they see the curly signature: Dr. Truleloo.

They say in town that she has eyes on the tips of her fingers. When she runs them over the patient, she sees clearly whatever's going on inside.

But most of Dr. Truleloo's medicines aren't available in any pharmacy in the world. She herself is the doctor, the medicine, the pharmacy.

My efforts to unravel more secrets about her friend did not meet with particular victory. "A mouth isn't for eating; a mouth is for staying silent."

Nevertheless, she showed some consideration for my efforts, and so she did tell me that if not for her friend, the same thing would have happened to her as did to her neighbor, who lay down healthy and got up dead. One day my grandma's liver suddenly swelled up. She had already knocked the dust out of her burial shrouds with a rolling pin when her friend came to her on her own two feet, bringing a powder: ground bark from the righteous-convert tree. The illness disappeared as thoroughly as if she, Grandma, had never had a liver.

She gave the landowner Vernihora a frog's tongue to slip under the shirt of his wife Katarzina so that she'd talk in her sleep. But what exactly Katarzina would say or unburden herself with in her sleep, she wouldn't tell me.

There was a remarkably strange story about a guy who laid out his pedigree right when he walked in: he was born in Baltermantz.

With her long lashes, Dr. Truleloo brushed the old age off him. "What do you want to tell me, Reb Murderer?"

Grandma commented that he was shaken right down to his heels.

VII

It was a windy day when we agreed to visit Grandma's friend. Fall was already on its way. A cloud shook off a bit of rain, like a dog coming out of the river shaking off water.

Grandma dressed up in two capes, one over the other. After all, it was chilly out. The top one gave off a dull, dark dazzle of old silver, the color of a kiddush cup in an orphaned house. I'd be a liar if I depended on my imagination to tell you what the cape underneath looked like.

A shawl was thrown over Grandma's shoulders—she had knit it herself when she got engaged.

The hairpin in her bun didn't scare me now.

Grandma coughed in my ear. "I'm not Pinte the rich lady, but you'll help me carry the basket for my friend. A plate of criminadl, a loaf of half-silken bread, and a jar of real bees' honey."

VIII

The friend lived beyond the glassworks in a hut of red clay. Getting there was uphill. Wooden, hollowed-out steps like bread troughs. Her visitors kneaded out their sicknesses.

A ray of sun with cut-open veins, sliced by the mounds of glassware around the factory, illuminated a brass plate on a door: "Madam Dr. Truleloo."

I wasn't lucky enough to see her alive so that she could exorcise my summer-birds. When the door opened with a sigh, Dr. Truleloo was lying stretched out on the floor, wrapped in a holiday cape, which Grandma had surely given her as a gift. Clay shards on her eyes, two wax candles at her head.

"Plup plup plup," murmured Grandma's blue lips, "her two blind daughters are shining at her head."

I thought: "Not lit by her two blind daughters, but by the ringdoves of my friend Lipe."

1986

KIRA KIRALINA

The past got lost in tomorrow. Let's hear what it has to tell us.

Years fly faster than days. But they wait for a bit at the edge of an abyss to let me throw my lasso over them and retrieve them before it is too late and they splinter along with my glance.

My flying lasso doesn't let them fall. Outliving the living is my painful joy.

Her name is Kira Kiralina. Probably no one knows her real name now. That's how her name is carved on the midair tombstone of crematorium smoke.

If there's any dead person who remembers her true name as a girl, they should give a knock on my forehead!

Why is her name Kira Kiralina? In the scout group we both belonged to, she was the first to read Panait Istrati's novel. Couldn't stop bragging about the fact that she read it, and also about her love for the main character: Kira Kiralina. So that's what her name came to be.

She was the most peppery girl, and not just in my circles. It wasn't because her father, Meirem on Troker Street, was a pepper seller. Even if he had a shop of the commonest herring she would still have had a honeyed flavor. She was thin, polished, flexible as the wind, like the slim, sprouting cattails in the green lake.

The girls whispered that the ancestors of the pepper seller's daughter were twisted. But that was born of jealousy, from the fact that an angel, mistakenly thinking she was a boy, gave her a punch in the nose when she was born, so her nose had a crooked angle to it that made the boys crazy.

I'm not dazzled by her nose. Let it nose how it wants. She does not exert a magnetic attraction on me, making me move in her direction when we're out for a swim, with her topsy-turvy smile that starts in her toes and rolls up like a wave to her red-haired head, lighting up the layers of her hair. Maybe my lack of attraction comes from her bragging that all the boys are head over heels for her and she loves—no one.

My nonchalance toward Kira Kiralina becomes dangerous though. Turns into a kind of stalking hatred.

I want to run away from her, but I don't have anyone to run away to. I want to run away from myself—and don't have anyone to run away from myself to either.

But a mysterious adventure occurs.

One evening, during a scouting jaunt among the end-of-summer poppy tracks, we wander our way up to the Żejmiana River. There in the grove of young-and-old fir trees, we decide to spend the night on the hill by the river's banks.

Grandmotherly shadows hunch among the trees, picking berries to take along to sunset.

The sunset loves hairy red raspberries.

As usual, people are heaping up dried-out twigs for a campfire. The flaming end of the sunset lights it; the night stays with us in the forest.

The plash of water silver in the earth's open veins.

The sharp odor of sap fills my every limb.

The campfire jumps off the hill into the Żejmiana. Naked, the fire is also wearing a topsy-turvy smile from its toes to its red head and layers of hair.

The campfire swims in the Żejmiana without going out.

Every person is a riddle that is better left unsolved. Even a boy.

Suddenly, someone inside me growls out through a horn: "Kira Kiralina, leave the boys and come here. I'll get you to sleep."

Barefoot, but without the barefoot tricks (that's what we called girls' flirting), she comes over and sits on the dewy grass opposite me. Tousled hair lit by the fire.

A scorpion stabs me in the buzzing horn in my insides. Someone else is in terrible pain inside of me. Possessed by the pain of that other, I stab her through with fierce glances: "Tell me, disgusting girl, who do you really love?"

No one sees or hears if Kira Kiralina is laughing or crying. Her face is veiled by her tousled red hair.

"Tell me. I'm ordering you."

"Yeah. I love—"

For the first, the second, the third time: Who? His name!

"Kira Kiralina." She lies drowsing in the grass.

I don't know whether she's pretending or not. Is this one of her famous pranks? People shake her, people slap her cheeks, and she stays asleep. She's doused with cold water; asleep. The moon itself is curious and tries to open her eye with a finger; asleep. I roll her into the weeds where the grandmotherly shadows picked raspberries, and I almost roll her off the mountain and into the Żejmiana, where people are swimming after the naked campfire; asleep.

The buzzing horn in my insides that put her to sleep before can't undrowse her.

Breathlessly, I run with someone else into the village for a doctor. No doctor, just some kind of quack. We have to carry him in our arms, he's so old. He blows the call of a rooster into her mouth. Only then does she open her guiltless eyes.

1986

THE PROPHECY OF THE INNER EYE

Her name is Badanna. A face carved out of gray salt, sitting on what looked like one little person stacked on top of another. Her protector was the mother of all mothers: fear.

During the first night of the yellow panic, a night that lasted two full years, Badanna found a thorny place to lay her head in a destroyed apartment on Strashun Street.

Into that same smashed-up apartment, during that same panic, I was also kicked by an iron hoof. The area soon filled up with unknown faces, like drowned people at the bottom of a well, illuminated from above by a ray of moonlight. They were all sunken in my memory as a faceless family. Only Badanna's face, carved out of gray salt on top of one little person grown out of another, stayed distinct, present.

Though a short, tiny woman, a tiny elder, Badanna became a hideout for her only child, Leibele. She wanted to get him back in her belly so that nothing bad would happen to him, God forbid. But Leibele happened to have disappeared somewhere when the yellow panic approached. And Leibele's hideout in his mother's belly was empty.

When I was a boy I read that primitive farmers in remote areas of China, who had never seen a clock and didn't even know that such a thing existed, knew about time and its turnings no less than people who own such devices. Picking up a pet cat by the back of the neck, the Chinese farmer knows exactly how time is turning at that moment by the bright green sparkle in the clockfaces of its pupils.

I turned into that kind of Chinese cat for Badanna, not just for orientation in time but also for the turnings of place and fate.

In a gaping pause between being and not being, Badanna gets up on her blocky legs and looks at her reflection in my pupils in order to see how her only child is getting along. "My Leibele is not used to war. Let him at least get out of it safely."

I tell Badanna that when the yellow panic was approaching, her Leibele "made boot tracks"—ran clear to the other side of the war.

Smiling sparks play in her gray furrows.

And another instance: "What's that place where my Leibele, he should be well, eventually got himself settled?"

I tell Badanna about a locale in my dream. Her Leibele found a place in a hut where I came of age: near the Irtysh River, in Siberia.

The sound of "Siberia" takes a bit of time to get into her brain. When it gets in, Badanna grabs her head with her short-fingered little hands. "I heard there are deep freezes there. If my Leibele catches a chill, God forbid, who will put a hot brick next to his feet and bring a saucer of preserves to his lips?"

A knot of dream images unravels in me. My voice is mine, but at the same time it comes from somewhere distant: "If you cover up with a bearskin you'll be as healthy as a bear. It's not like there aren't any trees in Siberia, either. They're tall. Reach up to the stars. You can warm up half the winter with the wood from one of those trees."

Badanna was gone the next morning, disappeared from the smashed-up apartment. But praise be to the eternal—she shows up again. Now white-haired, as if a tree from where Leibele had run away to had bent over her and covered her with snow from its branches.

"There's no telling what a foolish woman will babble." She demands justice again from the prophecy of my inner eye. "If Leibele marries, will he find a bride in that land, a Jewish girl?"

Badanna's belief in the prophecy of my pupils, my visionary power and omniscience, completely enchants me. I start believing in the powers that Badanna believes in: "Leibele got engaged already."

"Is she beautiful?"

My tongue becomes a paintbrush and depicts the beauty of Leibele's fiancée in detail.

Badanna unwraps something golden from a rag. "Here's a wedding ring. It's got to be rolled over to him."

When the ring is rolling from Vilna to Siberia, another question: "What's Leibele's fiancée's name? I must know."

"Her name is Gutle."

"A weird name. Maybe it's Gitele?"

"No, Gutle."

Dressed up in three strands of pearls over a dress of black shrouds, which Badanna found in an attic, she stares out the window into the distance. Her hands over her face of gray salt, as if she were making the blessing over the Shabbos candles. She no longer demands justice from the prophecy of my pupils. She sees Leibele between her fingers. He and his bride under a canopy of stars.

1986

IN MEMORY OF AN AMULET

I

On a visit to Paris, I got a phone call quite early in the morning; it was a girl's voice, or a woman's, in Russian, peppered here and there with half-Yiddish words, signs of an ancestry that was petering out.

From her tongue twisters I was given to understand that the person on the other end of the receiver was also in Paris and was flying back tomorrow to the city of my youth. She was a dancer, and her last recital was here, tonight. A friend told her I was in Paris and what hotel I was in. She *had* to see me. She gave me two options: either three in the afternoon or after her dance recital, whichever was more suitable.

To my question if I might learn her name and the reason she must see me, she answered that I've probably encountered her name and picture in magazines and newspapers. I still didn't guess who she was, but she said it was of life-and-death importance for us to meet.

I breathed in iron courage, and I answered (like an innocent man, hearing his sentence): "My dear unknown woman, I'll meet you at three in the afternoon at Café Ronsard, near Metro Maubert, in the Latin Quarter."

II

I had already gotten to Café Ronsard a couple of hours earlier to think over the strangeness of the unknown dancer: it's life and death to her.

Time heals all wounds? Time is itself a wound! But let's have patience for impatience. I am a longtime guest at the table where unseen fingers are playing piano on my black-and-white nerves; I even wrote poems in praise of the waiter, a long, tall guy with a necktie who hadn't aged in 25 years, and likewise the ringing of his coins hadn't changed either.

I like to have dates here with myself. Ronsard! The great French poet of the 16th century. No worries; I can sit bent over a table under his glory.

There are other reasons that, for years, I've been attracted to the Village Ronsard—that's the full name of the café. I witness twice a week how a small market is quickly and expertly set up with all sorts of fruit and other produce. In those orchards and gardens that provide those products, sparkling jewels grow, and they melt in your mouth. The saleswomen, who praise their merchandise for ladies carrying baskets, could act in the Comédie-Française. One who I named Tzipke Fayer keeps tossing and catching her sun oranges. She could be in the circus. And while the piquant odors are at war with each other, it's all tasty.

The palette of colors at the Ronsard becomes particularly lively when the rain comes down to take its portion. Clouds bring the aromas of pharmacies to heal words.

III

I'm chatting away about a waiter, a market, and the rain, but the voice of the girl or woman on the other end of the receiver is still drilling away. Now it's in my ear. A weird fly of Titus.

Death and life, sins and good deeds are inscribed on the same scroll. I unroll it—and myself—very, very carefully, so it doesn't crumble into bits.

Look—a shining hand over the scroll that's unrolling inside me. The nails are long, sharp, and as if just dipped in blood.

A young warmth like fresh milk draws a breath over me. "Zdravstvuyte."

The café is quite empty. It's after lunch. Even the ensemble that plays at the market has left the scene. The area is washed clean by galloping water. The dancer sits on the chair that I had set aside for her, facing me at my table. A young woman who has time as her servant. Dressed lightly, for summer, with a path to her two treasures. A wide-brimmed, woven hat, with a bunch of cherries pinned to the side, shadows her face.

"It's easy to recognize a dream." I feel her hand in mine, and neither hurries to free itself.

With a hasty movement she takes off her hat as if shaking off the remains of the rain, letting it hang off the back of the chair. Then she lights a cigarette with a small lighter. The cigarette smoke, full of desire, stays woven in her hair, which takes on the colors of the start of the sunset under light clouds.

"What will you drink?"

"Make it a cognac."

Now I will be silent, embalm my words in my tongue. Let the unknown woman speak—the blush of the cognac has already reddened her face.

"I said I have to see you because it's a matter of death and life. I am the daughter of Anita, whose name is certainly not unfamiliar to you. In a certain sense you are my father, though my true father is someone else. My mother told me that you saved her, so it's easy to figure: I was born thanks to you."

My internal scroll unrolls even more, but I'll only be able to read and understand all of its secrets and riddles when I rise from the dead. One secret reveals itself to me right now, though. Anita's daughter is a reincarnation of her mother. Her eyes are Anita's; I wrote about them in *Poems from My Diary*: "If God were to create only their darkest green / he'd still be the same God. How can they disappear?" But my words remain embalmed on my tongue. I won't even ask her name again and whether her mother is alive. Everything is already written on the scroll.

The dancer plucks a single cherry off the bunch pinned to her hat and puts it into my gaping mouth with a cherry smile. Like a bolt of lightning on a blue summer day, the thought runs through my mind: it's the "cherry of remembrance," the name of an old, longer poem of mine. Who knows in what enchantment this cherry has been submerged. Its magic poison will soon take effect in me, and I'll become young against my will, to yet again and again fail to understand why an angel might enjoy my suffering. I'll become young against my will to live and relive what has already happened.

IV

On the dancer's bare arm I notice a scar from a pox vaccine administered years ago, which now looks like her little fingernail. A sign that this woman was once a child. I saw this mark on her mother when she was 16. I remember what I thought then: it's charming to see this on a pretty girl, but only for a pretty girl. We were both walled in then.

One evening when the sunset was bringing its sacrifices of cloud incense above, while mixing the people of the walled-in alleys below in its crucible with crazed haste, I saw Anita at a white wall, the only remains of a building that had collapsed.

I knew that today was our last sunset. I knew it would be of no help to intone in that moment, "Let the sun stand still over the ghetto."

Through the crowd tumbling like rocks down a mountain, I made my way to the white wall where Anita stood frozen in fear. I kissed her and swore: "This kiss will be your amulet. Don't give it away to anyone anywhere. You'll bring it back yourself. Give me your hand."

V

"Another cognac?"

The dancer's earrings swing: no. She can't mix one drink with another—another spirit with the drink of ecstasy that intoxicates her when she dances. Her last concert was tonight.

Yes, my amulet saved her mother. She gave her word and didn't want to depart from this world as a liar.

"When she ran naked in the snow, your amulet warmed her feet. When she was driven to a funeral pyre, the amulet melted into tears that extinguished the fire. She drank water from a canal in which dead bodies were floating, and chewed horse meat from a carcass, but the amulet made that food tasty. The amulet enabled her to flee from Klooga. She was found in a swamp swarming with snakes, shot through one lung. Blood poured from her mouth when they brought her home barely alive. Your amulet healed her. She married the officer who pulled her out of the swamp swarming with snakes. She didn't hand him your amulet."

I sense terror. This story shouldn't end melodramatically: *Here's a kiss; my mother asked me . . .*

The dancer gets up, dons her broad-brimmed summer hat missing a cherry, and hands again do not hurry to part. "Come to my recital tonight. I'll dance the last kiss for death and life."

1986

BALLAD OF THE WOODEN PEOPLE

1

Ever since the end of the Second World War, people have appeared in my hometown with small aluminum briefcases swinging from yokes on their backs, hammered and pounded out of the carcasses of airplanes that were shot down and fell to earth nose first, like kamikazes.

When I returned to my hometown from Moscow, after the encounter with my dead mother at the crater of Ponar—which was still giving off purple smoke—I got myself that kind of briefcase for a nominal cost, and I put inside it what my memory no longer had room for.

The briefcase accompanied me through cities and countries and stopped off with me in the Land of Israel.

Since the house I live in is not crowned with an attic, for all those years the briefcase made its home in the curve between ceiling and door, nestled together with a partisan's hat, a wooden spoon, and a mess tin.

When a bolt of lightning split open a dream one night, I saw inside that briefcase. I rose like a moonwalker to that curve and took it down from its other planet. An angry grinding of teeth, and the top cover gave way.

It was like opening my own grave and saying hello to my own skeleton.

Among written materials there was a broken watch without a glass or hands that my mother had gotten me for my bar mitzvah and that always shows exactly the right time, and among old letters (including a letter written on bark, peeled off a birch tree in a shining mythical locale) there quivered a piece of paper with stamped, green-yellow-violet spots, like a sucked-out and dried-up violet that you find sometimes in an old book bought for a song at an antique store. The letters, in their uphill and downhill course, looking like what a kid learning how to write would create, became clearer and clearer:

Twenty-two of us women are in the hospital outside Moscow.
During the death march from the camp in February 1945, when the Red
Army approached, we fell exhausted
in the snow. We were brought here with frozen
limbs. Most people had to have an arm, a leg
amputated, sometimes both.
We have a serious request for you: please make sure
to do what you can for us to be provided with wooden
arms and legs, so we can somehow make our way
home, home.
I apologize that my words are jumping like blind
birds over branches. I'm writing them with my mouth . . .
with a pencil between my teeth.
Greetings from the armless and legless but hot-blooded
women of the ward: Yudis, Michelle, Jablonka,
Rosette, Selma, Temerl, Angelina, Caroline—and
Bubele from Gaon Street.
Your ex-girlfriend Paike

II

Now I know for certain that the oysters at the bottom of the briefcase contain
hidden pearls that must not be touched.

I lock the briefcase. Enough searching its bowels. I put it at the head of the
bed.

I read my lit thoughts in the dark: Where am I? (*Who* is a different question.
Always the same and always different!) Yes, here I am again at my Aunt Malkah's
in Moscow on Rusakovske Street. After encountering my dead mother at Ponar, I
come back to my temporary home, to my Aunt Malkah.

It's winter, 1945.

"I'm sorry that my blind words are jumping like birds over branches"—tattooed on the cracked mirror. While I'm looking at it, they jump out of the crack
from their silver captivity and pick and beak me in the face.

I'm embarrassed by my writing hand, and I don't know what to write Paike. "A letter should be transmitted by dreams or be written on dream paper so that the creator of dreams can be the mail carrier" is what I'm thinking.

Here are the friends who have been won, whose words still survive. My lit thoughts illuminate their faces.

I run out with the letter at dawn. My words do jump like blind birds on branches and pick at me. Everybody gets an official answer to their query. Each person gets almost the exact same one. Thousands of armless and legless soldiers are waiting, generals too.

III

As Malkah's oldest son, the "unsuccessful" one, Bereh, says, "I don't care if the Messiah speaks Greek, as long as I hear his voice."

I'm definitely hearing his voice, not Greek but Russian: So can I say kaddish?

A man takes shape from the voice. A thin, collapsed face, chalk-colored. A black hat. And his clothes are blacker than his shadow, though the summer is sunnily naked, like Adam and Eve before they tasted of the Tree of Knowledge. No, like Adam and Eve if they had tasted of the Tree of Death.

The man in black asks me, at the smoking crater in Ponar during the encounter with my dead mother, if I could say kaddish.

"Yes, I can," I answer him. "Just tell me, for whom?"

"My father's name is Leonid Markovich. For my father."

I say kaddish for his father. A white cloth drapes his pupils in funeral shrouds.

"If you're in Moscow, drop in. Here's my card."

He bows before the crater, takes a few steps backward, and vanishes in his car, which is waiting there for him near the torn wire.

I admit I hadn't looked at the card before, but now an unfamiliar urge told me to go look for it. Who is the man in black whose pupils don white shrouds?

Senses aren't tricksters. The man in black was quite a high-up official in a ministry.

He sends his driver after me, in double-breasted brass buttons.

I tell him the reason for my visit. Read Paike's letters. Translating to Russian as I read them.

"Read them in Yiddish; I understand it," he murmurs.

I read: "I'm sorry that my words are jumping like blind birds over branches. I'm writing them with my mouth, with a pencil between my teeth."

I notice his face turning the color of chalk, as at the encounter at Ponar.

"This woman comes from the same city as your father. The other women there are also possessed by the same yearning: for wooden arms and legs. Even Bubele of Gaon Street."

IV

The door opens for a row of wooden people who are coming to say farewell to me. It's a forest with branches in the house and the roots outside. Paike is the first one. I recognize her right away, her lips swollen with young blood.

I press her wooden forklike hand, like one of flesh and bone. And here are her friends: Yudis, Michelle, Jablonka, Rosette, Selma, Temerl, Caroline . . . Bubele from Gaon Street is downstairs on a three-wheeler.

Birds from various locales come and sing while flying overhead.

The most beautiful women in the world!

They extend wooden hands to me. Branches grow out from their shoulders: arms with rare fruit.

I accompany them down the stairs.

The forest is moving homeward, home.

Bubele, the enchanted forest girl, in front.

Paike takes me under her arm.

"What tortures me the most: Is Bome Zaytshik still alive? If so, are his arms wooden too? If not, he won't love me, because he won't want to embrace me."

1986

THE WOMAN WITH SOMEONE ELSE'S FACE

I

I didn't exchange a single word with my neighbor on the other side of the wall, or her husband either.

When running into one another on the way in, on the stairs or on the street, even in a café, it's a nod of the head and that's it. Obligation met. Me, her, and him—the same thing.

Very rarely did they loose their tongues in my presence, and when they did, the sounds of Spanish tickled my ear. Their cat (a she-cat, with whiskers) meowed in Cervantes' language too.

I knew their names from the doorplate: Clara and Manuel. Manuel blessed with a considerable hunchback, though I shouldn't give him the evil eye. And whenever I met Clara, the same thought awoke: she has someone else's face. I don't know who that someone else is. I don't even know who the first someone is.

On a late fall night, my neighbor on the other side of the wall broke the silence between us. She walked into my place without ceremony, like an old acquaintance, and with the voice of a broken string, thin and refined, requested that I come the next day to her husband's funeral.

She didn't say it in Spanish but in a language that I'm close with. But that language was also aquiver with Spanish melody. "Manuel didn't curse death. He just gave it the finger—then he was no more."

II

I remember that cemetery from when it was first born, and now it's blessed with grandmothers, grandfathers, and grandchildren.

Count the fingers—some of them shot off—of two disabled soldiers. That's how many people, including me, Clara, and the gravedigger too, showed up grave-side.

A black veil rained over Clara's face.

After the memorial prayer, two people were left at the mound of clay: Clara and me. The mound was like Manuel's hunchback. I could swear that Clara thought so too.

Both our feet, mine and Clara's, were stuck in the moist clay around the mound. The clay, I thought, unites us. The food for our eternal diet.

Clara bent over and laid to sleep a bouquet of chrysanthemums on the mound of clay. Then she came close to me, free of the clay's gravitational pull. "I don't know all those people who just made themselves scarce. They were Manuel's associates. He played bridge with them. My friends also came to the funeral, but they aren't anywhere to be seen."

I looked around. Maybe her friends are hiding behind the tombstones? But I didn't notice any living thing behind them.

"Do you know who my friends are here? My tears." Tiny lightning bolts flew to and fro behind the black rain of her veil.

Soon the rain growled for real. Its drops skipped and jumped over the mound of clay like fish through the torn fabric of a heavy net pulled out of the water.

"I'll take you home. I'm familiar with the address." I took her by the arm.

Hearing the sound of the rain over the cemetery, I thought, "It's not the sound of rain but the dead waging war underground. How can one find out who won the war?"

The black veil over Clara's face spread, blowing over us both, blowing over the entire cemetery. It began to get dark before the storm.

III

When Clara unlocked the door and we walked into her apartment, she took off her black veil and her face got brighter. Like a pearl removed from its shell.

I sat down at a small table encrusted with Aztec gods. A portrait of Manuel was on the wall across the room. Much younger than when I met him. A scythelike mustache. Lapels hung with medals. No sign of a hunchback.

Clara went into the kitchen, rummaged around for a bit, and emerged standing straight while holding two cups of coffee. The color of the chrysanthemums on the mound of clay quivered on her face. She sat down on the other side of the table. Lightning flashed in her eyes again after a sip of the black beverage. "I know what you might be thinking."

"It's what we're both thinking. For many years you wore your black veil inside, and during the funeral you pulled it out from under your skin and put it on the outside."

"That's enough thinking about what you shouldn't. Reading other people's minds. It's better to read some digits." Clara rolled up a sleeve of her light blouse and stretched out her ivory arm.

I read the digits on her arm, tattooed with a blue different from all other blues.

"It's good that we don't know each other, though we can read each other's minds." Clara concealed the numbers under her sleeve. "I knew what you were thinking about me when our glances silently collided: when the sun dries out mud, it doesn't get muddy."

"No, Clara, that didn't come to my mind. Here's what I thought: you're a woman with someone else's face."

"If you could think that, may the invisible wall between us shatter into pieces!" With both fists she pounded on the mercury in the table's decorative overlay, making it roll in all directions. "No one has ever revealed a more horrible truth. If you could think that, I'll undress my lips for you."

IV

There were four of us in the room: Clara, me, the portrait of Manuel, and the cat with her mannish whiskers. Clara, who probably didn't want any witnesses, suggested we sit on the glassed-in balcony behind its brocade curtains.

She brought two fresh cups of coffee. It wouldn't surprise me if she were drowning her friends, her tears, while drinking.

"The longer I live," Clara began, "the stronger is my belief that I haven't yet been born. Rather, inside me there lives a life that is not mine. They say about someone who commits suicide that they took their own life, but in reality they took their own death. I'll speak more clearly very soon. If I don't say these things right now, I soon won't be able to speak in this world. Like I already said, I'll undress my lips for you."

"I've never heard that expression."

"It's not mine. That's what they say where I come from."

"But the naked lips are yours."

"Probably."

The telephone rings. Clara hurries behind the curtains, then returns.

"A bridge partner of Manuel's. He wants to come comfort me. I told him not today, I'm sick. I took the phone off the hook so we won't be bothered."

Suddenly hail—ice locusts—began attacking the glassed-in balcony, quickly devouring the electric lamps. When the lights turned on again, the locusts dripped off the windowpanes and the wings stopped. Another woman was now sitting across from me: the woman with someone else's face.

"Now I'm the real Clara." She gave a smile split in two. "Only the past, which doesn't exist, lasts forever. Previously I was my best friend, Hella, a friend from my childhood. We were both only daughters to our parents. Except for my mother I didn't love anyone as much as her, Hella with the blond hair and blond soul, so to speak.

"It is quite near to the truth to say that we shared our breaths in the death camp. Even a devil knows not to be a traitor, but I betrayed her. When they burned my mother to ash I couldn't live anymore. I ran to the electric wires so that I could also be burned to death. I wasn't so lucky, though. The guards with their electric dogs thought I wanted to flee from the camp, so they caught me alive and sentenced me to hang. How old was I then? Eighteen. And though life is short and death is so very long, I didn't care. As long as I could be redeemed. If the Angel of Death had revealed himself to me, I would have given him a kiss.

"But my luck left me then, too. When the officer called out my number in front of that crowd of women that they had driven together with whips, Hella suddenly dashed to the gallows. One woman gagged me, another bit into my shoulder, and before I knew it Hella was swinging between the ground and death.

"That was when her face grew into me. I survived and live now with someone else's face."

V

Clara turned out the light on the balcony. "I don't want you to see two women when only one is talking to you. There's also another reason it's better this way: if the neighbors see a light, they'll come up."

No sign of the hail remained.

The night looked into the balcony with all of its stars.

I cut through our silence. "Maybe I should turn out the stars too? See how low they are, how close to us? They don't even need to break the windows to come in here."

"No, they saved me when I wanted to live."

"How's that?"

"Most of the women in the camp lay there dead in a pit. I was dead and half alive.

"At night the pit gleamed from the jewels, which the victims had hidden. She who had undressed her lips for you floated out of the ground's shark mouth. It was hard to distinguish between the scattered diamonds and the scattered stars. The temptation was real. It's true: Hella wanted to test me. But I passed the test, grabbed a bunch of stars, and ran away with them. I was swallowed up and concealed by . . . a forest."

VI

"In the camp Hella told me about her father's youngest brother, who lived in a Spanish-speaking country. I told her about my aunt in another country. We etched their names and addresses into our memory.

"As a survivor, I wanted to sample the honeyed taste of nothing. Why were human beings created? I asked myself that continuously. And I answered: so that they can go on asking.

"I was like a sealed bottle bearing the secret of a sunken ship, which the last sailor had managed to seal and launch onto the waves. Where will the waves rock me away to, whose hands will pull me out and reveal the secret of my life?

"By then, my aunt was already in paradise, where all aunts go sooner or later. I wrote to the youngest brother of Hella's father and described, cruelly and unsentimentally, how Hella grabbed the noose from me.

"I got a telegram from him very quickly: stay where I am (I was then holed up with the other liberated people in Landsberg); he's flying to see me.

"Did my letter really disturb him that much? I didn't need to consider it for long—he was here. His intention, I understood, wasn't only to see Hella's best friend but also for me to have the honor of seeing him. Short, broad, his head came up to my chin. Balding head, mousy gray. If he had just put on a hat—but no. If his beard had been trimmed, combed out, without tangles—no. If he were to put on a wide coat so that the top of his hunchback weren't poking out—nope. And if all that weren't enough, he brought a gift to our first meeting: a severe asthma attack, which made me fear he was done for. To top it all off, it was two nearly silent people who were meeting. I didn't understand his Spanish, and neither did he understand the two languages that I spoke. It was remarkable that we managed to understand each other. If we were both without tongues, we still would have understood each other. As you can guess, that was Manuel.

"His brutal pride in his balding, mouse-gray head, his crazy beard, his pointy hunchback, and his asthma attack actually attracted me to him. His being related to Hella also played a role. I admit that if he were an impressive man I wouldn't have been able to get close to him.

"It didn't even bother me that his occupation in his Spanish-speaking country was raising horses. Right after his asthma attack, he showed me a series of pictures of his horses, going on about them in his language, peppered with Yiddish, with greater adoration than one hears even from the most loving male heroes in romances.

"Manuel brought me with him to his Spanish-speaking country. I became his wife.

"We divided up our roles. Manuel raised horses and I wrote my memoirs. For one reader: Hella.

"I didn't give him any children. Yes, Manuel boasted to me that he had a wonderful son, Cesar. This was a horse of his who had won the grand prize at the horse races three times. But a tragedy occurred after the third victory. Cesar fell and broke both forelegs. He was embalmed and put in a mausoleum constructed specially for him. The people of that land didn't stop kneeling to him, admiring their favorite son.

"I don't have any complaints against Manuel. He saved some love for me too. During a ceremony in which he was presented with a medal for his horse breeding, he called out ecstatically while the president was there, 'If there's no God, my wife is God!'"

VII

I can't believe that the night is already in two outside, the day dawning over dry land like the Exodus.

Clara is drowsing, eyes open, on the chair. Her face is shining like embers in white ash. Now it's Clara. Now it's Hella. Maybe she put a sleeping pill in her coffee?

I am thirsty to keep hearing her story. She had undressed her lips for me, but she wouldn't do it again. But I'll have to stifle my egotism and let her rest. I cover her up with a shawl and retreat a few steps.

Clara is startled. "Dear friend or neighbor, don't leave me in my aloneness, in my doubleness. I'm nearly finished. You're a writer; how is it that you're not curious about the fate of the hundreds of pages of my memoir?"

"Clara, you must believe me that I forced my powerful curiosity to be silent. Don't think that I'll ask you for them to read, to find joy in your wounds. I have enough of my own."

"You had the right to ask. Anyway, you should know. So listen. As I was telling you, Manuel and I divided up our roles. Him, breeding horses. Me, writing memoirs. After the revolution in the country we had been living in, we returned Manuel's beloved horses to it, legs up. Cesar lost his throne as well. They launched him out of his mausoleum. The uncaring public knelt for a new hero, one with two legs.

"Manuel remembered that he had studied in a cheder once and that we have a nation of our own. So just as quickly as he had flown to me in Landsberg and took me to the Spanish-speaking ends of the earth, we left his dead horses there and flew to the Land of Israel.

"There's a Chinese saying: once you get on a lion to ride it, you're afraid of getting off. The saying is also relevant for me, though I wasn't riding on a lion but a horse.

"And what about the fate of my hundreds of pages of memoirs? I wrote them for one person, for Hella. On the eve of our departure from that country, I read all of those pages for Hella, and when I finished reading, I burned them. Of course. Why leave a will or instructions for others to burn them, like Kafka? His best friend Max Brod stuck his tongue out at him."

1986

CARPIE THIMBLE

I

How long has it been since I saw or heard from my landsman? More years than since I was born. What does "saw or heard" mean, though? I actually did see-or-hear him on the last night at the last sunset, which gurgled down the horizon looking for a straw to grasp on to. But of course that was in the kingdom where every human being is a citizen and no one knows the kingdom's name. There's no other choice than to call it: Dream.

This happens to me not infrequently. First a painter sketches out a face, a sunset in my dream kingdom. A storm or composition. The real dream picture is revealed later. If life has any reality, I should say.

Who and what am I talking about? I'm talking about the fact that my landsman, the hero or antihero of this story, is a living person who jumped out of my dream picture that an artist painted that last night.

II

Since he's called Carpie Thimble it would fit if he were a tailor, or at least the descendant of a clan of tailors. Nothing of the sort. He tells me that his name has no connection to his profession or that of his father, nor his grands and great-grands.

"What do you do, Carpie?"

"Nothing."

"A brilliant profession. And what do you live off of?"

"Off of nothingery."

"So you don't approve of working, you prefer to bum around?"

"Let my servants work for me."

"Who are your servants?"

"Sun, Moon, Earth, rain. They work for me day and night without a penny. A bird sings for me for free. I applaud."

"And how can you live without something to eat? Even a bird has to have a nibble between songs. It's not a birdbrain, after all."

Thus did a conversation start to come together between the two of us when we met on the beach in Tel Aviv.

The sunset gurgled out its last wave. Swimmers were still doing the freestyle in the sea. Others were rolling about in the sand in their birthday suit or putting on shining moonsilk. Like heirs of the drowned sunset, streetlamps turned on up and down the promenade. Strolling spectators devoured the nakedness of those who weren't able to get away from the water's magnet.

I remembered feeling that I was being unfair to my landsman, as my thoughts fluttered around those who weren't able to resist the water's pull. "Carpie, come with me to Jaffa if you have time. I promised to come to a gallery where a friend of mine is exhibiting his pictures. The show opens today. We can both go to the gallery, if you like painting. We can take a stroll and chat along the way."

Carpie's eyebrows scrunched up like a hedgehog. "Anyone who tells you 'I don't have time' isn't worthy of having time."

My landsman put a pistol finger to my forehead. "About what you asked earlier; how can I live without something to eat? Since they took out my wisdom teeth I've gotten smarter. I've stopped eating."

Once he discharged that quote with his pistol finger, it got easier for him to unravel his thoughts. "Like all so-called human children, for many years I was a murderer of chickens, goats, cattle, until—until a fork that I had stuck into a chicken's gizzard suddenly burst out laughing one fine day and started stabbing at me while I was eating. The knife helped too. I barely escaped with my life. That fork and knife were the messengers of the slaughtered fowl and all God's other creatures. Yes, they were the avenging messengers for shedding innocent blood and taking pleasure from the victims. From that day on, I vowed neither to murder innocent creatures nor to be an accomplice in their murder. I also stopped eating bread, because stalks are cut with a scythe—as you know—and bread is cut with a knife. So I appended to that first vow a vow regarding bread. Only then did the fork and knife forgive me, and things got a lot better for me. I live from nothingery."

III

The fires of Jaffa blossomed and grew larger before our eyes like shining mushrooms. We sat down to rest a bit on a flat rock on the beach, which was facing the leaning Hassan Bek Mosque. The rock gave off a warmth, as if a fragment of sun were preserved underneath. A wave listened to the shell of my ear and picked up the cry of the sea.

When we got up and started off again in the direction of Jaffa, I put a naive question to my landsman: "Nevertheless, my brother, I see from your face that you have had something to nourish yourself. Unless you've already risen from the dead and eaten the food of the resurrected, I don't know what it could be."

"Of course I have some nourishment. Of course I eat. What are you thinking? I eat glass. Only glass. The first pogrom in our city provided me—absolutely free, unrequested—with my first glass breakfast. A frosted layer of shattered windowpanes fell on streets and alleys. It looked like the manna in the desert once upon a time. Would you believe me? I tasted, chewed, swallowed, and was sated. I didn't collect the heavenly bread and drop it into a bag for the next day. I was sure that the manna would fall the next day as well. I wasn't mistaken.

"I cut through dozens of towns. The same layer had fallen in all of them. Indeed, I didn't go hungry anywhere. You must know that each kind of glass has a particular flavor. You say 'wine,' but there are all sorts of wine. Sweet, sour, Carmel, Burgundy. You have to be a connoisseur. The same is true of glass. A piece of blue glass is something to savor. A red piece tastes like cherries.

"I didn't have a choice in the forests, and so I sated my hunger with grass, weeds, wild nuts, and beads of rowanberries. Frogs and woodpeckers I let live. I made an agreement with the worms: I won't eat you, you won't gorge yourself on me.

"When the war ended, I became a glass eater again. I even displayed the amazing feat at Cirque Medrano. They would bring three glasses of tea on a tray. I'd add sugar, three slices of lemon, then drink up the tea and crunch up and swallow the glasses. Someone in the audience yelled that I was cheating, the glasses were made of sugar. Three fresh glasses were brought and I asked the unbeliever to come up to the podium, pick a glass, drink the tea, and eat the glass. Then he wouldn't yell out 'cheater' anymore. It cost him half of his tongue. And I'd drink up and eat the other two glasses.

"Eating glass isn't something just anyone can do. You have to learn the art. But it's worth it. A glass eater never gets sick. Microbes have no control over him. Just feel these muscles: iron wheels! Don't be scared; you won't get stabbed."

IV

Carpie Thimble got braver and tugged at my sleeve. "You're also among the unbelievers. You're not the first and won't be the last. No matter—you'll be convinced. I'm thirsty. Let's go in and have something to drink."

We went to a miserable establishment. "Just a glass of tea," he asked the boy doing duty as a waiter.

My landsman put two teaspoons of sugar in his tea, mixed it, dropped in a slice of lemon, drank it, and then ate up the glass like an apple.

He cut the air with his diamond smile. "Oh, PS: You should know who you have the honor of speaking with. It's not Carpie from before. It's Carpie the founder of a sect of glass eaters. My students and Hasidim already number in the hundreds. It would be right if you joined too."

The gallery flamed up like a fire in an alley of Old Jaffa. Gray enthusiasts were drawn there. Among them, painters with their anticipatory opinions that the pictures would be too old fashioned.

Before we went in, my landsman again put a pistol finger to my temple. "It's true, eating glass isn't something anyone can do. It's an art you have to learn."

1986

THE DYING MAN'S BEDSIDE

It's not a white angel bargaining with a dark one at the dying man's bedside; rather, it's a man kneaded out of dirt and clay who listens to the incoherent stammering at the dying man's bedside.

A golden leech, the sun had already sucked all the blood from his face.

Elye the Chimneysweep is saying farewell. His fingers, charred kindling held together only by the char, search over the arms of his only friend, looking for a place to hang on.

"You're still born yesterday, kid, huh?"

The kid is now a grandfather, but Elye the Chimneysweep is the same as he was then: a moonwalker who treads over the snows of frozen-together roofs, and tied to a rope thrown over his shoulders is a bucket with a boy born yesterday.

Elye the Chimneysweep picks his way, wandering over the roofs' black snow, the bucket tied to a rope over his shoulder, and in the bucket: a child anointed with soot.

The houses below are fenced in with rings of fire.

"You're still born yesterday, kid, huh?"

The man of dirt and clay, who listens to the incoherent stammering at the dying man's bedside, doesn't know what to answer. But he knows that Elye the Chimneysweep pulled him out of a chimney, anointed him with soot from the bucket, broke through the rings of fire below, and brought him to a farmer, where the good woman raised him in a stall with warm cattle.

"Boy, beat the *Al Chet* without mercy for the sins on my heart. I have sinned! I didn't save your sister from another chimney."

The man at the bedside can no longer rein in his galloping silence. "Elye, you yourself told me not long ago that the roofs had become slippery snakes; you fell off of them with me and got all busted up. I got lucky. The metal of the bucket protected me like a coat of armor. How were you supposed to climb up from the fiery rings below?"

"If that's the way it is, kid, I'll take a question with me on my journey. Why wasn't God a chimneysweep, then?"

1986

THE TASTE OF BIRDS' MILK

I

Somewhere among the news and newsletters that come to me thick and fast from all corners of the world I fixated on a name surrounded by a black border: Bere-Leib. A name I recognized.

A fragment of time popped off time's axle, turned over and over, and fell to a stop at my feet, like a hub that came off and rolled downhill. Let other memories start howling like dogs off their chain! I'll talk about that fragment of time that rolled to a stop. And you, Bere-Leib, in the world of truth, will hear me and remember something that happened in the world of deception, where we met and I played a strange part in your love affair.

II

As suddenly as I saw your name bordered in black, that's how suddenly I caught a glimpse of you so many years ago in the Strashun Library, if years have an order to them.

The library's patrons were eager for stars. They also come to the Strashun Library to read, but the library was too full and couldn't accept them, so they had to be satisfied with staying outside where they read the unrolled snow scroll.

Both long tables in the library's reading hall are bordered with eager faces. It's terribly quiet here, even though the readers' thoughts are laughing, crying, fighting, and shouting. The pages, turned by silken fingers, are also of silk. You can hear a snowflake fall outside. You can hear hair grow.

Here's where I read and studied, mostly in winter, from afternoon till late at night, from the opening of the library's heavy front door till a little bell drives off the silence with its cat o' nine tails of sound: good night.

During one of those reading sessions, when my mind became a hive for the entrances and exits of the glowing bees of *Also sprach Zarathustra* and I lifted my head to digest the bitter honey, I saw your unknown face across from me—difficult to digest. So much pain in its creases, in its pale skin, garlic-colored like an ascetic.

Who is that young man, a perfect orphan, not reading or studying but just turning the pages? Which evil spirit doesn't let him come further inside? Maybe he's browsing himself, reading himself, and I can't see it? I see only the desperation pecking at his temples.

It was the same thing tomorrow and the next day. Wherever I sat, you were there across from me. You were nothing but a messenger to darken the Torah of Zarathustra. I decided that I had to meet my opposite number. When the bell lashed the silence with its cat o' nine tails of sound, and people got up to exit between the tables, I kept my eye on you so as not to lose you.

Past the iron gates with the two lamps where two stars have moved in, you turned left onto Jews Street and into the night. The moonlit windowpane was overgrown with a forest of frost. Your starving shadow was more warmly dressed than you. Because I am a curious person by nature, I followed your footsteps through the warren of alleys. Suddenly I saw you collapse into a snowbank next to a gate, and its white piano keys wept underneath you.

Then and there we made our acquaintance on a winter's night on a snowbank.

III

"Bere-Leib, Bear-Lion, your parents must have had a sense of humor when they yoked you to two animals at your birth. Perhaps the animals helped bear your tortured soul?"

I found out on that night that you fled from the city of Slonim to Vilna, and that your father is a miller, his years worn away between the millstones. You were his right hand at the mill near the city. Your head was full of soaring birds then, and until the tragedy (at that time I didn't know what tragedy it was) the birds would sing inside you. Now you live near that snowbank in a baker's store. Not only doesn't he charge you rent, you also get a few extra golden coins from him for your expertise in the different kinds of flour carried into the bakery by the porters on their flour-covered backs.

You get more talkative after a couple more weeks, when we're on more familiar terms. When I ask why you had collapsed into a snowdrift, you answer, "Because I want to take my own life and I don't know how."

"You're saying that you've never died?"

"Don't laugh at me. If you help me take my own life I'll never forget you."

"Bere-Leib, shake your secrets out of your pocket. You said just now, 'Until the tragedy.' What sort of tragedy?"

"I'm in love."

"Since when is being in love a tragedy?"

"Her father is a goldsmith, and he doesn't approve of it. He got as stubborn as a billy goat. 'The miller's son isn't for you. Your black braids will quickly turn white from the dust of his mill.' She wanted to run away with me, but she preferred her father, more's the pity."

"Who's the 'she,' who is that beauty you want to sacrifice yourself for?"

"Her name is Mindeh."

"You want to take your own life because of a girl with a name like that? I couldn't even fall in love with a princess with that name."

"Her lips taste like birds' milk."

I had great esteem for you on hearing such an expression. "Bere-Leib, I'll perform magic and bring her to you, in your room at the baker's."

"You don't know her father."

"Even if ten fathers stand in the way, they won't be able to stop her. I'll write Mindeh such a fiery love letter she'll light up and come here right away. Bere-Leib, you'll write it with your own handwriting so she doesn't suspect anything. But it's of prime importance for you to tell me about the girl, about you both, your love, as many details as possible: what she looks like, what jewelry the goldsmith's daughter decks herself out in, what sort of thing she usually likes to eat, are her ears cold or warm—and other particulars. I also need to know if you ever gave her a compliment that her lips taste like birds' milk."

"I did."

"Bere-Leib, I'll write her a love letter that soars like an eagle."

I piled up my thoughts like pitchforking hay and wrote the love letter for your sake. I blew into that letter all my passion and jealousy for someone else. Lines of poems that were hatching in me also took part. You, Bere-Leib, signed and sealed it in an envelope and sent it off with luck to Mindeh.

The love letter did make Mindeh take off like an eagle. She's here. A girl with integrity, she didn't touch her father's jewelry or gold work. She only brought her love. It didn't bother the baker that you lived together in his room.

The most beautiful woman carries her own skeleton inside. Sometimes two. But I must tell you that when you brought Mindeh to get my opinion of her, I asked forgiveness in my heart for the unjustified complaints I had about her because of her name. A girl—who's attractive and keeps attracting. Young, pink-cheeked, with a charming duet of shyness and lack of embarrassment.

You, Bere-Leib, Mindeh's fiancé, were no longer recognizable. You had looked like a totally orphaned orphan; now you were a handsome man. The outside changed too. Spring was galloping its way to you with its green wedding canopy.

Quickly you managed to disappear. The secret of the love letter remained with us both, only with us.

IV

Since you disappeared you've sprang out of my memory. What was left of my city the earth swallowed up, and I remained a witness. What do I do? Write stories.

Stories tend to fly off over the entire world. People read them—someone says to someone else, let's invite that author. Let's get our hands on him.

Thus it was that I traveled to a strange land. The people there eagerly came to see what I had to say. Who was the first to greet me with a warm hello? You, Bere-Leib! I recognized in the blink of an eye that you were both the same and had aged, making you appear to be your own ancestor. The garlic color of your face had gotten darker, but it was still there.

"You were sent again by an angel," you said with a happy nervousness, in the voice of a rooster trumpeting out the sunset. "Tomorrow is the wedding of our youngest daughter, whose name you probably won't have any problems with. Her name is Pearl. I can't imagine that you would be in town and miss her wedding."

"Mazel tov, Bere-Leib," I answered. "Of course I'll come. Mostly I want to see your family and, of course, Mindeh. Yes, tomorrow I'm telling my stories in front of an audience, but as soon as the wedding of words, or their funeral, is finished, I'll hurry to your happy occasion. I'll make an effort to speak for as little time as possible."

I kept my word and abbreviated my words. My chief greeter, a renowned cardiologist, was friendly and hospitable, taking me in his limousine to your daughter's wedding—in a restaurant that was shining and murmuring across the street from us, like a waterfall.

I was not late. Music was playing, and they were leading the bride and groom to the chuppah. You tugged my sleeve toward the chuppah, wanting me to witness the event. Here's Mindeh. Her father was right. She had turned white from your flour dust. She looks like my aunt, I thought, who I've never seen.

The real wedding was celebrated at your abode, where people gathered together later: the young couple, brothers, sisters, grandkids, parents of the bride and groom, and close friends, with me at the head. Everyone again sat down at tables covered with all sorts of delicacies. You put me at a special table between you and Mindeh.

Suddenly I felt a shiver run over my entire body. I didn't believe my eyes. Have they taken leave of their senses? A black frost broke into the salon, and its breath extinguished the lamps and chandeliers. Only two stars were left shining in two lanterns atop an iron gate. A moon overgrown with trees of frost. You slipped through the ghetto alleys in a tattered coat, me following in your footsteps.

"Our guest drank too much; he probably doesn't know not to mix Martell with wine," I heard someone murmur as I drowsed off.

The lamps and chandeliers went on again and I felt the wedding in my bones.

V

I could finish the story right here, Bere-Leib. You know the next installment. But I want for us both to hear it from both sides of life.

The goldsmith's daughter didn't keep silent at the wedding. Suddenly she stood up, and with her rosy cheeks, with an ounce of resemblance to the one you brought for my opinion, she began to orate: "I want my dear guest to know that I lived a happy life with my husband. I gave him children, and he—whatever I desired he gave me. I have only one complaint about him: he never listened to my pleading and cajoling: 'Bere-Leib, you're a talented writer; why don't you pick up a pen?' If he had listened to his wife, he would now be as famous as our dear guest. I've kept a letter he wrote me, which tore me out of my house, away from my own father. Children are present, so I can't read all of it out loud, but just a few lines. 'Your lips taste like birds' milk.' Or, 'I love your small ears, one of which is cold and the other like fire.' Or . . ."

Here is where you stood up. Your face was again the light silver color of garlic skin. Your trembling hands too. Like a fish tossed out onto the sand you opened your mouth, and with all your might were silent.

1986

SOLDIER BOOTS

We, your feet, also have a story to tell.

Are hands preferable because they hold a pen, or because they hold a knife? Because they caress or strangle? We have our own digits, and they don't cause anyone harm. They have never tested their nails on anyone's neck.

Even if we were to tell a thousand little secrets, your right hand couldn't catch us. But our fate is to serve you slavishly. You've rarely mentioned us positively. It's hard to know, though, whose imprints will last longer: hands' or feet's.

Do you know that feet dream? Yearn? Pray?

That winter the snow wasn't snow at all but a lime kiln heated by a frosty conflagration.

Unprotected and barefoot, because in panicked flight you weren't able to put boots on us, we both—your twin feet—fled from the traps and nets that your enemy had spread out over the region.

We ran through one village, then another. Not "as if" we had been shot: we were.

In places, the snow warmed up under us and melted into tears.

But we were just imagining it. We were insanely desperate. If we weren't soon provided with shoes or boots, then the red that was flowing in us would freeze up; your breath wouldn't be able to fan our last sparks.

Did we ever envy the wolf under the stars who needs no clothing on his paws!

The hunger for a warm breath was stronger than the hunger in your guts.

But our prayer was heard: one night, when the silence bent under a wolf's groan, we shuffled into a stall next to a snow-covered hut.

The door wasn't chained shut.

A horse was sleeping standing up in a crown of moonlight.

In truth, we have never seen an angel's eye. You haven't either. But when the horse opened its merciful eyes, they seemed to be angelic.

That horse, which must certainly have been waiting for us, bent its crowned head, and with its warm, sweet steam it thawed and set flowing the red stream in our veins.

When the sunrise laid its ax into the stall's roofbeam, you yourself saw that the anointed horse's forefeet wore soldier boots.

The horse stretched out one leg, then the other. You took them off. The boots were precisely our size.

Then, our lord, we both helped you mount the anointed horse, and you were able to ride away on him—and keep riding till this very day.

1987

THE NO-ONE

I

This brief incident occurred many years ago, but the past is a real and tangible thing for me. It beats in my consciousness, as if my consciousness were my heart. The beating isn't really because of me, but rather it has to do with a neighbor of mine who lived in the same courtyard next to the Viliya River.

Because no one knew what to call that Jewish man, they called him The No-One, or just No-One. Other people, when addressing him, used to call him Mister Neighbor. The pharmacist in the courtyard called him Neighbor Sir.

He lived at the end of the courtyard, nearest the storage spaces where the neighbors kept their old rags and a great deal of birch logs that they bought from farmers in fall for the oncoming winter.

Standing guard at the entrance to the home of The No-One and his wife (who did have a name, Wooden Blume) was a wild pear tree whose pears brought enjoyment only to the crows.

The only chimney from which no curl of smoke ever issued in winter was the chimney that The No-One and his wife, Wooden Blume, lived under.

II

I thought about it for a long time and finally figured out why the nameless neighbor's chimney has a smokeless soul. It's because The No-One is a kind of smoke himself!

And if that's the case—my thoughts continued—The No-One's parents must have been fire! But it's still a puzzle why their descendant, my neighbor, is without a name.

In our courtyard, people overhear Wooden Blume calling him, but not like people are wont to do, or even like people call their cats and dogs. She calls him "he." "Is he hungry, hmm?" "Does he want a bath?"

It happens that one night someone knocks on our door above the creaking stairs. I jump out of bed (where I'm reading a book) and ask with sweet curiosity: "Who is it?"

I pick up a coughing answer on the other side of our door, which hangs on one hinge. "No-One."

Though I know that it's my neighbor from the other side of the wild pear tree, I feign ignorance. "Who's knocking? What name?"

The person behind the door feigns even more ignorance. "I said No-One. Let me in."

"If it's No-One, I don't have anyone to let in," I say with playful impertinence, but I immediately feel merciful and take off the bolt.

His mustache—the color of carob—turns gold from the oil lamp hanging across from me. He smells strongly of whiskey.

How can a puff of smoke be drunk? But then again, who should be drunk if not a puff of smoke?

"How can I help you, neighbor?" I ask and slide a chair in his direction.

"Could you by any chance loan me a needle?"

Another time he asks: "I need an onion."

And a third time: "Maybe you can loan me a star? I'll give it back."

III

People told all sorts of stories about our courtyard neighbor No-One and his wife Wooden Blume.

A. Blume gave birth to three wooden children from him, two girls and a boy. Both girls were burned up under the chuppah, and the boy—is the wild pear tree at the end of the courtyard.

B. No-One is a moonwalker. He was seen on a moonlit night floating over the city's roofs, playing a little violin. Nobody is astonished at the moon itself floating over the city's roofs and playing a little violin.

C. Our crazy neighbor behind the wild pear tree was sentenced to death for shooting some big shot. But as they were leading him to be hanged, the gallows disappeared.

I don't know which of the stories contained a spark of truth. But I am ready to swear in this world and the next that they involved the same character who knocked on the door of my ghetto hideout.

Snow was dead on the ground in the fenced-in area. Bloodhounds strained on their chains, pulling toward quivering dreams.

The knock at the hideout didn't scare me then. It was recognizable. I even thought that I was at home at the top of the creaking stairs.

Nevertheless, through a crack I asked the same question as I had long ago.

"No-One." I heard his reincarnated voice. I let him in.

I recognized him when I lit a match. It was the same man. Only the mustache had changed: two sharpened sickles.

His words have no fear of being cut by the sickles.

"I'm setting the city on fire tonight. Enough sitting around at home! Into the woods! Into the woods!"

Was what was burning at dawn our fenced territory or the four-sided sun?

1988

SUNFLOWERS

I

What I'm about to tell you happened in the late '50s, when hacked-down trees from the Polish forest breached dams and floated into the Jews' land with a strange haste.

Their roots dug even deeper into the earthy darkness and took an oath to never climb again toward the sun—not until the Messiah comes.

At that time, dozens of refugees who carried their manuscripts with them were making their way to me, the editor of *Di goldene keyt*, in my fenced-off corner atop gray stairs worn smooth by footsteps. They were like ants with miniature eggs in their jaws. Their cargo was a treasury of eternal memories, diaries of their deathly experiences during war and Holocaust, which if all were printed and bound would be a library of the richest wounds.

I refined my ability to sense whether a submission was appropriate for the journal after leafing through a few pages of a handwritten manuscript, a diary, a description. Because I couldn't read and live through all of them. I confess now those sins, my errors. But without those errors I wouldn't confess.

II

On a day when summer changed its colors to fall and the scent of ripe sea waves landed on my palate, while seated at the small desk in my editorial office I felt the touch of someone's skin on my left hand, which was resting on a book. Autumn's greeting. A fall leaf veined in scarlet had flown in through the window with a "good morning." A thought needled my brain. But then I heard a "good morning" said by a woman's voice.

Before I lifted my eyes to the woman's face, they first stopped on the pattern of small sunflowers that seemed to be blossoming on her dress. But the woman gave a start, and the small sunflowers on her old-fashioned dress blew in the wind.

Above the sunflowers I saw a head that was more like a cloud of hair. A thin lock of hair floated across her face; behind it her eyes went out and then glowed again, like nighttime fireflies in forest moss.

"Let's introduce ourselves," the woman began, her voice like a hoarse songbird. "My name is Lisa. I don't know how I should talk to the editor, who I remember as being somewhere between a little boy and a boy. How polite do I have to be? But in any case, no matter how, we're talking to each other, and I want to tell you one thing right away to ease your mind. They can call me what they want, but I'm not a writer. I can't even read what is inscribed in me and can never be erased, unless one can print a bitter silence for a blind reader."

I locked the door so we wouldn't be bothered, and I brought the chair on the other side of the table over to mine, so that no wooden divider would separate me and the woman. "Lisa is a name I recognize. But I don't recall from where and when it wandered into my memory. Let's talk as friends, so my memory will have mercy on me."

Her cloud of hair fluttered over my eyelashes, leaving a haze over them.

"I'll help you remember who Lisa is. I was the best friend of your sister Etele, who died at 13 of encephalitis. Her brain was full of higher mathematics and philosophy. She was more learned than her teachers, who used to come to your mother to admire Etele. They'd never had a student like her before.

"Yes, such a brain had to burn bright and be consumed. The last time I saw you was at Etele's funeral. You wrote something with a stick in the sand of her grave."

Lisa stood up. Her firefly eyes turned into fractured tears. "If you don't remember me, maybe you remember the sunflowers on my dress. The dress was definitely longer then, but apart from my face, my figure has stayed the same. I've been wearing the same dress for years. There's a reason. Where can we talk where we won't be overheard? Walls have ears. Fish do, too."

"God has ears too, I think," I wanted to say. But what I said was, "If so, Lisa, let's go downstairs and find a private place without ears."

When I went to unlock the door, Lisa skipped in front of me and reached the doorknob first. "I'm no writer, but I did bring something for the editor, a collection of lovely poems written in Russian. They aren't mine, no. They're Etele's. Your sister gave them to me before they took her to the hospital, where they couldn't extinguish her brain inflammation. I couldn't save my only child—but Etele's Russian poems? Those I could."

Then Lisa took out from under the lining of her old-fashioned handbag a packet of poems tied with a red ribbon, giving it to me. "But I want a lot for them. Some smart advice."

III

As soon as Etele's writing tied with the red ribbon was placed under my control, I felt a kind of sisterliness to Lisa.

The painful joy of owning concrete proof of the existence of my sister Etele, that my sister was once really living, made me more alive too.

Now, where my sister's friend had been hidden all those years, a little cell has opened up in my memory. I clearly see Lisa coming to our house in a dress covered with small sunflowers. Of course it's not me she's coming to see but Etele. But before both of them close ranks, I manage to caress her branchlike braids.

The second half of the day prevails over the first. Summer begins to become accustomed to its defeat.

I come across acquaintances, but I act like I don't see them. I see only Lisa with her branchlike braids.

Sobriety burst like a cork from a bottle of whiskey. "Lisa, where should we go? I'll let you take me to a world without ears. Maybe you want me to take you home, and there you'll tell me what no one is supposed to hear? But your walls have ears too!"

Again I hear the voice of a hoarse songbird. "I have no home. Maybe it's more truthful to say that the whole city is my home, the country is my home, unless I were to wander off into a desert. But it would be incredibly presumptuous of me to ask something like that of you. If not just your legs but your head is able to, let's go. You said yourself that we'll find ourselves a corner."

IV

We traversed half the city, both there and back. The air filtered down over us like pink flour. Maybe we should sit down for a bit in a small park? Maybe in a movie theater? God forbid, film actors are murderers.

I was barely able to cajole her into having a bite of something. Afterward we again set out across the city. That's how we made it to Tel Aviv's port neighborhood, walking, hiking really, down streets and alleyways. We boarded a broken-down wooden ship piled high with rusted iron. An anchor hung from the starboard side. It occurred to me that the backwards anchor in the water's green mirror was keeping the ship moored to the stony land. Lisa made a place for herself in a corner of the ship over a heap of rotting cable. I sat to her left on the rings of a sawed-down tree, and from her mouth I heard words that assumed flesh and bone before my eyes. Here is the terrible tale that I heard from my sister's friend.

Her parents didn't ask her if she wanted to be born. Neither did the father of her child ask her if she loved him, or if she wanted a child from him. If a woman got married earlier, she wouldn't get married later. How is it that Lisa, who studied art and philosophy, came to marry a soccer player, and with such haste to boot? She only saw him playing once. They were cheering and carrying him away for scoring the most goals off the opposing team.

Her birth, Lisa believes, wasn't any biological accomplishment. A cow is born too. Out of respect to Etele, she shouldn't have fallen head over heels for the soccer player. If she were to live ten lives and die ten deaths, she still wouldn't understand things having to do with man and wife. She let herself be shaped by him, like a piece of glowing iron under hammer and tongs.

Her life was not doubled through her husband, says Lisa, but through her daughter, Tillie. When Tillie hung on her neck, she became a living medallion. She felt thankful to her husband then. But the soccer player disappeared when Tillie was still nursing. The medallion, which shone like a diamond at her neck, knew nothing of this.

When she and her mother were walled up like lepers, Tillie was leaping into her third year. Lisa was sure that the world's evil was aimed at her daughter alone.

Together with her child, Lisa made it through the wall that enclosed them, and a noble young Polish woman, with whom Lisa had studied art and philosophy, took the child into her protection.

Yes, when Lisa said farewell to her living medallion, she had deliberately put on that same dress with the little sunflowers that she's wearing now. She did it with her hundredth sense: if their separation were to last a very long time, and Lisa returned with a mangled face, or blind, Tillie would be able to recognize her mother from the sunflowers on her dress.

Lisa went back inside the walls after saying farewell to her daughter, and she covered up the dress under a pile of junk where some Russian poems were rolled up too.

She doesn't want to say how she managed to avoid being burned up on the pyres of the camp in Klooga. She was, in fact, but she kept living.

When Lisa returned to the ruined city, not a breath remained of her home. The house of the Polish woman, and with it the woman and Tillie both, cut down—as with a scythe. She was told that it was hit by a bomb. But the attic where Etele's poems were curled up in the dress with the little sunflowers clouded to her. Not my word but Lisa's. "Clouded to her."

She cursed the thought that Tillie was no longer alive. Since then, throughout summer, winter, autumn, and spring, she has wandered through different countries, always wearing the same dress, which she can't take off since it has become her skin.

V

On the ship, Lisa clearly forgot that fish have ears. Or maybe she didn't forget and was just sure that the fish in the sea were sleeping, not hearing a word.

Before us, the sea looked like it had been through a mass murder. Most waves had breathed their last, while others gasped with difficulty and tried to hold on to a gleam of moonlight.

"I'll finish soon. Be patient and keep listening. You're not a stranger; you're Etele's brother. I finally found my daughter on the other side of the country. I saw her on the street. An older, distinguished man was holding her under her arm. Noticing a woman walking in a dress with little sunflowers, she cried out, "Oh!" She even turned around. But the man pulled her away and both of them disappeared into the crowd. They appeared again, but they were very far away."

Lisa tracked the two of them like a dog more human than its owner.

No, she wasn't mistaken; it was him, the soccer player, and his wife was Tillie. They live in a neighborhood near Bat Yam that's under construction. The street is still young and doesn't have a name. The houses are only stamped with big black numbers.

She can't blame either of them. When Tillie was still a girl, her father had to flee from their city in Poland to Russia. When they met in Poland after the war, he was probably about forty years old and Tillie wasn't twenty yet. Lisa believes that they didn't know, and maybe even today don't know, who they are. When the noble Polish woman took Tillie in to protect her, her daughter's name was polonized too. Her protector became her mother.

Lisa got hired as a cleaning woman in the neighborhood near Bat Yam, so she was lucky enough to be able to look at her child from a distance, which made her happy, if you can say that, seeing her child and her grandchild together, a girl who looked just like Tillie did when the noble Polish woman took her in to protect her.

Lisa lifted her head from her knees, and a shining heavenly body cut through the night and extinguished itself.

This was the right moment for her to say, "Every end has a beginning, and every beginning expires in its longing for the end."

I felt her hand on mine. "Now I'm waiting for your wise advice."

VI

Somewhere, a wave turned gray from fear. The sunflowers rose on Lisa's dress. "You owe me wise advice. Should I tell them who I am and who they are, or . . ."

After the "or" an abyss gaped for a couple of seconds. Lisa leaped over it with another question, quite a different one. "Can you remember what you wrote with a stick on Etele's grave?"

"I wrote on the sand of her grave the word FOREVER."

Lisa's hand on mine turned soft as sand. "Yes, I also remember the mark your stick made. But listen to me again. Should I tell the soccer player and his wife-daughter in what crucible they were formed, they and I together, or should I disappear forever—so you'll be the only one in the world who holds my secret?"

Lisa said this quietly and deliberately, as if she were telling me a story from a novel she had read.

A voice (mine? not mine?) answered her. "I'm not smart enough to give you the wise advice you demand, but I have a friend in Jerusalem whose wisdom and intelligence are unsurpassed. Let me ask him for advice . . ."

Lisa burst out laughing for the first time. Her laughter skipped over the water like stones. "King Solomon is still alive in Jerusalem?"

1987

AUTHOR AND TRANSLATOR

Avrom Sutzkever (1913–2010) spent his childhood in Siberia and emerged as a writer in the burgeoning literary circles of Jewish Vilna. In the Vilna Ghetto, he wrote poetry as a means of survival. As a member of what became known as the Paper Brigade, he helped to save Jewish cultural treasures from Nazi destruction. After the war, he became an influential advocate and activist for Yiddish culture, as well as a symbol of resistance through acts such as his testimony at the Nuremberg trials. He founded the Yiddish literary journal *Di goldene keyt* (*The Golden Chain*) and in 1985 received the Israel Prize for Yiddish literature.

Zackary Sholem Berger is a multilingual poet and translator. He has published multiple books of his own Yiddish, English, and Hebrew poetry. He has also translated among these languages in a variety of genres for children and adults, and for secular and Hasidic audiences. His translations of Yiddish poetry have appeared in *Poetry* magazine, the *Forward*, and other publications. He was a 2013 Yiddish Book Center Translation Fellow. A doctor by profession, he lives in Baltimore with his Yiddish-speaking family.

ABOUT THE YIDDISH BOOK CENTER

The Yiddish Book Center is a nonprofit organization working to recover, celebrate, and regenerate Yiddish and modern Jewish literature and culture.

The million books recovered by the Yiddish Book Center represent Jews' first sustained literary and cultural encounter with the modern world. The books are a window on the past thousand years of Jewish history, a precursor to modern Jewish writing in English, Hebrew, and other languages, and a springboard for new creativity. Since its founding in 1980, the Center has launched a wide range of bibliographic, educational, and cultural programs to share these treasures with the wider world.

White Goat Press
White Goat Press publishes new English translations of Yiddish literature.

Titles currently available from White Goat Press:

Seeds in the Desert
by Mendel Mann
translated by Heather Valencia

Warsaw Stories
by Hersh Dovid Nomberg
translated by Daniel Kennedy

In eynem: **The New Yiddish Textbook**
by Asya Vaisman Schulman, Jordan Brown, and Mikhl Yashinsky

To learn more, visit yiddishbookcenter.org/in-translation